SL BEAUMONT

Shadow of Doubt

For my family with much love

Contents

I   Part One

Chapter 1   3
Chapter 2   17
Chapter 3   24
Chapter 4   30
Chapter 5   34
Chapter 6   41
Chapter 7   51
Chapter 8   58
Chapter 9   65
Chapter 10   72
Chapter 11   75
Chapter 12   77
Chapter 13   84
Chapter 14   92
Chapter 15   94
Chapter 16   98
Chapter 17   106
Chapter 18   115
Chapter 19   124
Chapter 20   128
Chapter 21   133
Chapter 22   143

Chapter 23	153
Chapter 24	159
Chapter 25	161
Chapter 26	169
Chapter 27	172
Chapter 28	180
Chapter 29	191

II   Part Two

Chapter 30	199
Chapter 31	201
Chapter 32	211
Chapter 33	215
Chapter 34	222
Chapter 35	226
Chapter 36	236
Chapter 37	243
Chapter 38	251
Chapter 39	255
Chapter 40	260
Chapter 41	264
Chapter 42	272
Chapter 43	282
Chapter 44	288
Chapter 45	298
Chapter 46	310
Chapter 47	316
Chapter 48	325
Epilogue	337
Acknowledgements	341

Author's Note   343
Also by SL Beaumont   344

I

Part One

Chapter 1

"For God's sake, get one of the others to do it," I said, exasperated, as I looked up from my computer at my boss who was leaning on the wall of my cubicle.

"No. It's your turn," Andrew replied turning away, signaling an end to the conversation.

I sighed and stood up, stretching my back. Three hours straight sitting at a desk wasn't good. I had been hoping to squeeze in a trip to the gym after work to loosen everything up, but it looked like my evening was going in entirely another direction.

Hesitating only for a moment, I followed Andrew down the row to his cubicle, not willing to give in quite so easily. Andrew was a heavyset man in his mid-thirties. His thinning hair was cropped close to his head, but did nothing to detract from his good looks. He oozed charm and ruled his team of accountants and analysts in the derivatives division of the investment bank, Dobson Stone, with a mixture of fear and admiration. To be on Andrew's good side was like being bathed in the warmth of sunshine, but do wrong by him and it felt like being exposed to the iciest of winters. Fortunately, I had only ever felt the heat of summer, which gave me the opportunity to push the boundaries. And now was when I needed one of those opportunities.

"Come on, Andrew. You know that you're going to employ him anyway." I flashed my most winning smile at him. "Let's just skip this bit."

'This bit' was the tradition in the team of finally vetting any new recruit by taking them out to a local watering hole and doing a 'social' interview. The derivatives team was a close knit, play hard, work hard group and Andrew was a big fan of team players. Ever since the disastrous recruitment of an accountant named Peter, who had been hired without the social interview, Andrew had deemed it mandatory. Peter had passed all of the other interview stages with flying colors, but once he joined the team his lack of humor, aversion to socializing with his colleagues and propensity to back stab had caused major problems.

"Need to make sure he's not another Peter, Jess. And besides, William seems like the kind of guy who will appreciate a pretty face." Andrew grinned, knowing full well that the latter comment would annoy me and distract me from my argument.

Putting my hands on my hips, I scowled at him and practically hissed, "I can't believe you just said that. I will report you to the Diversity Committee. Maybe select me for my knowledge of the business or my social charm, but because of my looks? Give me a break."

Andrew threw back his head and roared with laughter. He had one of those loud laughs which made people stop what they were doing and look in his direction, in case they were missing something really good. Jimmy looked up from the next cubicle, catching the end of my rant. He and fellow Antipodean Dave were always quick with a quip and up for anything. They were usually behind the many practical jokes that went on at the office and they never, ever, missed an opportunity to wind someone up.

"Watch out, Scotty is about to blow," Jimmy called out to anyone in the team who was listening. Jimmy had an open, friendly face. At the tender age of twenty-four, he already had smile lines surrounding his mischievous eyes. He had the physique of the champion fighters in his family, but not the temperament. Andrew and I both glared at him. Still grinning, he held his hands up as if to protect himself and sat down again.

"Machiavelli's Wine Bar, seven pm," Andrew instructed and turned to pick up his ringing phone. I was dismissed with a wave of his hand.

I returned to my cubicle muttering about the appropriateness of the venue, and picked up my mobile to call my husband Colin. He answered on the second ring.

"Make it quick, Jess. I'm having a crazy day."

"I have to work late, a recruitment interview in a pub of all things," I said.

"Which one?"

"Machiavelli's."

"Okay. Good. Gotta go." He was gone. I wasn't even sure that he had heard me.

Jimmy and Dave stopped by my desk as I was shutting down my computer at the end of the day. Dave was the opposite of Jimmy physically, short and slight with a mop of messy blond hair, but he shared his friend's sense of fun.

"Where are you meeting him?" Dave asked, picking up my stapler and twirling it around.

"At Machiavelli's up by St. Paul's," I replied, taking the stapler from his hands and replacing it on the desk, only to have him pick up my hole punch instead. "I will know which kleptomaniac to come after if I come in tomorrow and there are stationery items missing," I warned him with a grin.

Dave simply laughed, putting the hole punch back in its place, and swiped my favorite pen instead. I shook my head at him. He was incorrigible.

"We'll be at The Tower if you wanna meet after," Jimmy said, naming the pub closest to the office as we walked towards the bank of lifts to take us down to the lobby entrance of the building.

"Okay, see you there in fifteen minutes," I said, only half joking. Seriously, I was going to get this over and done with as quickly as possible.

* * *

The rain had stopped and the early evening sun bathed the city in a soft glow. The old fashioned wrought iron streetlamps that lined the road towards St. Paul's Cathedral hadn't yet turned on. Machiavelli's was on a corner and had floor-to-ceiling plate glass windows wrapping around both street views. It was already busy for a Wednesday night, with groups of men and women dressed in business attire gathered around tables chatting and laughing.

I stepped off the street and entered through the open doors.

The bar itself was brightly lit with strings of tiny lights draped from one corner of the room to the other and back again forming a crisscross pattern across the entire ceiling. The heels of my shoes beat out a loud rap on the polished wooden floor, as I walked towards the bar, my eyes scanning the room. Andrew had said that William Johnston was tall and dark-haired. "You should have made him wear a rose," I had suggested to Andrew as I was leaving the office, which had only earned me a glare; at this rate summer would be turning into autumn.

Ah, that had to be him, leaning against the bar, fiddling with his mobile phone. He was tall, as Andrew had described, with thick dark hair, which curled over his collar and hung across his forehead. He was well dressed in a dark blue suit. As if aware of my scrutiny, he straightened up and looked towards me with a questioning tilt of his head. Over-confident, I thought, deciding in that instant that I disliked him. I stopped in front of him.

"William?" I asked, returning his cool questioning gaze.

"You must be Jessica." His accent was English, well-educated. I shook his hand. "Call me Will. Can I get you a drink?"

"I think it's me that's supposed to offer that. What can I get you?" I asked.

"A Becks then, please, Jessica," he replied leaning back against the bar and studying me.

I signaled to the nearest barman. "A bottle of Becks and a skinny gin and tonic please."

We found a couple of empty armchairs in one corner and Will turned on the charm. First, he helped me take my raincoat off and laid it over the back of my chair, then he waited until I had sat down before taking a seat himself. Old manners, unusual in the politically correct equal opportunity business world, but still, I refused to be charmed. I wasn't here to make friends. Will adjusted the cuffs of his pale blue double-cuff shirt beneath his suit jacket. His cufflinks were gold dice; I noted the satirical choice for a career in investment banking, where so much was speculative.

"So, what's this then? Get me drunk and see if I will spill all my deep, dark secrets?" He smiled.

"Actually, it would save me a lot of time and money, if we can skip the drunken bit and you just tell me your secrets," I replied.

Will leaned forward and looked up at me with a glint in his blue eyes. "So, Jessica, what exactly *would* you like to know?"

I spluttered on my drink. Holy crap, this guy was super confident. Flirting with the interviewer didn't usually get you a job.

I sat back in my chair and tried to adopt a neutral expression and ignore the fact that he had my attention. "Well, why don't you tell me a bit about yourself?"

"Okay, I grew up in Sussex. Obtained my Maths degree from UCL and Chartered Accountancy with EY," he answered. "But I'm sure you know all that."

I had expected him to wax lyrical about himself, given that I had left him with such an open-ended question. The fact that he didn't, showed he was clever. There was more to him than just the charm. I finished my drink as we chatted a little about the work he had done and who we both knew at EY.

"Anyway, enough about me. How did a nice Scottish girl like you end up working in the cut-throat world of investment banking?" Will asked.

Okay, so maybe I was wrong. There was that awful charm again.

"Who said anything about me being nice?" I growled.

Will, to his credit, laughed and raised his empty bottle. "Next round is definitely on me," he said.

I looked at my watch and acquiesced. It would be rude to end the interview after just twenty minutes, even if I did consider it a farce. "Okay, but just one. I have to get going."

Will nodded and made his way to the bar. I watched him go. He had broad shoulders and carried himself in a way that spoke of someone at ease in their own skin. He stopped and shook hands with a guy standing at a tall table and leaned over, kissing the cheek of the woman with him. As much as I hated to admit it, he would be a good fit in the team. Easy to get on with and charming enough to deal with the odd difficult trader. I didn't have to like him. Hell, I didn't really have to even work with him. My job here was done.

"So. What else are you supposed to glean from me tonight?" he asked with a grin as he placed my drink on the little table between our chairs.

I sat twisting my wedding and engagement rings around on my finger. "Nothing, I think I'm done. I guess you'll be hearing from Andrew tomorrow. Do you have any questions for me?"

Will tilted his head, a little smile playing around his lips. "Just one."

"Sure, fire away."

"Will you have dinner with me?" he asked.

I wasn't expecting that. "No," I replied, trying not to sound prim. "You do realize that I am married?"

Will nodded and shrugged his shoulders. "Just thought I'd

9

ask," he replied.

* * *

I arrived at The Tower around eight pm. The doors of the old pub were wide open and Jimmy and Dave were holding court out front, surrounded by a group of people. From the peals of laughter coming from their audience, it sounded like they were trying to outdo each other with the funniest anecdotes; nothing new there. Jimmy caught my eye as I walked closer and broke away from the group to greet me.

"Hey, Jess, how did it go? William? Verdict?" he asked.

"He has the charm of a prince and the morals of an alley cat. He will be a perfect fit," I answered.

Jimmy looked stunned for a moment, before a grin spread across his face.

"Did he try to hit on you?"

I must have looked uncomfortable because he slipped a friendly arm around my shoulders and turned me towards the doors leading into the bar.

"Didn't you tell him about the strapping Scotsman that you have tucked away at home?"

I laughed. "No, it wasn't like that."

Jimmy signaled to the barman. "My friend here needs a G and T pronto."

The barman obliged, upending a blue bottle into a measuring cup just as a loud boom sounded and the pub shook. The cup slipped from the barman's fingers with a clatter. Bottles in the refrigerators behind the counter and those on the shelf against the wall behind the bar rattled. Empty glasses tipped over on an adjacent table and several bottles of spirits skidded off the end of the bar, splintering into shards as they hit the wooden floor. Clear liquid ran across the boards following the slope of the floor towards the door. With a shriek, I grabbed on to the edge of the bar for support.

There was an eerie silence for a moment as everyone looked at each other with a mixture of confusion and concern.

"What the hell was that?" Jimmy said. "An earthquake?"

"Jim," Dave shouted from outside.

Jimmy and I looked at each other for a second before rushing through the door to join Dave.

"Look." He pointed up the road to where an enormous cloud of smoke and dust rose into the dusky sky. The screech of brakes sounded as traffic pulled to an abrupt stop on the busy road. Then loud splintering crashes could be heard as brick, timber and metal returned to earth and the awful sound of human suffering rose above the din.

We started running up the road in the direction of the blast. Jimmy and Dave, not hampered by shoes with three inch heels, raced ahead of me, covering the two blocks in no time. By the time I joined them, the first survivors were staggering from what remained of the Kings Arms Hotel, covered in white powder from fractured concrete and plaster.

"What the—" began Dave.

We stood frozen to the spot and watched as two figures stepped from the rubble into the road, leaning on one another to stay upright. Both had blood running down their faces from cuts to their heads. Behind them a woman took a few lurching steps before collapsing beside a broken wooden bar stool with a feeble cry for help. A dazed man stepped over her, crossed the road and kept walking, his gaze unfocused. Two young women stumbled out of the wreckage, clinging to one another, their clothes torn and dusty, each missing a high-heeled shoe, so that they appeared to be engaged in an elaborate twisting dance routine. A man pushed past them calling for help, blood squirting from beneath the hand he pressed into his shoulder where his arm would once have been. Another man remained seated at an outdoor table, his hand still wrapped around a half-full pint of beer. On his lap sat one of the pub's many colorful hanging baskets, the reds, blues and greens of the flowers and foliage in stark contrast to the chalky white powder which covered the man's hair and clothes. What remained of his drinking companions lay scattered around him, like a macabre human jigsaw. The man stared into space with a blank expression.

"Oh my God," I said, covering my mouth with my hand as I took in the horrific scene, struggling to comprehend the wreckage.

All around us people began rising from where they had taken cover moments earlier. There were desperate shouts as some hurried towards the wounded, whilst others held back, unsure what to do faced with such devastation. As I looked around, I noticed some people begin filming the carnage on their mobile phones.

Dave rushed forward and took the arm of one of the young women, while Jimmy went to the aid of her friend and helped them to sit down on the edge of the curb. They were shaking uncontrollably, so I took my raincoat off and draped it around the shoulders of the one nearest to me.

The wail of sirens from emergency responders racing to the scene began to get louder as they approached from all directions. A single police car pulled to a stop beside us and two young police officers alighted, donning their hats as they stepped out. Their faces displayed horrified expressions as they surveyed the chaos, but these were soon replaced by grim determination as they strode forward and took charge. One officer directed those of us helping the injured to lead them to an open outdoor square across the road from the scene, whilst the second officer tried to contain the spectators.

"Help is on the way," he called. "We need to make certain that there isn't a second device or a gas leak before going in." Jimmy, who'd been climbing into the rubble to assist the injured, now stepped back and looked around with a helpless expression. "I know," the officer said understanding his reaction. "But until we know what we are dealing with we don't want any further casualties."

"It was a car bomb," a man in the growing crowd called out, pointing to the almost unrecognizable mangled remains of a vehicle lying on its side up against the broken windows of a neighboring building, which until a few minutes earlier had been a lunch-time sandwich bar. "I saw it light up seconds before the explosion."

"Okay, sir. Don't go anywhere. We'll need a statement from you," the officer replied before relaying the information through to headquarters on his shoulder-mounted radio.

"Jessica." I turned towards the voice. Will jogged across the road to join me. "Are you okay?"

"These poor people, they were just having a drink like we were earlier," I said, wringing my hands and watching as a team of fireman leapt from their truck, unwinding a hose to deal with a small blaze that smoldered at the rear of the site.

Will nodded. "I know."

I looked up at him. His brow was furrowed and he looked as distraught as I felt.

"Who would do such a thing? In the heart of London?" I asked.

Jimmy and Dave returned from helping the two young women to an ambulance that had just arrived. Dave handed me back my raincoat.

"Will, this is Jimmy and Dave, two of your new colleagues," I said.

"G'day, mate," Jimmy said as he hurried past us and back towards the remains of the pub. "Can you give us a hand with this guy?" he called over his shoulder.

"Sure," Will replied, following him and taking the other side of a solidly built injured man who had staggered from the pub. Between them, Jimmy and Will helped him across the road to the square where more ambulances and paramedics were beginning to arrive.

The smell of smoke and rotten wood intermingled with something sweet and sickly hit me as I helped an older woman away from the debris to relative safety. I wrinkled my nose and looked skywards; sunset was upon us. I noticed a police van arrive and several officers begin setting up spotlights on tripods pointed at what remained of the pub.

We were busy for the next twenty minutes, helping the walking wounded from the ruins across the road to the square to be triaged and assisting the small handful of police officers to set up barriers until more of their colleagues arrived. At one point I found myself moving odd shoes, bags, documents and other personal objects thrown by the blast into the street, to an area at the edge of the square. The bomb squad arrived and we were all moved back from the site. We were beginning to feel surplus to requirements when a police officer approached us.

"Anyone else is going to need either a stretcher or a body bag," he said with a grim expression. "Thanks for your assistance, but I'll need you back behind the barrier now. Leave your details with the officer over there as we'll need statements from you all."

We nodded and walked across to the officer holding a tablet, at the edge of police cordon, and gave our names and contact details. I looked down at my white shirt; it had a blood stain on the sleeve and black marks across the front. I went to pull my raincoat on but noticed that it had drops of blood across the shoulders. I shuddered. I looked at my hands, they were blackened too. I hiccupped, the beginnings of a sob.

"Come on," Jimmy said, taking my arm. "Let's head back to The Tower, I need a stiff drink after that. Will, mate, join us?"

* * *

As we ducked under the hastily erected police cordon, a block back from the scene we noticed Aditi Sharma, the petite dark-haired BBC reporter, standing alongside the crews of a several other television networks, awaiting the signal from her cameraman as he counted her in. We paused to listen.

"I'm reporting live from the scene of a devastating terrorist attack in the heart of London tonight." Aditi paused and looked behind her at the remains of the pub, a smoldering pile of brick and plaster, dotted with a number of white sheets, covering the bodies of the dead. "Eye witnesses tell me that a car bomb exploded outside the Kings Arms Hotel on Cheapside at 8.05 pm tonight. No one has yet claimed responsibility for the attack at one of the City's popular after work venues. There is currently no official death toll, but I understand that there are already eighteen confirmed dead and many more injured."

Aditi pressed her right hand to the earpiece in her ear as the news anchor in the studio asked her a question. A moment later she nodded.

"Another incidence of home grown terror? We're hearing those rumors here too. This is the third attack since the outcome of the Brexit referendum, but as yet there's been no official comment. Witnesses describe the two men who parked the van containing the bomb and walked away ten minutes before the explosion, as white and in their twenties. We understand that police teams are pulling the street CCTV footage as we speak."

She paused, listening before continuing. "At this point no one has claimed responsibility, so we have no idea as to the motive behind the attack, but there is some speculation that this incident may be related to the recent Trafalgar Square and Windsor bombings. However, it does seem that this was a much larger device, so authorities will be desperately hoping that this isn't an escalation of violence."

Chapter 2

September 18

The hairs on the back of my neck stood to attention as I joined the crowds of office workers riding to the top of the escalator and striding across the shabby tiled ticket hall, and passed the armed police officers to exit the London Underground station. I glanced around me trying to shake the uneasy feeling I'd had since leaving the flat. Out on the street, a procession of black cabs, red double-decker buses and ubiquitous white vans streamed by as I waited for the lights to change. The sky was a slate grey dome, foretelling the winter that was just around the corner. I shivered and looked sideways at the people around me also waiting to cross the road. All suited and booted ready for another day at a desk, many scrolling through messages on their phones, others chatting with a colleague that they'd caught up with on the journey from home.

Still, the feeling of being surveilled wouldn't leave me and my gaze drifted across the road to where a high-visibility-vested workman wearing a white hard hat lazed against the window sill of a pub eating his breakfast from a paper bag. A straggly blond ponytail extended from beneath his hat and despite his nonchalant stance, there was something watchful and alert about him. The green walking man sign illuminated and I crossed the intersection still studying the workman. As I got closer I did a double take. I could have sworn he'd been at Sloane Square when I got on the tube twenty minutes earlier. The man caught my gaze for a brief instant and screwing up the paper bag, tossed it in a nearby bin before turning and hurrying away, pulling his phone from his pocket as he disappeared around the corner. I gave my head a shake; no one was following me. I was being stupid. It wasn't the first time I'd felt such paranoia and each time I put it down to a weird reaction to what I'd seen at Cheapside. I should probably have talked to someone to get my head straight, but Colin's reaction to anyone having any sort of therapy was derision, so I hadn't.

I joined Dave in the queue for coffee at the bank's lobby café. The café, situated in one corner of the wide marble foyer, consisted of a single counter topped by a large shiny stainless steel espresso machine and a cabinet filled with an assortment of pastries. Clusters of small round white tables and chairs were scattered in a loose circle around the counter, with several two-seater sofas along the wall.

"Jess, are you okay, mate?" Dave asked in his Australian drawl, turning and peering at me. "You look like you've seen a ghost or something." His dark suit was a little crumpled and his hair looked as though it hadn't seen a comb that morning. His shoes were scuffed, and he had several days' growth covering his jaw. I marveled at his blatant unprofessionalism.

I gave a weak smile. "Nothing a coffee won't fix."

"Tell me about it," he said, grabbing his takeout cup from

the counter and giving the barista a nod of thanks. "You're not alone; even though it's been a couple of months a lot of people are still a bit jumpy after Cheapside."

"I know," I replied. "Although the much larger police presence is supposed to make us feel safer, right?"

"Apparently."

"Morning, Jess. Hey, Dave."

I turned as Will joined us. By contrast, his hair was still a little damp, but combed and styled; his shirt and suit were crease-free and his shoes shone. I glanced at Dave, but he seemed oblivious to the difference. Just as well he was so good at his job. He nodded to Will and wandered off towards the bank of elevators.

"How have you settled in, Will?" I asked handing a few coins to the barista, who knew my order by heart.

"Good. Jimmy has taken me under his wing," he replied.

"I'm sure he has. Just watch your liver, he's a dangerous person to know," I joked.

Will smiled. "How are things on the Euro team?"

"Just the usual. It's on a different scale to what you'll be seeing on the US dollar book. You have the volume but we often have a little more complexity."

"Can you show me sometime?" he asked, flashing a devastating smile at me. I wondered if he realized how much he used it to get what he wanted. Part of me wanted to say no, just to see his reaction, but being churlish wasn't really in my nature. Besides, Will had been nothing but friendly since he'd arrived, often stopping by my desk for a quick chat each morning. It wasn't his fault that he was naturally charming, I needed to give him a break.

"Sure, I'd be happy to," I replied.

"Great. Tell you what. I'm sure I'll be volunteered to do the coffee run mid-morning, I'll get you one to say thanks in advance," he said. "Skinny cappuccino, right?"

We travelled in the lift up to our floor together. I dumped my bag beside my desk and followed Will into the large meeting room at one side of the floor for our weekly team meeting.

Most people were already seated around the enormous wooden board table and I slid into a spare chair beside my friend Marie.

"You're late," she said, rolling her straight dark hair into an elegant topknot.

"I couldn't face this without coffee," I said wiggling my cup.

She grinned at me as Andrew strode into the room, closing the door behind him and lowered his large frame into his usual seat at the head of the table.

"Just a couple of things this week, people," he began. "Internal audit have given me their timetable."

There was a collective groan, but Andrew held up his hand. "Necessary evil, folks. And we have two of the middle office team visiting from New York later in the week, I trust you'll make them welcome."

"That sounds like you just offered to put your card behind the bar at The Tower," Jimmy said as everyone laughed.

"One final item, the analytics whizz-kids have come up with a new derivative product that's ready be tested. They need two people to run the testing, check that the systems, settlements etc. can handle it, make sure that it's priced accurately and incorporated into the bank's trading strategies correctly," Andrew said. "And following that, you'll be required to educate the front office traders."

Several side conversations broke out. A new financial product was always a source of excitement in any investment bank. It was a cut-throat industry and any competitive advantage was useful. In-house, being a new product expert was a good thing, as your expertise and advice was often sought, making you a more valuable commodity and less likely to fall victim to the restructuring cuts that regularly sliced through the banks.

"Are you looking for volunteers?" Ramesh, one of my team, asked.

"That's good of you," Andrew replied eyeballing him. Ramesh shrank back in his chair under the scrutiny. "I will need you to step up and cover Jess. She's going to lead the testing."

There were several murmurs, both supportive and disgruntled, around the table.

I was delighted, as I had begun to feel the need for a new challenge. However, my delight was short-lived.

"Mmm... who to work with you?" Andrew mused, although I could tell he was teasing me, and had already decided. I just couldn't quite see what the joke was. "I think Will could learn a thing or two from you."

"Great, thanks, boss." Across the table from me, Will was enthusiastic.

Jimmy caught my eye and waggled his eyebrows suggestively, while beside him Dave winked at me. I scowled at them. What was going on here?

"Okay, back to work, you lot. Jess and Will stay behind." Andrew dismissed the team.

Passing behind me, my colleague Rachel, leaned close to my ear and whispered, "Ooh, a couple of weeks alone in a room

21

with Will, lucky you."

I blushed and busied myself sorting through my papers, while Will sat there with a satisfied smile.

Andrew ran through the testing plan and the timetable. We were to spend half of each day on the project for the next month, as well as covering the bare bones of our existing roles. As we gathered up the notes and left the meeting room, I took Andrew to one side.

"Why Will? I could have done with someone a little more experienced," I asked.

"Jess, he has a Maths degree, he will be able to test the analytics in his sleep. And besides, I thought it might be a good team bonding exercise for you. I do recall that you had reservations about him. This way, you can get to know him a little better and put them to rest."

"Gee, thanks," I muttered heading back to my desk to plan my work handover for the next month.

* * *

"What the hell was that all about this morning?" I said to Jimmy as we walked out of the building and into the cool night air at the end of the day.

He grinned. "Ah come on, just teasing you, Jess. Everyone knows Will is sweet on you." This was news to me and my face must have showed it because he continued. "Buying you coffee, stopping by your desk to chat during the day and he's always asking about you."

"Oh, Jimmy, people could say the same about us," I retorted, and mimicking his Kiwi accent I added. "Always buying me a gin and tonic, making sure I get into a cab safely at night…"

Jimmy patted my arm. "Not the same, Jess, and you know it."

Chapter 3

October 25

My phone chimed with several missed messages as I stepped out of the tube station and onto the crowded footpath for the short walk to the office. After a month of long days, the new product had been launched and all systems were operational. I'd had a well-earned night out with Rachel and Marie, and I'd overslept. My head was a little dusty and I was chugging down the first of what I suspected would be several strong coffees. Sighing, wishing that I was still tucked up in bed, I waited for the light to change so that I could cross. I pulled my phone from my bag and glanced at the screen. Will had been calling while I was underground. I listened to the first of his messages.

'Where are you? JP is looking for you!'

Shit. Jean-Pierre Roux was the very French, very arrogant and very powerful Head of Trading at the bank. He scared most people silly. Being summoned to his office to explain something was never good. But to have him come looking for you was disastrous.

I called Will back.

"Where the hell are you?" he answered.

"Late. What the heck does he want?"

"Dunno, Jess, but you better get here soon. I have stalled him, but I don't know for how long."

"Shit, I'm nearly there."

I entered the lobby of the building at speed and ran across the marble floor towards the bank of lifts at the rear of the vast atrium, waving my access pass at the security guard who held an entry gate open for me when he saw my haste. I acknowledged him with a grim smile.

"Come on, come on," I urged the elevators, punching the lift call button several times with my finger, but the metal doors remained resolutely closed and I watched in frustration as the lights above each set of doors illuminated showing the elevators to be climbing, rather than returning to the lobby. My phone rang.

"He just called again. I told him you were on your way to his office now. I'll meet you at the lifts on his floor," Will said.

"Thank you," I breathed, hanging up. Just as I was contemplating heading for the stairwell behind the lifts, one arrived.

I took a few steading breaths on the ride up to the eighteenth floor and shucked my raincoat ready to hand over to Will.

The lift doors opened and he was waiting for me with an anxious smile. I handed him my coat and bag.

"What does he want? It's not the new product, is it? It should be working fine, we've tested everything over the last month," I said.

Will shrugged. "He didn't say."

"How do I look?" I asked running my hands over my hips. Typical, just the day I hadn't worn a business suit. The ruby red and black wrap dress looked fabulous with my knee-high

25

black boots and ribbed tights, but it felt a little frivolous and with too much cleavage on display to wear into the Head of Trading's office.

"Great," he muttered. "Now, off you go. I'll wait here." He gave me a little push towards the trading floor.

I took a deep breath and tapped the intercom next to the doors.

"Yes," a disembodied voice asked.

"Jessica McDonald to see JP," I said hearing my voice sound a little high-pitched. I cleared my throat.

The automatic door leading onto the noisy open plan trading floor swished open as my access was granted. I stepped into a cavernous space filled with row upon row of desks and computers. Some of the traders were sitting in front of their screens and others were standing, either talking on their phones or shouting across the rows at one another. The noise was quite unbelievable. It reminded me of the volume of a school playground at interval but trebled.

Set on a mezzanine level at the far side of the floor were three glass-fronted offices, belonging to the Head of Investment Banking, the Head of Asset Management and the Head of Trading. I took a deep breath and started walking down the wide corridor separating the rows of desks. On a quiet day, this was known as the catwalk and it took a brave person to walk it, but as luck would have it, it wasn't a quiet day, so no one gave me a second glance. However, JP stood at the window of his office watching me walk down, tapping his fingers on the window ledge.

I will not run. I will not run. I chanted to myself. I refused to let him see that he intimidated me, especially if I was about to be fired.

After what seemed like the final walk of a death row inmate, I was at the steps leading up to the mezzanine. My heart was beating so hard in my chest, it felt as if it would hammer right out. I took a deep breath and climbed the stairs, knocking on JP's open door when I reached the landing at the top.

"How kind of you to join me, Ms. McDonald." JP's voice was dripping with sarcasm.

JP was solidly built with dark hair slicked back from his face and coming to rest just above the collar of his expensive looking double-cuff shirt. His eyes were sharp and intelligent, and he exuded power. *Not a man to cross*, I thought with a little frisson of fear. His office reflected his personality. Minimalist, stark almost, there was nothing on the walls to give any hint of the man. His frosted glass desk was empty, except for a computer screen.

"My apologies, I understand that you've been looking for me. How can I help?" I belatedly realized that Will hadn't told me what excuse he had used to stall JP, so I decided not to offer one, in case we contradicted one another.

"See this trading floor." JP turned to look through the floor-to-ceiling window, the buzz of the staff muffled by the glass. "It's the second largest in London. The amount of money that we can make or lose in a single day is staggering," he said in lightly accented English, waving a hand to indicate the breadth of the floor laid out below him. Diamond studs twinkled at his cuffs as his arm moved, no doubt very real and very expensive.

I nodded, unsure where this was heading.

"Have a seat," JP said and motioned to the chair opposite his desk. "Now, this new product of yours," he began, sitting down in the large black leather chair behind his desk.

I felt my stomach go into free fall. *Had something gone wrong? It couldn't have. We tested everything. Just how much money had we lost?*

"Well, of course I can't take all the credit..." I began as I perched on the edge of the chair; time to start damage control.

JP waved his hand to silence me. "Well, from what the trading teams tell me, it was the best product launch they have had. Apparently, you pitched it perfectly, so everyone understood how to price and hedge it, so much so that we have won the GSK Pharmaceutical derivatives business from Goldman's. A big coup, which will open the door for the investment bankers to do further work with them." I tensed waiting for the other shoe to drop. JP was not known for praise without a backhand. He stood, holding out his hand to me. "So well done and keep up the good work. You can pass that on to your team too." I was being dismissed.

Hardly daring to breathe, I shook his hand. "Thank you."

Once again, I had to tell myself not to run back across the trading floor.

Back at the lifts, Will was pacing. He turned as the door swished open and I burst through. "Well?"

I broke into a grin. "He wanted to congratulate us on a fantastic product launch. Apparently, the traders have successfully used it to win some business from Goldman's and he's holding us partly responsible."

Will grabbed my hands and together we began jumping up and down like a couple of ten-year-olds, complete with stupid grins on our faces. It was only the sound of a lift arriving that broke us apart. Will scooped up my coat and bag from a chair on the landing and handed them to me. Together we got into the lift down to our floor, still grinning like idiots.

As we descended, I turned to look at him. "Thanks for covering for me with JP. I owe you."

He smiled. "Anytime, Jess. I've got your back."

As the doors opened on our floor, Will leaned over and said in a low voice, "And you didn't need to worry about how you look, you are stunning in that dress." He brushed past me and out of the lift. I stood there open-mouthed as the doors began closing on me. I felt a blush rising from my toes to the top of my head and a strange feeling settling in my stomach. I jumped out before the doors closed to be greeted by some of my colleagues, eager to know what JP had wanted.

"Oh you know, he's cost cutting. He wanted me to suggest which one of you should be let go," I replied.

Jimmy followed me to my desk. "Seriously, Jess. You don't get tracked down by JP unless there is a big problem." Over his shoulder I could see Andrew grinning.

"What did you know about this, Andrew?" I called over to him, ignoring Jimmy.

"I told him that you should hear it from the boss himself," he replied.

"Thank you," I said smiling at him. I turned back to Jimmy. "JP was really happy with the new product launch. It has gained us some market share in the Pharmac industry already."

Jimmy looked pleased for me. "That's cool, Jess. You should know that Will really covered your arse with JP this morning."

"Thanks, Jim. I know, I owe him big time," I acknowledged.

Chapter 4

I had just walked up the four flights of stairs to our flat and unlocked the door later that evening when my mobile rang. We had moved into the light and sunny top floor apartment in a red-brick Victorian block near the King's Road in the summer. I dumped my bag on the narrow hall table just inside the door and retrieved my phone. A photo of Colin's face taken at our wedding six years earlier lit up the screen as the incoming call icon flashed.

"Hi, how much longer are you going to be?" I asked. "I have something to celebrate."

"I'm going to be late. We've had some trouble," he said.

"What's happened?" I asked as concern from the tone of his voice knotted my stomach.

"We've had a break-in. I need to check that everything is secure." He sounded distant.

"Be careful, won't you. It's still not a great area, you might have to up your security," I said.

There was a pause as Colin said something to someone in the background.

"Don't wait up." He hung up without saying goodbye.

* * *

I was dozing on the couch around 11:30 pm when I heard Colin's key turn in the lock. I stood, stretched and walked into the little reception area to greet him.

"I told you not to wait up," he said running his hand through his wavy hair. It was more auburn than ginger and over recent months I'd noticed the first signs of grey at his temples. He had the type of skin that never tanned and his tidy beard had a definite Gallic tone.

"S'okay," I said and then gasped as I took in his disheveled appearance. "Colin, what happened?"

His left eye was puffy and almost closed over and dried blood was smeared around the backs of his hands.

"It's worse than it looks." He brushed past me into the kitchen.

"Seriously?"

"It's fine, Jess. Don't fuss," he replied.

"At least let me clean you up. What happened? I thought you said it was just a break-in?" I said following him, pulling a packet of frozen peas from the freezer and handing them over, indicating that he should put them on his eye.

"It was a break-in. I almost had the guy too, but he got away." He winced as he applied the icy bag to his eye.

I poured some warm water into a bowl and added a few drops of antiseptic and using a clean cloth, began dabbing at the knuckles on his right hand. It must have stung, but he was stoic and sat still at the tiny kitchen table beside the window letting me work. I patted his hand dry with a clean cloth and applied first aid cream and band aids to the deeper cuts.

"Thanks. Florence." He stood, pulling himself to his full six feet four inches in height and strode from the room. Several seconds later, I heard him talking on the phone in the study. I tidied up the kitchen and switching the light off, stood in the doorway of the study waiting for him to finish.

"Who do you think it was? Just local kids?" I asked.

"No. The guy I almost caught appeared to be older. Well-dressed. Professional. No. I'm thinking corporate espionage. I'm in the running for a large new contract and I think someone is trying to undercut me," he replied.

"Colin, that's awful. Have you contacted the police?"

"Already being taken care of."

"When can I come and visit, I'm dying to see the new warehouse?" I asked.

Colin shook his head. "Not yet, the renovation work isn't finished."

"Well, on a happier note, I had a major success at work today," I said.

"Really? Did your balance sheet balance?" he said without looking up.

"Ha, ha. No, remember that new product that I've been working on with Will, the new guy?" Colin looked up with a blank expression. "Well, it's been a huge success and we've won some important business because of it," I continued, but not before I noticed the slight change in his expression.

"So what do you get out of it?" he asked.

"I got called to the Head of Trading's office and congratu-lated," I said with a grin.

Colin looked incredulous. "I wouldn't call a pat on your head a *major* success," he said emphasizing the word major with sarcasm.

"Well it will reflect in my bonus later in the year," I added, his taunt stinging.

Colin waved his hand dismissing me. "We'll see, they'll have forgotten by then."

"Don't be mean," I said pushing off the door frame and turning away as tears smarted in my eyes. "Why can't you be happy for me, for once?"

"I'm just being honest. Would you rather I lie?" Colin asked.

I shrugged and began walking away.

"Hey, Jess," he called after me. "Were you in the study earlier?"

I paused and turned back toward him. "Yeah, just paying a couple of bills and filing some paperwork."

Colin studied me. "I hope you weren't snooping in my stuff."

"Snooping?"

"I brought home some sensitive commercial documents to review and they've been moved."

I rolled my eyes at him. "I didn't touch your stuff. Besides, I'm your wife. It wouldn't matter if I did."

"Just don't, alright." He held my gaze for a moment before pushing past me and walking down the hall into the bedroom.

I watched his retreating figure and shook my head wondering what had possessed him.

Chapter 5

October 26

After-work drinks were in full swing at The Tower, the tiny two-roomed pub on the corner opposite the bank that was our team's regular haunt. Whilst a number of modern wine bars had sprung up in the area, The Tower had clung firmly to its historic roots, right down to its ancient wooden bar and cozy corner tables.

"It's still not as busy as it used to be," Rachel said looking around. "Bloody terrorists."

"It's what they want, isn't it?" Dave said. "To disrupt our way of life, make us scared."

"I think Londoners are a pretty resilient bunch," I said. "I read last week that theatre numbers are back up and it's getting harder to get tables at the best restaurants again."

"Good, we can't let them win," Dave agreed.

A little while later, Jimmy was regaling us with a tale of drunken debauchery following the New Zealand Rugby team, the All Blacks', win over England, the previous weekend when I felt a hand on my shoulder. I looked up and Colin was standing beside me.

"Hi. This is a surprise," I said. Colin never, I mean never, joined me for after work drinks. I had long since stopped inviting him. He kissed my cheek and removed his jacket, tossing it over a nearby chair. The conversation lulled as my colleagues eyed Colin as though some exotic creature had been catapulted into our midst.

"I think you know everyone," I trailed off. Dave came to my rescue, shaking Colin's hand. "How are ya, mate? I'd hate to see the other guy," he said peering at Colin's face.

Marie and Rachel murmured "Hi." Jimmy leaned across and shook Colin's hand. But Colin's attention was directed at Will.

"I don't think we've met," he said.

"Will." William introduced himself.

"Nasty cut," Colin commented looking at the back of Will's hand.

"Yeah, that's what you get for fighting with a window, they always win." Will laughed. Colin studied him unsmiling.

I stood dumbstruck, knowing I should offer to get Colin a beer, but also not wanting to miss what felt like an impending train wreck. Colin was in one of his moods, I could just sense it. What was he doing here?

"A beer would nice, Jess," he said.

"Sure, sorry," I murmured, turning and pushing my way through the crowd to the bar. It wasn't until I got there that I realized that I hadn't offered to get anyone else a drink. *Shit*. He had thrown me, turning up like this. Luckily Marie arrived at my side a moment later with everyone's order.

"You okay, you've gone very pale?" she asked.

"Yeah, fine," I replied, forcing a smile.

"Sure? Unusual for Colin to turn up," she said.

"Isn't it just," I said. My heart was racing. "Can you go back to the others? I hate to think what he's saying in my absence. Y'know he can come across badly at times."

"Sure, Jess." She gave me a sympathetic look and slipped back through the crowd.

I sighed as I waited to be served. Colin could especially be an arse in a group where he wasn't comfortable and given his attitude towards those 'wanker bankers that you work with', I just knew that this wouldn't be his finest moment. I shook my head and admonished myself no sooner had the thought formed. I shouldn't be thinking those kinds of thoughts about my husband. I should be glad that he was here. It was just that I had worked so hard to build my own identity at work, separate from the Mrs. Colin McDonald that the rest of the world seemed to only see me as, and I liked that person better. I didn't want her undermined.

I carried the drinks back to our group. They were laughing as I arrived.

Colin took his beer from me without thanks. "I was just telling them what a disaster you are in the kitchen." He laughed.

I bristled. "I wouldn't say I'm that bad."

"What about the half-cooked birthday cake or that dreadful roast dinner?" He raised his eyebrows at me.

I looked at him for a moment willing him to stop whatever he thought he was doing. Out of the corner of my eye, I saw an unspecified emotion pass across Will's face and a look of thunder take residence on Marie's. So I did all I could think to do and laughed at myself. "Ah, you got me there." I couldn't explain that the oven was playing up when I made the birthday cake, we got a new one shortly after, and the roast was burnt because he was at the golf club for three hours longer than he said he would be and I fell asleep on the sofa waiting for him.

"So you Englishmen have shot yourselves in the foot voting to leave the EU," Colin said, turning to Will as Andrew joined us. "From what I hear the banking sector will be the first to relocate to Frankfurt. You'll all be speaking German before you know it."

"Yeah, I still can't believe the outcome," Andrew said. "That's democracy at work, I suppose."

"I wouldn't say that," Colin said. "Scotland overwhelmingly voted to stay in the EU, yet we're going to be dragged into this mess with you lot."

"It was a whole country vote," Andrew added.

"Was it though? The sooner Scotland breaks away and saves itself, the better."

I spent the next half hour on edge, my evening ruined. Once Colin got into a nationalism debate there was no distracting him. I had spent many an evening at various pubs in Edinburgh while at university listening to him debate the merits of independence from England.

"Jess, who does your dad work for?" Colin asked during a lull in the conversation a little while later.

I looked at him puzzled. "He's a partner in his law firm, you know that."

"What I meant was who are his clients? Does he work for the government or private sector?"

"I don't really know to be honest," I said. "I think mainly corporates, but I can ask him. Why?"

I noticed that Will had ceased his conversation with Jimmy and was listening with undisguised interest.

"Nothing. Just a couple of mates going into business who

need some legal advice," Colin replied.

"Point them his way. I'm sure he can find someone to help if he isn't the right person."

Colin drained his beer. "Okay, let's go, Jess. I have an early meeting tomorrow." I still had half a gin and tonic in my hand. Colin pulled his jacket on and turned towards the door. I sighed and looked around for somewhere to leave my drink.

"I don't think Jess has finished," Will said in a quiet voice.

Colin went very still and turned to look at Will, head cocked, as though sizing him up. Colin was a big guy, broad as well as tall, but Will had a similar physique. After several seconds Colin shifted his gaze to me. "Hurry up then."

"I'm done," I said placing my glass on an adjacent table and gathering my things. "See you all tomorrow."

Colin put his arm around me and ushered me out onto the street. As soon as we were outside, I turned on him.

"What was that all about?"

"What?" he replied.

"Putting me down like that in front of everyone."

"Oh, Jess, stop being so sensitive. I was having a joke, for God's sake, trying to fit in with your banking mates."

"At my expense," I replied.

"Whatever. I'm sorry that I bothered to come. I see you're still hanging out with that loud-mouthed Kiwi," he added. "And who's the English guy think he is? I don't like him."

We travelled home in silence.

* * *

I arrived home to an empty house early the next evening. Colin had left me a scribbled note on the kitchen table.

'Gone to Dubai re new contract. Be two or three days.'

I was a little ashamed to find that I was relieved. I was still hurt from his comments over the previous few days and all I wanted was a long soak in a hot bath and an evening to myself.

I was up to my neck in raspberry scented bubbles when the phone rang. Fortunately I had taken it into the bathroom with me, so grabbing a hand towel off the rail next to the bath, I dried one hand, and answered it.

A hysterical woman half screamed, half sobbed at me down the line.

"Hold on. Calm down. Who is this?"

"Mmmmuumm," the voice answered sobbing.

My stomach plummeted. My mother was the world's worst drama queen, but this was extreme even for her.

"Mum, deep breath. What's wrong?"

"You need to come. It's your dad," she managed to say.

"What about Dad? Put him on,' I suggested.

"Can't. He's d-dead," she whispered followed by uncontrollable sobbing.

Knowing I would get no more out of her I clicked 'end' on the handset and leapt from the bath. I dried myself, dressed and packed a weekend bag in record time. I called the car service we used for work and ordered a car to take me to Heathrow. Only then did I dial Mum and Dad's number.

One of my aunts answered.

"What's going on? Is Dad really dead? What's happened?"

"Oh, Jessie. He is, lovey. Heart attack," she answered with a heavy sigh.

"Oh God, no. I'm on my way," I replied.

I hung up the phone as the room spun. Dad couldn't be dead. I had only talked to him on the phone the previous afternoon. In fact, we'd made plans to go to see a play in the West End when he was down on business in a couple of weeks. I realized with a start that I'd been supposed to organize the tickets today, but I had been busy and I'd forgotten.

I slid down the wall in the hallway and sat on the floor, waiting for my driver to buzz the intercom. I felt like crying, but the tears wouldn't come. I grabbed my mobile and called Colin. His phone went straight to voicemail. He was probably still in the air. I hung up. It wasn't the sort of news that you left a voice message about. I really needed him, so I phoned back and left a voicemail for him to call me as soon as he got my message.

Twenty minutes later, I was in a car on the way to Heathrow.

"Business trip, love?" the driver, a portly middle-aged man, enquired.

"No… my dad has just died," I replied in a flat voice.

I stared unseeing out of the window as we wound our way through the London traffic.

Chapter 6

October 27

I managed to get a standby ticket on the next flight to Edinburgh, and so two hours later I found myself standing at Mum and Dad's house, not wanting to go in, but knowing that sooner or later I would have to. The porch light shining above the red front door of the two-storied grey brick semi was usually a warming, welcoming sight, but not tonight. I knocked. I'm not sure why. I usually just walked straight in. It was still my family home, after all. My aunt Doreen, Dad's sister, opened the door, red-eyed. She enveloped me in a smothering hug as she dragged me across the doorstep.

"Eileen," she called. "Jessica's here." At which point my mother sobbed and crumpled to the floor.

Colin called at midnight, once I'd managed to shoo most of the mourners out the door and back to their own homes. I looked at Dad's liquor cabinet. I would have to restock it tomorrow. Some people; a wake was just an excuse to get drunk. I had tucked Mum into bed an hour earlier with a sleeping tablet after she had become hysterical again.

Colin was of course shocked to hear about Dad.

"I'm so sorry," he said. "What happened?"

"He had a heart attack at work. His assistant found him slumped over his desk during the afternoon. Of course, none of them knew how to do CPR, so they all just stood around, watching him die, until the ambulance arrived," I said.

"I'm sure it wouldn't have been like that at all," Colin said in a soothing tone.

"I need you. When can you get here?" I asked, the words catching in my throat.

"Oh, Jess," he said. "I should be able to get away tomorrow night. When's the funeral?"

"Well that's just it," I said. "I have to organize it. Mum's gone completely to pieces. I'm meeting the minister in the morning."

"Okay, darling. Let's talk after that. I'm so sorry," Colin said.

"I wish you were here," I replied.

I didn't sleep much that night and the next day was a whirl of visitors and funeral planning. Once we returned from the undertaker, Mum took to her bed, and did her entertaining from there, like some bloody duchess. Of course, I had to redo her hair and makeup before anyone was allowed up the stairs.

My cousin Lucas arrived in the afternoon and offered to help, so I dispatched him to the liquor store with a list. I knew there would be another round of mourners that night.

I finally got to talk to Colin at four in the afternoon.

"Hey, love, how's it all going?" he asked.

"Madness. What time is your flight?"

"Well, that's the thing," he hedged. "Negotiations here are

on a knife edge and I have a series of meetings tomorrow and Friday."

I shook my head; not comprehending what he was saying. "Didn't you tell them that your father-in-law has just died?"

"Yes, but you sound like you have it all under control and I should be able to make it for the funeral on Saturday," he said.

"Who said anything about the funeral being on Saturday?"

"Well, I assumed…"

"Well, you assumed wrong. It's on Friday. You'll just have to postpone the negotiation."

"Calm down, Jess. I know you've had a shock and all, but it's not that simple."

I hung up and didn't answer any of his calls for the rest of the day.

The next morning, an enormous bouquet of flowers arrived for me and one for Mum, both from Colin. Aunt Doreen rescued mine from the rubbish bin in the kitchen.

I called the minister to see if there was any chance of moving the funeral to Saturday, but the church was fully booked with weddings, so we would have to go ahead on Friday or wait another week. I took a deep breath and phoned Colin.

"Did you get the flowers?" he asked, as if that would bring Dad back.

"Yes. Now when are you coming?" I asked, not quite ready to forgive.

"Sunday morning, Jess. I can't get away any sooner. I'm really sorry." He sounded contrite.

"Colin, it's my dad." My voice cracked.

"I know, Jess, and he would understand."

I had to give him that. Dad was a workaholic too.

"This negotiation is critical for the future of the company, our future," he continued.

Hell, how can you argue with the future? I took a deep breath and knew that I would have to just deal with this on my own. Grieve later.

"Okay, I will see you at home on Sunday night. Don't bother coming here. I have to be back for work next week," I replied.

"Jessie, I'm sorry. I'll make this up to you," he said before hanging up.

* * *

The funeral service passed in a daze. Mum, of course, wailed throughout, but to my perverse delight the old stone church was packed. Dad was really well thought of in the community and highly respected in his profession. I walked, or should I say, half carried Mum behind the coffin out of the church to the waiting hearse. As we passed the last pew, I did a double take. Will was sitting there. He gave me a gentle smile. Beside him, Marie was sobbing and dabbing her eyes with a tissue.

The tightness in my chest eased a tiny bit. After I helped Mum into the waiting car, I sought them out in the crowd of mourners, who were being shepherded into the church hall by Aunt Doreen.

"Thanks for coming," I said pulling my sunglasses off my head and covering my eyes, which I knew were puffy and red from lack of sleep.

"Of course, Jess," Will replied squeezing my arm. "We're so sorry for your loss."

Marie threw her arms around me and hugged me tight.

"Hey, I have to go. Cemetery and all that. Will you be here later? When's your flight back?" I asked.

"Tomorrow or Sunday, whatever you need," Will replied.

"Good. I need someone to get drunk with," I said.

"Unfortunately, I have to go back shortly, it's my grandmother's eightieth birthday tomorrow. I'd love to stay and keep you company. I'm sorry," Marie apologized.

"It's okay. Thank you so much for coming," I replied, hugging her again.

Will's eyes scanned the crowd. "Where's Colin?" he asked, as the funeral director tapped me on the shoulder and nodded towards the cars.

"Dubai," I said.

"What?" The look on Will's face was one of disbelief. He and Marie exchanged glances.

* * *

I arrived back from the cemetery to find the wake in full swing. Lucas and Will were behind a makeshift bar in the church hall acting as unofficial barmen. Two of my middle-aged aunts were propped up against it, flirting with them. It was the first time I had smiled in what seemed like days. Will caught my eye as I walked over to them. I could feel a bubble of really inappropriate hysterical laughter rising in my throat.

"A quick whiskey, barman," I asked. Lucas obliged and I knocked it back in one go. It hit the spot burning its way down into my stomach and somehow settling the hysteria. I let out a deep sigh.

"How are you?" Will came out from behind the bar and enveloped me in a hug. "Everyone has been saying how amazing you have been. That you singlehandedly organized everything because your mum was so distraught."

"I'm exhausted," I said, leaning into him. "I think we should pack up here and head back to Mum and Dad's with the stragglers."

"Okay, close the bar," Will announced to Lucas and together we began moving glasses, tea cups and plates to the kitchen at the back of the hall.

Will loaded up the dishwasher as I did the rounds, accepting condolences and listening to little anecdotes about Dad. I kept looking around the hall for him. It just didn't seem right that he wasn't here with all of his family and friends.

With the help of a couple of difficult to locate, sober drivers and several taxis, the more dedicated mourners made their way back to the house to polish off the remains of Dad's restocked liquor cabinet.

"Bloody hell." Will leaned back against the front door as we waved off the last of what can only be described as the revelers, several hours later. "Your parents' family and friends sure know how to drink."

I look at him wide-eyed for a moment before giggling at the inappropriateness of both the drinkers and his statement.

"Jessica?" my mother called in a pathetic voice from the front room. I took a deep breath and went to her.

"Do you want me to help you up to bed, Mum?" I offered.

"Yes please, dear. And one of those little pills you gave me last night would help steady my nerves," she said in a sad, pleading voice.

"Okay, Mum. Come on," I said helping her up from her

chair and propelling her towards the stairs.

"Oh, Jessie. He's really gone, hasn't he?" She stared at me, a look of horror taking residence on her face as though the reality of his death had just hit her again.

"He has, Mum. It's just awful." I pulled her into my arms and we clung to one another.

After I had her tucked up in bed, I returned downstairs to find Will in the front room going through Dad's CD collection, selecting some music to play.

"Fancy a nightcap?" I asked, from the doorway. Without waiting for his reply, I detoured into the kitchen to retrieve a particularly good bottle of red that someone had arrived with earlier, which I had hidden.

I pulled the cork and poured a big glass each. We collapsed onto the sofa, the long day catching up on us both, and sat in companionable silence listening to vintage Simple Minds. After a while, I realized that I was leaning against his shoulder and he was absentmindedly playing with a lock of my hair. I straightened up and moved to the opposite end of the couch, where I sat cross-legged looking at him.

"Do you want to talk about your dad, Jess?" he asked. "He sounds like a hell of guy from all the stories that I heard today."

"He was the best, Will. He always supported me so much. In fact it was he who encouraged me academically. He was delighted when my penchant for numbers had become apparent. I was good at it and I enjoyed the sense of satisfaction from using mathematical concepts to solve problems," I said.

"I know what you mean," Will agreed. "The rules and the fact that there is always a solution."

I nodded. "Pity life isn't as straightforward."

"What about your mother?"

"She's completely different. I think that she had somehow missed the wave of feminism. She was working in the typing pool of a law firm in Edinburgh when she met Dad who was a fresh-faced, newly qualified solicitor. As soon as they married, she stopped working and played house until I came along. I asked her once, if there wasn't something else that she wanted to do with her life and she looked at me like I was mad. "Why? I have everything that I ever wanted right here," she told me."

Will smiled and we were silent for a moment.

"I can't quite grasp that he's gone, even though we've just had his funeral and buried him." I paused. "I loved him so much, but I just can't seem to shed more than the odd tear."

"It's because you've had to take charge and organize everything. It hasn't hit you yet. You probably won't start to grieve until you get back to London and stop rushing around," he said.

I knew he was right, but that didn't make it any easier. I felt like I was letting my father down somehow by not crying over him as my mother spent the last few days doing.

"When did you become so wise?" I asked.

"Just call me Obi Wan Kenobi," he said in a serious voice.

"I always think of you as looking more like Yoda." Lame joke, but it was all I had.

Will feigned hurt at the comment, which made me smile.

"How is your mum going to cope, Jess? Is she always like this?" he asked after a moment.

"What? A drama queen? Yeah, she is. I don't know how she'll cope. At least he will have left everything set up for her financially, so she won't have to worry." The thought crossed my mind that sometimes lawyers were the last to tidy their own affairs. I prayed Dad wasn't one of those.

It had been an inspired decision on my part to stash the wine, it was very good. We talked and drank. Well, I talked, and Will listened until the wee hours. I think we went through Dad's entire Simple Minds, Beatles and Rolling Stones collection.

"Can I ask why Colin isn't here, Jess?" Will asked at one point.

"The company's need was greater than mine," I replied in a small sad voice.

A dark look crossed Will's face.

I jumped up and topped up our glasses.

* * *

I woke to find myself cocooned by a strong male body. I froze as I realized that Will and I had fallen asleep on the couch. I looked over at the clock on the mantelpiece. 6:30 am. Oh shit. Will was sleeping like a baby, so I extricated myself so as not to wake him and sat up. My head was pounding. God, why did polishing off that bottle of wine seem like such a good idea last night?

I grabbed a woolen throw that was draped over the back of one of the armchairs and laid it over Will before tiptoeing from the room. I crept up the stairs avoiding the center tread of steps three, six and eight, which I knew from experience as a teenager sneaking in after curfew creaked horribly. I went into the bathroom, swigged down a couple of paracetamol and then crawled into my own bed.

A knock on my door awakened me a little later. I sat up rubbing my eyes and Will walked in carrying a mug of tea.

"Hey, sleepyhead. I thought you might need this," he smiled setting the cup down on my bedside table. "How's your head?"

"Pounding. There's paracetamol in the bathroom if you need some," I replied.

"No. I'm okay," he smiled sitting down on the edge of my bed. "What time did you come to bed?"

"Six-thirty, what is it now?"

"It's nine. Do you mean you slept on the couch with me until then?"

"Sshhh…" I put my fingers to my lips and pointed down the hall towards Mum's room.

"It's okay, I've been downstairs having breakfast with her," he replied.

"Look, I think I unloaded on you last night. I was a bit drunk, so can I plead extenuating circumstances and have you just ignore everything I said?" I begged.

Will got a wicked look in his eye. "Do I have to? You are really quite entertaining when you're drunk."

I held my hands over my face. "Enough. Please just ignore me." I was mortified. "Now shoo. I need to get up and find where I left my self-respect," I said, chasing him from the bedroom.

His laughter followed him back down the stairs.

Chapter 7

November 20

The next few weeks flew past in a rush. Not only was work busy, but I was flying up to Edinburgh each weekend to help Mum sort through Dad's things, although really it was to keep her company as much as anything. As I hoped, he had left everything well set up for her, but she was struggling to get going again.

A couple of weekends after Dad died, I answered a knock at Mum's door. It was one of Dad's business partners, a thin man with a kind face and a booming laugh.

"Mr. Rawlings," I said, opening the door wide.

"Jess, how are you doing?" he asked.

"Still getting over the shock, to be honest. I keep expecting him to just walk in the door. Would you like to come in?" I asked.

"Another time, Jess, but I wanted to drop this around." He passed the cardboard file box he was holding across to me. "We've had a clear out of your dad's office. These are most of his personal things. Emily, his assistant, will drop around anything else."

"Thank you, I guess life goes on, doesn't it," I said.

Mr. Rawlings reached out and gave my shoulder a squeeze. "I'm so sorry, Jess. There's a letter in there, addressed to you, which we found locked in his desk drawer."

"Oh, thank you."

He gave a tight smile and said goodbye. I watched him walk down the little path and through the wrought iron front gate before I closed the door.

I took the box straight into Dad's study and sat it on the large mahogany desk. The room still had his smell, a mixture of the cologne he wore and something else that was just Dad. This was his favorite room. Book-lined with a large armchair and lamp in one corner and his desk with two guest chairs in front of the window. It was just as Dad had left it. Organized and tidy. A yellow legal pad front and center on the desk, with two Mont Blanc pens resting at the top, a framed photograph of the three of us taken at my university graduation ceremony, a stylish desk lamp and a working replica dial telephone that had been a birthday gift from me one year.

I began emptying the box. Another family photograph, a small engraved desk clock, two large bound law books, several framed certificates and at the bottom an envelope addressed to me. I lifted it out and turned it over in my hands. The words 'check, Nancy' were written on the back. I smiled as tears filled in my eyes and a lump formed in my chest. Dad was referring to my childhood love of mystery novels, anything written by Enid Blyton, the Nancy Drew books, and so on. He and I had spent one summer communicating through coded messages, simple alpha numeric codes, but surprisingly effective. Mum would find notes written in code around the house and shake her head at us, as though we were crazy.

As I examined the envelope in my hand, I noticed a single silvery strand of hair caught under the tape which sealed the flap. I flicked on the desk lamp and held it under the light; it was intact. The envelope hadn't been opened since Dad had sealed it.

I sat down in his big leather chair and pulled his letter opener from the drawer, sliced the envelope open and drew out a handwritten letter. Something dropped from the envelope, bounced off my lap and fell to the floor. I bent and picked it up; a small silver key.

I slipped it into my pocket as I sat back and read the letter.

Jessica, my dArling girl.

Hopefully, you will never have to read this. If you do, then something has happened to me. I aM so sorry. I have been trying to protect you, but there are some things that you need to know.

The key is for a safety depoSit box—I'll leave it up to you to woRk out where in case anyone else should read this letter—I'm sure you will have determined if that's been the case, by now, my cleveR girl!

Things are not what they seem. Be careful who you trust—everyone has secrets, particularly those closest to you. I don't have all the answers so I'm passing my Quest on to you.

I love you always. Look after your mother.

Dad xx

I sat back, my father's letter folded once again in my hands and tears pouring down my cheeks.

Be careful who you trust, what did he mean by that? A

sudden coldness came over me. Dad must have thought his life was in danger, otherwise he wouldn't have written this. Holy shit. Was he murdered?

I felt nauseous. No. This was crazy. Wasn't it? I wiped my face and opened the top right-hand drawer of the desk and lifted out his business card file and flicked through until I found the card of our family GP, one of Dad's oldest friends. His personal mobile number was handwritten on the back. Taking my mobile from the back pocket of my jeans, I keyed in the number. Dr. Sorrenson answered after three rings. Upon hearing my name, he sighed.

"Ah, Jessica. I am so sorry for your loss. I didn't get to talk to you at the funeral. Your father was a fine, fine man."

"Thank you, Doc. Had you seen him recently? Was he in good health?" I asked.

There was a pause and the sound of keys being tapped on a keyboard. "Yes, I saw him two months ago. Fit as a fiddle. Perhaps a little more exercise and a little less whiskey, but nothing to worry about. Let's look here." Dr. Sorrenson was reading his notes off a computer screen. "Blood work all good."

"So he wasn't a prime candidate for a heart attack, then?" I asked.

"No. I certainly wouldn't have classified him as anywhere near high risk."

"Mmm…" I said, my mind moving at speed. "And because it seemed natural, there was no autopsy, was there?"

"Jessica, it's normal in these situations to look for answers where there perhaps aren't any. It's not unusual for seemingly healthy people of a certain age to suddenly take ill," Dr. Sorrenson began in gentle tones.

"Look, I know all that," I interrupted, "but he left me a letter, written recently, in the event of his untimely death." My voice caught on the last word. "He thought his life might be in danger."

There was silence on the line. "What do his colleagues say, Jess?" Dr. Sorrenson asked.

"You are the first person I have mentioned this to," I replied.

"Leave it with me, Jess. I will see what I can find out. I do know that the doctor who pronounced his death is out of the country for a few weeks, but I'll catch up with him for coffee when he returns. I'll let you know what he says."

I thanked him and tapped end on the call, pushing the chair back from Dad's desk. The key in my pocket dug into me and I fished it out, holding it up to the light. Safety deposit box, but where? I turned it over in my hands. Something tugged at my memory, but it wouldn't come. I pocketed it again as my mother called from the kitchen.

I knew that Mum had been itching to say something to me all weekend, but it wasn't until we sat at the counter having a cup of tea, that she came out with it.

"Everything alright with you and Colin?" she asked.

I was surprised. "Sure, why do you ask?"

"Well, you've been here the last three weekends in a row without him and he hasn't called you once," she replied.

My immediate response was to defend him, but I hesitated. "I don't know, Mum," I replied. It was something that had occurred to me also, but I had dismissed it as silly. He was really busy and would have spent each weekend that I was away, with his head down, working. But hearing someone else mention it, I allowed myself to give it some airplay. "We do seem to be drifting a bit, but I guess that's only natural."

"When was the last time you went away together, just the two of you?" she asked.

I paused. I had been to Spain for a week earlier in the year with Rachel and Marie. I'd had several business trips to New York, which I'd extended slightly to spend some time with a university friend who lived there, but Colin and I hadn't even had a weekend away. "Probably last Christmas, when we came here for a few days."

Mum frowned. "You have to work at being married, Jess. It doesn't just happen. You have to plan things together, do things together."

I nodded as a lump formed in my throat. The thought of a week away on holiday with Colin no longer excited me like it used to. I'd really rather have another trip abroad with the girls. Did that mean we were in trouble?

"Are you still having sex?" Mum asked.

"Okay, this conversation is over," I said, standing and putting my cup in the sink and beating a hasty retreat. There was no way I was discussing my sex life with my mother. *Ew.* Although, a nagging little voice at the back of my head told me that it had been many weeks.

* * *

I searched every inch of Dad's study for a clue to where the safety deposit box might be. Perhaps the clue was in his office at the law firm. But no sooner did I have the thought, than I dismissed it. His office had been cleared out. Someone else was in there now. The idea left a bitter taste. How quickly

56

life just moves on, even when a larger than life figure, such as my father, leaves it.

It wasn't until Sunday morning, as I was leaving church with my mother, that it came to me.

I had stopped at the door, waiting to shake hands with the minister, when I spied the offering box on its carved wooden pedestal, standing behind the back pew, as if tempting us to deposit a further cash donation before leaving the church. The box had a shiny key hole in the side. A sudden thought hit me as I studied it. Dad would have already left me the clue to the whereabouts of the safety deposit box, I had just missed it.

I tore up the stairs to my old room when we got back to the house and pulled his letter from the bottom of my overnight bag. I opened it again and this time found what I was looking for. How did I not see that earlier?

Scattered throughout the handwritten text were capital letters in the middle of sentences where they shouldn't be and in the top right hand corner of the letter, was the code breaker, A3. I grabbed a piece of paper and copied the capital letters in the order that they appeared in the text of the letter: A M S R R Q. I could crack the code in my head. A3 meant move the letter A to the third letter of the alphabet. Dad and I had used a far more complex system of codes to send each other messages in the past. Either he was in a hurry when he wrote this one or he wanted to make certain that I would remember how to translate it. So, A=C, M=O, S=U, R=T and Q=S.

COUTTS

The safety deposit box was at Coutts Bank.

Chapter 8

November 22

Coutts Bank is located on The Strand. From the moment you are ushered through the glass doors by the dapper doorman, you enter a world of quiet prosperity. Soft carpet underfoot, plants with shiny green leaves, muted lighting. The paintings adorning the beige walls looked like the real deal.

I had telephoned earlier and booked an appointment to view the safety deposit box, so all I had to do was show the receptionist my identification and provide the box number. On the plane back to London, I had studied Dad's letter further and realized that the date written in its DD/MM/YY format actually made no sense. 45/23/72 had to be the box number. I wasn't turning out to be the smart code breaker that Dad assumed me to be.

A door opened and a stylish woman around my age emerged to take me to a bank of elevators. We travelled to the eighth floor where she deposited me in a small room with a desk and two chairs while she retrieved my box. The woman returned several minutes later carrying a black rectangular metal box.

It had two key holes.

"Now, your key please?" she asked. I produced it from my handbag and inserted it into the lock she indicated. She inserted a key of her own into the second lock and the lid of the box popped open. The woman stepped back.

"I will leave you. Just press the button here on the desk when you are finished or if you need anything," she said.

"Thank you," I replied.

I waited until she had closed the door behind her, before I reached to open the lid fully. A sudden thought occurred to me. Would there be cameras in this room? I glanced around. I couldn't see any. Why was I being paranoid?

I'm not entirely sure what I was expecting, but the stack of envelopes and papers were initially something of a letdown. I lifted the first envelope out and opened it. It contained a death certificate. It was for the accidental death of a woman by the name of Catriona Mackie on 30 May 1998. She was just twenty-three years old.

I frowned and put it to one side. I had never heard of her. Next in the box was a grainy photo of six teenage boys and an older guy wearing a cap, whose face was obscured by his hand holding a cigarette to his lips. The boys were dressed in fatigues, holding semi-automatic rifles and grinning for the camera. I turned the photo over; written in block capitals on the back were the words 'The Unit'. I put the photo to one side. The next envelope out of the box contained a birth certificate. Colin's. I frowned. This made no sense. Why would Dad go to such lengths to give this to me? I studied the document as a name jumped out. Colin's mother was listed as Catriona Mackie. The space for his father's name was left blank. I picked up the death certificate and made the connection. The dead woman was his birth mother.

I knew that Colin had been adopted. I did a quick calculation in my head. Catriona would only have been seventeen when she had him. I wondered if Colin even knew who his birth mother was or that she was dead? It was something we'd never discussed.

I picked up the photo again. One of the boys was looking up at the older man, saying something. I peered at it. It looked like a teenage Colin, the same side profile that I saw every day. I didn't recognize any of the other boys.

I wondered whether I should show this to Colin, but something made me hesitate. Surely Dad would have shown Colin the old photo when he was last in London a few weeks ago. Why hadn't he? I trusted my father's judgement. I would wait too.

The next two envelopes were something of a surprise. Each contained a stack of £20 notes, at a guess, £1,000 in each. I turned the envelopes over. Dad had written, *Emergency Fund*, on the outside. Weird.

The next bundle of papers was secured with a bulldog clip and had a handwritten page on legal paper attached. I recognized it as coming from the type of legal pad that Dad always kept on his desk in the study at home. I swallowed the lump that appeared in my throat and brushed a stray tear from my cheek as I noted Dad's small neat hand writing. I studied the page. At first, I thought it was a family tree, until I realized it contained the names of companies with solid lines linking them indicating ownership and dotted lines indicating money movement. It was like a labyrinth.

Two names jumped out, Loch Freight Logistics International Ltd and Labour For Hire Ltd, both Colin's companies.

What was going on here? What was Dad looking into Colin's businesses for?

Beneath the handwritten chart was a thick document. I scanned the front pages. It looked like a copy of a British government contract with a company called Mendelson.

I shook my head. None of this made any sense.

The final items in the box were three newspaper clippings from our student days with photos of Colin on the podium at several different Scottish Independence rallies with a number of other individuals including the current First Minister of Scotland.

I sat back, still unsure exactly what the 'quest' was that Dad had left me and why. He obviously had been looking into Colin's businesses along with a number of other associated companies and trusts at the time of his death, but what Colin's mother's death certificate, an old photo of Colin and news clippings had to do with anything, I wasn't sure.

I repacked the certificates, photo, newspaper clippings and cash back into the metal box, and closed the lid, locking it and removing my key. I slipped the documents into my bag to read later.

* * *

Colin came up to Edinburgh with me the following weekend and received a very cool welcome from Mum.

"How nice of you to finally come and pay your respects, son-in-law," she said when we walked in the door.

He leaned over and kissed her cheek before launching into

a grand apology.

"It was just as well that nice friend of Jessica's was able to come to the funeral. I don't know what we would have done without him," Mum said when he'd finished.

"Who was that?" Colin asked.

"Will and Marie came to the funeral," I said in a quiet voice.

"What? Will from your work?"

I nodded.

Colin frowned, but said nothing else about it until we were in the plane on the way home on Sunday night.

"God, that house is awful without your dad. I don't think I want to go there again," he said.

I looked at him in surprise. "How do you think it feels to me? You can't say that."

"Well it's true. Why did Will come? Did you invite him?" he said.

"No, you don't invite people to a funeral, Colin. I turned around at the end of the service and he and Marie were sitting there," I explained. "Mum was right though; he was a great help. Rolled his sleeves up and got on with it."

"I'm sure he did," muttered Colin. "I didn't realize that you knew him that well or did the bank send him as their representative?"

"No, we're good friends," I said.

Colin sat in silence for a while peering at his laptop screen as I flicked through the latest *Red* magazine that I'd picked up at the airport.

"Has he been to our flat?" he asked.

"Who?" I murmured, engrossed in an article.

"Will," Colin replied.

"No."

"Mmm... You will have to watch him. Single guy sniffing around you," Colin advised.

"Oh you are so gross sometimes. He's my friend. That's all," I responded, hating Colin in that moment, for making my friendship with Will sound so tawdry.

I looked across at him typing away on the keyboard of his laptop and considered again how little he involved me in anything that he did of late, business or otherwise. Perhaps he just didn't want to burden me with his work issues when I was grieving for Dad. But perhaps Mum was right. I looked at our life. We didn't plan anything together, we almost never went out together, just the two of us. If we did go out, it was usually with his mates. He was hardly at home; he only ate and slept there. I wondered if he had someone else, but there was no evidence of that.

I realized with a start that I actually didn't really care and that scared me more than anything. What I was feeling was anger; anger at Dad for dying and leaving me too soon and anger at Colin for not being there when I needed him the most. Colin looked up and caught me staring at him.

"What?"

"What are you working on?"

He closed the lid of his laptop. "Just work stuff. Why?"

"Just wondered. Anything I can help with?"

He shook his head. "No." His voice was sharp and his posture tense, as though he was ready to pounce.

"You'd tell me if anything was wrong," I added.

"Nothing is wrong, Jess."

I looked sideways at him. "Do you miss your student politics days?"

"That's an odd question," he said. "But yeah, I do. When

63

we move back to Scotland I will get involved in local politics again."

"I didn't realize that we were moving back to Scotland," I said, shaking my head in dismay.

"Of course, that was always the plan."

"Nice of you to mention it," I said. "But I don't want to leave London."

"Not yet, but you will when the time is right."

Chapter 9

November 24

Positano was a rustic Italian restaurant crowded with wooden tables covered in red and white checked tablecloths topped with tea lights flickering in glass jars. Framed photos of iconic Italian scenes covered the walls and classical music played in the background from wall mounted speakers. The waiter took our orders and returned with a glass of red wine each.

"How are you getting on?" Marie asked, her dark eyes, rimmed with kohl looked concerned.

I sighed. "Okay, I guess. Everything feels like hard work all of a sudden. I still can't believe that Dad's gone."

Marie reached across the table and gave my hand a squeeze. "It must be so hard."

"Yeah, especially as life just seems to carry on. There's still work to do at the bank and Colin is absorbed with his businesses, yet Dad's no longer with us," I said.

"I realized the other night that I don't know anything about how you and Colin got together," Marie said, removing the clip holding her mane of thick black hair in place and shaking it free.

"You mean, you wondered how I ended up with such an arse?" I said.

Marie blushed.

"He really is a very sweet guy, but he's just got a lot going on at the moment with expanding his business and he's very stressed."

Marie nodded and smiled. "So what's the scoop? How did he sweep you off your feet?"

"Not much to tell really, I was in my third year at Edinburgh University when our paths first crossed. Colin was the president of a student group supporting Scottish Independence. He was on the local TV news often as the media could always count on him for a juicy soundbite. The fact that he was a tall, good looking man, passionate about his country, didn't hurt either."

"The makings of a politician," Marie said.

"I was the opposite, just your average student. My wardrobe consisted of short colorful skirts with black tights, Doc Marten boots and a black duffle coat to ward out the bone chilling Edinburgh cold. Bits and pieces picked up from the vintage clothing stalls at the market," I explained.

"Oh God, I can just picture you." Marie laughed.

"For some reason, I attracted Colin's attention at an Independence rally. I'd had an unfortunate episode at a cheap student hairdresser that week and my hair was burgundy. Seriously, I was hard to miss. Anyway, Scottish Independence wasn't really something that I'd given much thought to, but my flat mates were going, so I went along. Colin, of course, had been asked to address the crowd. He was quite something," I said.

"I'm sure," Marie murmured.

"No really. Everything he said made perfect sense and he wound the crowd up into frenzy of righteous indignation with seeming ease. On one hand he sounded like one of us, Scottish, but at the same time his choice of words, phrases set him apart."

"Future leader in the making," Marie suggested.

"Something like that. Anyway, later that night I was on my second glass of cider at a party in a damp, cramped flat on George Street, when he wandered over and asked, 'do you think we made a difference today?' I didn't realize that he was talking to me until I looked behind me to find no one there. Of course, he found that hilarious and we ended up chatting for ages. As the party started winding down, I looked around for my friends, only to find that they had all left without me. Colin came to my rescue and walked me home."

"I bet he did." Marie laughed.

"My flat was only four blocks from the party and Colin continued to regale me with stories about the injustice of English control of Scottish economic interests. At my door he said goodnight and gave me a chaste kiss on the cheek. I was smitten, not only was this guy intelligent and interesting, he didn't expect me to sleep with him after I had only just met him."

"Smart move on his part," Marie said.

"Yeah," I agreed. "Good way to differentiate yourself from the other sleazy students. And that's it. We started seeing each other. It wasn't a hugely passionate beginning, more of a slow burn, but we very quickly blended into each other's lives and getting married when we'd both finished our degrees seemed like the logical next move. He'd been adopted as a baby and was keen to be part of a larger family."

Marie nodded. "So no fireworks then."

"There were enough," I replied. "Anyway, what about you? I imagine you have left a trail of broken hearts?"

Marie laughed again. "Oh yeah. Where to begin? Hey, I meant to ask you about Will getting that job on the trading floor."

"Yeah, I know. Good move for him. There was an opening for a new equities analyst," I said. "And, I've also got job news."

"Yeah?"

"I'm changing jobs too. I'm going to lead the new product analysts."

"What? The nerds on level three?"

"Not nerds. They're a bunch of extremely bright techy guys who spend their days inventing new cunning and devious ways for the bank to make money," I said. "My role will be coordinating the testing and installation components of any new product."

"That's great, Jess. You're ready for a new challenge."

"Yeah, I'm a little nervous about keeping up with the technical details—these guys are the rocket scientists after all," I admitted.

Marie laughed. "Yeah, but you're no slouch when it comes to understanding the math and the systems. Your biggest challenge is going to be selling the new ideas to the bunch of sceptics that sit on the trading floor."

"Oh God, I know. I'm well in over my head," I replied.

* * *

My phone rang just as I arrived back at my desk.

"I hear congratulations are in order."

"Thanks, Will. How's your new job going?"

"Good so far. Hey, I'm missing our coffee breaks, though. Do you want to have lunch instead?" he said.

"Good idea."

"Can you do Tuesdays?"

"Like each week?"

"Yeah, let's make it a regular thing," Will replied.

I smiled down the phone. "Sure."

* * *

"I'm glad you decided to come along tonight," Rachel shouted over the noise of the music as we leaned against the mezzanine railing at the club in Covent Garden, having a drink and watching people throwing themselves around the dancefloor below. "How are you getting on? How's your mum doing?"

I shrugged. "They say it's supposed to get easier, but I'm yet to experience that." I spied Marie in the center of the dancers, hands in the air, singing along to the DJ. She looked up and waved to us to join her.

"Come on," Rachel said, downing her drink in one swallow and grabbing my hand.

"My feet are too sore from dancing. You go," I said shaking my head.

"If you're sure." Rachel turned away, her short peroxide blonde hair bouncing as she skipped down the stairs to join Marie.

Will and Andrew had their heads together, deep in conversation, at one end of a nearby booth. Will caught my eye and gave me a grin. I ordered a large glass of water from the bar and leaned on the railing again looking down at the Jimmy and Dave dancing like men possessed with Rachel and Marie.

"Hey, you. Tired of dancing?"

I turned and smiled as Will joined me. "No, but my feet are."

Will ran his hand through his thick dark hair and gazed at me for a long moment. "Jess, I've been meaning to ask you about that night?" I frowned, trying to grasp which night he was referring to. "When Colin joined us at The Tower for a drink," he prompted.

"Yeah?"

"Is he, uh… always like that?" Will asked.

"Like what?" I made my voice as unemotional as I could.

"A bully," Will said.

I said nothing. I wasn't sure what to say. *Yes, he is often like that, but I'm used to it,* or *no,* and come across as defending him. Instead, I turned my attention back to the dance floor.

Will leaned closer to me. "Why do you let him do it? Jess, you deserve so much better."

I was shocked to find tears stinging my eyes. Will's words had an echo of something my dad had said to me before my wedding.

"I'm fine," I said, turning away and grabbing my bag from under the table. "This is none of your business."

Will stepped in my path. "Jess, don't run away," he said. "It's like you are a possession to him. You are talented, smart, gorgeous, beautiful actually, and he just doesn't seem to see it."

"Oh and you do," I blurted, without thinking.

Will looked at me for a long moment. "Yeah, I do."

My mouth dropped open. The others returned to the table, chattering and laughing, at that moment.

"You two look like you have had a fight," Dave announced.

"Nah, Will's just talking about something he knows nothing about," I said, composure recovered.

Will pulled a face and shrugged. "How can I argue with that?"

Chapter 10

November 26

Colin and I had just been seated at his favorite Italian restaurant, on the corner near our flat, when his mobile phone pinged with an incoming text.

He sighed.

"Can we ignore our phones for an hour?" I asked.

He hesitated, before pulling it from his pocket and glancing at the screen. The blood drained from his face. "Uh… sure, good idea," he said replacing it.

I frowned. "You okay?"

He gave me a bright smile. "Yes. Now wine," he said picking up the wine list and ordering a bottle of Chianti from the waiter hovering near our table.

I watched, cringing inside, as Colin made an elaborate scene out of swirling, sniffing and finally tasting the wine, before nodding to the waiter that it was okay. It was just a garden variety Chianti, for God's sake, no need for the theatrics. I gave the waiter an apologetic look as he took our order, spaghetti marinara with a green salad for me, veal for Colin.

"So how's the new job?" Colin asked sitting back and

fiddling with the stem of his wine glass.

I did a double take. Colin never, I mean ever, asked about my job.

"It's good, it's going to be a challenge," I said. "Although, Brexit is a huge distraction with everyone so focused on trying to work out just what it will mean."

"They only have themselves to blame," he muttered and sat back drinking his wine and letting me talk, for once, but I had the feeling he wasn't really listening. His mind was elsewhere.

"What about you?" I asked. "Is the new business going okay?"

That seemed to shake him out of his reverie. "Yeah, it's great. There's just so much to do. At least now we've moved into the new warehouse. I can run both businesses from there."

"I'd love to come and see it," I said.

"Soon, once it's fully up and running."

"Did you ever find out who broke in?" I asked.

"No, but I have my suspicions." Colin shook his head as his phone chimed again and then a second time almost straight away.

"Jess, I am going to have to take this," he said.

I sighed. "Sure."

He pulled the phone from his pocket and with a grim set of his jaw, read his missed messages. With a sharp intake of breath, he stood. "I'm just going to have to make a quick call."

I watched as he paced up and down outside the restaurant, phone at his ear, rubbing his free hand across the back of his neck. I couldn't hear what he was saying, but it appeared that he was arguing with the person on the other end. He came back into the restaurant and was quiet for the rest of the meal. We skipped dessert, paid the bill and started walking home.

"That was nice to go out, just the two of us," I said, bumping his arm with my shoulder.

"Mm."

"I think I'm going to paint every wall in the flat pink with green stripes," I added.

"Whatever you like," he replied, tapping a message on his phone as we walked.

"Colin," I said, stopping and putting my hand on his arm. "Did you even hear what I just said?"

"What?" He looked up, annoyed at the interruption.

I shook my head. "Forget it. You are obviously somewhere else tonight."

"Yeah sorry, but I am going to have to go into the office, something has come up."

"Oh," I said. "Can I do anything?"

"No. I'll try not to be long."

Chapter 11

December 1

I spun around as a throat was cleared behind me. Will was standing there holding a lunch bag and a tray with two takeout coffees.

"I thought since you were too busy to have lunch with me, that I would bring lunch to you," he said.

I leapt to my feet, blushing. "Sorry, I haven't been avoiding you. I've been really busy," I said.

"Liar," he replied pulling a chair into my cubicle from a vacant desk. "So I have tuna mayo on wholegrain or roast beef. Which will it be?"

"Tuna," I mumbled and sat down again, completely outmaneuvered.

"Good. Here you go. How are things? Has Colin settled in at his new office? It's in that renovated complex down at Limehouse, isn't it?"

"Yeah. I guess. I haven't seen it yet," I replied. "He wants to wait until the fit-out is completely finished to show me."

Will's phone chimed with an incoming text as we finished our coffees. He pulled it from his pocket and glanced at the screen and frowned.

"Everything okay?" I asked.

"Looks like I need to go," he said. "Someone's been shorting various oil stocks all morning and it would now appear that they're focusing on one of the companies on my watch-list." He rose and wheeled his chair back into the cubicle opposite.

"Thanks for lunch. That was really kind of you," I said, turning in my seat and smiling.

"Sure, Jess. Same time next week?" he asked.

I nodded and turned back to my computer screen. But Will hadn't left. Next thing his cheek was inches from mine as he said in a low voice in my ear, "You can pretend that we didn't have that conversation the other night, but we both know we did. Let me know when you want to talk about it."

I froze. Shit!

Chapter 12

December 20

All of a sudden, it was Christmas week. I hadn't seen Will since we'd had lunch at my desk, which was a bonus. I still felt a little embarrassed about sleeping on him and pouring my heart out after Dad's funeral and we hadn't cleared the air from the argument at the club, but he was just something I couldn't deal with at the moment. The fact that he was spending a couple of weeks in the New York office couldn't have come at a better time, as far as I was concerned.

I was also aware that I hadn't stopped and properly accepted that Dad was dead. I didn't know how, and deep down I didn't want to. I kept expecting him to call for a chat and often found myself playing back the only voice message I had left on my mobile from him, recorded the day he died, just to hear his voice.

'Jessica, my darling girl, give me a call when you get this. I need to talk to you about something'.

Work had kept me busy with deadlines to meet before the holidays and I'd pushed the puzzle that Dad had left to the back of my mind. I really didn't feel all that festive so I managed to avoid most of the Christmas functions too.

However, on Friday, Rachel and Marie cornered me and insisted that I join them for a Christmas drink that night.

I knew it wasn't just a quiet drink with the girls as soon as I walked into Machiavelli's. Most of my friends were already seated around a huge table. Jimmy jumped up and called me over to a spare seat beside him. I shrugged off my overcoat and draped it over the back of the chair.

"How are you, kid?" He pulled me into a hug. "You've had a shitty few weeks."

"Yeah, I know, Jim. It seems like everything has lost its shine." I sighed, sitting down.

Marie placed a glass of bubbly in front of me and I sat back and listened to everyone's chatter. It was really soothing actually. A second drink appeared, when the first one was empty.

"Next round's mine," I called across the table to Marie, as the door of the bar opened and in walked Will.

"Hey. The traveler returns," Dave called, raising his hand to give him a high-five. Will grinned and shook a few hands, before his eyes settled on me. He tilted his head to one side and mouthed hello, before he was pulled into a conversation across the table from where I was seated. I sat studying him as he laughed, listening to one of Dave's stories.

I drained my glass and wandered up to the bar to get the next round. I also got a beer for Will and was about to deliver it to him when he appeared beside me at the bar.

"Hello, Jessica," he said formally as he leaned over and kissed my cheek, smirking at me.

"Hello, William," I replied in kind. "Here, this is for you," I said, handing him the bottle.

"Thanks. How are you doing? Is it getting any easier?" he asked, helping me to carry the rest of the drinks back to the table. My seat had been taken and I waved my hand at the girl sitting in it, as she went to move, signaling that she could stay. Will and I leaned against the wall at the end of the table.

"I've been spending each weekend with Mum, helping her sort through Dad's things," I said. "She thinks the sun shines out of your arse."

Will laughed. "Really? I bet she wouldn't think that if she knew that I'd slept with you on her couch."

"Will," I hissed, glancing around to make sure that no one had overheard him. "Slept being the operative word, nothing else."

Will put his hand on my arm. "I am just teasing you, Jess. I most certainly wouldn't have taken advantage of you in that state."

"Okay, moving swiftly on," I said, my cheeks getting warm. "Tell me all about New York?"

An hour or so later, having joined the others at the big table for a while, I yawned and decided to call it a night. I hadn't been sleeping at all well and the thought of a long hot bath and an early-ish bedtime was enticing.

I pulled my coat on and grabbed my bag, before jumping up and calling, "Merry Christmas, guys, I'm off." After waves and kisses, I pulled the door open and stepped into the cold night air. St Paul's gave off an eerie glow on the hill to my left. I could remember as a girl climbing up the 200 odd stairs to the Whispering Gallery with Dad, and my delight as we whispered messages to one another from opposite sides of the perfect sphere of the dome. I had taken Colin once, but he had such vertigo when we reached the gallery that he'd had to sit down and refused to play the game with me, miserable bastard.

I looked up at the fast moving clouds in the night sky and wondered if it would be a white Christmas. I buttoned my coat around me and started to walk towards the underground station.

"Jess, wait," a voice called. Will was hurrying up the street behind me, pulling his overcoat on. As he caught up to me he pulled a beanie from his pocket and slipped it on his head.

"I'll walk with you to the station," he said, linking my arm through his.

"Thanks, but you don't have to," I said, smiling. "I've found my way to the station plenty of times on my own." However, I was pleased to have his company and had been delighted to see him tonight. I realized with a jolt that I had really missed him over the last few weeks. I leaned into him and smiled.

We turned the corner and cut down a side street containing a curved row of Victorian buildings with grand entrance porches. The offices were silent at this time on a Friday night. Overhead there was a loud crack of thunder and all of a sudden the heavens opened. The rain came down in sheets, icy cold and sharp. I gave a cry of dismay and Will started running, pulling me along with him.

We skipped up the steps of the nearest building and took shelter under their porch.

"Yuk. Where did that come from?" I said, shaking the rain from my hair and pulling a face. Will took his gloves and hat off, stuffing them into his overcoat pocket and grinned back at me.

"Here, your face is all wet too," he said, reaching out and

running his dry hands over my wet cheeks. He paused, his hands cupping my face. The laughter died on us both, as his gaze went from my wet cheeks to my eyes and then dropped to my mouth. I bit my bottom lip and felt my own gaze mirroring his. He dipped his head and kissed me, a gentle brush of his lips on mine. He pulled back and studied my reaction, but didn't remove his hands. Before I could stop myself, I wound my hands around his neck and pulled him back down towards me and returned the kiss. Will backed me up until I was hard against the side wall of the porch. Then without breaking the kiss, he lifted me up and sat me on the wall, pushing my knees apart so that he could stand between them and pull me closer to him.

We stayed like that pressed together, tongues tangling, arms wrapped around one another, whilst out on the street the rain poured down. It was as though we were cocooned in our own little world, one where we suddenly couldn't get enough of each another. When we eventually broke for air, Will unbuttoned my overcoat and slipped his hands inside and around me, pulling me into an even closer embrace.

"Jess," he murmured into my hair.

I mirrored his movements, unbuttoning his overcoat and his suit jacket and sliding my hands underneath and over the hard curve of muscle on his chest. I slid my hands around his back and tilted my head up to look at him. After gazing into my eyes for a few seconds, he lowered his head towards mine again and gave me a kiss that had all sorts of unspoken desire wrapped in it. My body was responding to him in ways that somewhere at the very back of my mind I knew were wrong, but it, he, just felt so good.

"We shouldn't be doing this here. What if one of the others

comes past on their way to the tube?" I said.

"Look at the weather, Jess. No one is going out in this," he replied before kissing me again.

A little while later, the rain stopped. We had spent the entire time wrapped up in one another. We fitted together well, no awkward twisting of heads, no bumping of noses or teeth. I sighed and relaxed against him for a moment, knowing that what had been bubbling away underneath our friendship and building up over the past few months, had finally overflowed and would forever alter us.

"Um… that was amazing, but we shouldn't be doing this," I began.

"Don't tell me you didn't want me to kiss you?" Will's eyes flashed and he took a step back.

"You misunderstand me. I hadn't consciously decided that I wanted you to kiss me, but it was really nice." I made a grab for his lapel and pulled him back towards me.

"Nice?" he sneered but allowed me to pull him close. "Now I'm feeling insulted."

I grinned. "Yeah, it was okay." I shrugged, teasing him with the understatement.

He took my mouth again with his and left me in no doubt that his kisses were anything but nice. They were fantastic and utterly consuming and he knew it from my ragged breathing.

I reached my hand up and stroked his face. "Will. I can't do this. I'm married. And whatever you may think about my husband, I'm not the sort of woman to have an office affair. We can't allow this to happen again."

He pulled my head onto his chest and hugged me. "I know, Jess, and I'm sorry." We stayed like that for a few moments, his hand stroking my hair. He stepped back and lifted me down from the wall and started buttoning my overcoat back up. "Rain's stopped. Time to go home," he said in a heavy voice, his face unreadable.

I gave him an apologetic smile, but he avoided my gaze. Damn, I had hurt him.

We walked to the station, hands thrust into our own pockets, and ran for a waiting train. We found seats next to each other and rode in silence, neither of us knowing quite what to say. I was very aware that he was leaning towards me, his leg and arm pressed against mine, as if the simple contact was saying what he couldn't. If anyone read our body language, it would have been all too revealing. When the train pulled in at Sloane Square, I gave his hand a squeeze and jumped off without looking at him. His stop was further on at Earl's Court.

I walked the short distance from the station to my flat, my thoughts jumbled. *That was so wrong*, I chided myself. *What the hell were you thinking? You should have put a stop to it immediately*. But my racing blood, light heart and overactive mind won out over my guilty conscience. Whatever it was that had just happened, I felt amazing. I hadn't felt this good in months. I stopped walking for a moment and frowned as I analyzed my feelings. Actually, I didn't ever remember feeling this good.

Chapter 13

December 21

Colin was gone the next morning when I woke. I stretched and reveled in the fact that it was Saturday and I had the whole day to myself. A few domestics, maybe the gym and then shopping. My happy planning was brought to a screeching halt as memories of last night came crashing in. Oh God, I kissed Will. Or should I say, he thoroughly kissed me. I had never been kissed like it. Not by Colin, not by any of the previous teenage boyfriends that I'd dated. I remembered his hands on my face and his arms around me. There was no fumbling or groping, in fact he hadn't touched me anywhere inappropriate, yet I still felt utterly consumed by him. Lying in bed reliving his kisses in my head, my toes curled as I felt a flush run right through my body. This was going to have to be my guilty secret.

I wandered into the kitchen to make myself a coffee. There was a note on the kitchen counter from Colin.

'Playing golf all day. Remember dinner at Tartines 8pm. Don't be late'.

I was sitting at the little table in the kitchen with wintery sun streaming in, enjoying my coffee and cereal, when my phone chimed with an incoming text.

'We need to talk. Lunch—the Queen's Head? 12:30pm? Will'

Oh God. He regrets it. How much did he have to drink? Hardly anything from what I saw. What to wear? A million thoughts crashed around my head. I looked at my watch. It was already 11 am. I had to do this or it would be excruciatingly embarrassing the next time I saw him. I took a deep breath and tapped my reply.

'OK. See you there.'

After half an hour of tidying and other domestic chores to occupy my racing mind, I pulled on my boots, jacket and scarf. Locking the door behind me I skipped down the stairs and headed out. Colin wouldn't notice a tidy flat anyway.

I took my time wandering up the King's Road looking in shop windows. I couldn't really concentrate and didn't register any of the Christmas displays. I got more and more nervous the closer I got to Tyron Street.

It was just after 12:30 pm when I pushed open the door of the pub. A puff of warm air enveloped me as I stepped inside. The smell of roasting meat, beer and burning wood assaulted my senses. My eyes scanned the room, from the semi-circular bar in the center, to the tables and chairs grouped here and there. I let go of the breath that I was holding when I saw that Will was already waiting, seated at a table by the open fire. He jumped up as I walked over, and smiled.

"Hi, Jess," he said, kissing my cheek and taking my coat as I slipped it off. He draped it over the back of the chair nearest his. "Don't look so scared. It's just me."

I gave a nervous laugh. "I know. But it's you and at the same time, not you." I sat down beside him and forced myself to look into his eyes. I saw my own uncertainty mirrored.

He studied my reaction for a long moment. "Our friendship is important to me and I really don't want to mess that up. Can we spend time together without it being awkward?"

I gave him a half smile. "Of course." I felt a little stab of hurt. He regretted what had happened the previous night and he was right, of course. I sat back, putting a little distance between us.

Will held my gaze, his expression serious, and a slight frown creasing the skin between his eyes. I attempted to match his expression, but mine came out a little defiant or defensive, before I dropped my eyes and looked down at my clasped hands.

He leaned across and put this thumb and finger under my chin and encouraged me to look up again. "It's not that I didn't enjoy kissing you, Jess. I did. A lot."

My stupid heart swelled. I looked around the pub as I waged an internal battle. Despite it being lunchtime and the weekend before Christmas, it was still only half full. A couple of men at the next table were looking at us, clearly checking Will out. I did the same. He was wearing jeans and a dark blue cashmere jumper with the collar of a pale blue shirt showing underneath. The only other time I had seen him in anything other than a suit, was at the house the day after Dad's funeral. I decided that I really liked seeing him casual and relaxed. He really was very good looking, in a clean cut, chiseled kind of way. It was the mop of dark hair flopping over his forehead that gave the only clue to any lack of control on his part. Having experienced him letting go a little last night, I knew that there was a lot more passion in this man than I ever realized.

I looked into his eyes, then dropped my gaze to his lips.

"And if I am honest, I really enjoyed kissing you too."

Will's mouth broke into a grin. He leaned over and holding my face with one hand, pressed his lips to my lips for a few seconds and then rested his forehead against mine. "Oh, Jess," he murmured. "What am I going to do with you?"

A few crazy stray thoughts raced through my head, but I thought it wise to keep them to myself.

We ordered the pub special, a delicious ham and chicken pie, and sat chatting and laughing. Will's hand rested on my leg, just above my knee. He linked his fingers through mine when I finished eating. Everywhere he touched seemed to tingle. His eyes sparkled and I felt a warmth that I hadn't for months. After our plates were cleared away, he leaned over and whispered, "Let's go." He grabbed my hand and pulled me out of my seat and helped me on with my coat, his fingers lingering on my neck, as he pulled my hair free, causing a shiver to run through me. He smirked as he felt my reaction.

"I am so glad it's not just me," he said.

We caught the bus back to his place in Earl's Court. We sat close together on the top deck, his arm around me, holding me close in to his side. I closed my eyes and inhaled his peppery scent. On the street, the world continued along its merry way. People were wrapped up warm against the December cold in overcoats, scarves, hats and gloves, laden with shopping bags. Christmas trees, lights and decorations shone from every store window. The odd snow flurry floated silently past the window of the bus, adding to the picture postcard scene. I relaxed and leaned closer to Will, who responded by squeezing me harder and kissing the top of my head.

Will lived in a one-bedroom top floor flat in a row of terraced houses one road back from the underground station.

It was immaculate; simply decorated with white walls, leather couch, glass-top dining table, flat screen TV. There were no photos, nothing personal, it reminded me of a hotel suite in some ways.

Will watched me explore his home. I peeked in his little kitchen. It too was spotless. I felt him come up behind me and put his arms around me, pulling me back against him. I held my breath as he lifted my hair, exposing my neck. When he kissed a sensitive spot on my collarbone, I couldn't stop myself from moaning.

That was all it took. Suddenly I was on the move, being spun around to face him, lifted up and deposited on his bench top, his mouth finding mine. Like the previous evening, he pushed my knees apart, so that he could stand between them and pull me close. We kissed with the desperation of two people starved for each other's touch and I wound my hands in his hair and my legs around his waist, trying to pull him closer too. Breaking the kiss, he leaned back and unbuttoned my jacket, pushing it off my shoulders. I pulled my arms out, as he began unbuttoning my cardigan and slipping that off my shoulders too. The scoop neck black top that I had on underneath suddenly seemed too tight as I watched Will's eyes drift from my face to my cleavage. He bent his head and placed a gentle kiss on the soft mound of each breast. I sighed and leaned back as he kissed his way up my neck to regain my mouth. I untangled my hands from his hair and began to unbutton his shirt, mirroring his movements of a moment earlier. Stepping back, he discarded his shirt and pulled the t-shirt underneath over his head, dropping both on the floor.

I raised an eyebrow at him. Dropping clothes seemed almost wrong in this immaculate flat. Correctly reading my teasing expression he muttered, "Now is so not the time to be tidy."

I pulled him back to me using my legs and ran my hands over his broad chest and down his muscular arms. "Gorgeous," I breathed. My hands were too small to encircle his biceps.

He shook his head. "No, it's you who is gorgeous," he said, tugging at the hem of my t-shirt with a question in his eyes.

I raised my arms allowing him to pull it over my head. It joined his on the floor, and I flushed as he took in the sight of me sitting on his bench wearing just jeans and a black lacy bra. He stepped back and pulled off my boots and socks. I wrapped my legs around his waist again as we kissed and explored each other's bodies. He stood me up to unbutton my jeans and slide them down my legs.

Thank God I had worn matching underwear, although I don't think Will would have noticed. His hands and mouth were everywhere. I felt my bra slide off and hit the floor as he lowered his mouth very gently over one breast and then the other, teasing the nipples with his tongue. We made love there and then up against the bench in his kitchen, and again on the floor in the lounge before finally collapsing in his bed, only to rouse and make love again as the sun began setting in the sky.

"You are so beautiful," Will murmured afterwards as I lay across him, well and truly spent. His fingertips ran up and down my back and over the curve of my butt. His hand stilled on my hip. "I hated seeing you leave the pub with Colin that night," he said all of a sudden. "I know I had no right to, but I think it was then that I realized that I was in trouble where you were concerned."

I rolled onto my front and propped myself up on my elbows

looking at him. "Mmm… although I think we were in trouble a bit earlier than that." I smiled at him.

"You really are beautiful, Jess."

"Thank you." I blushed, dipping my head. "I guess I was lucky in the genetics department."

"You must get sick of being told that," Will said.

"What? That I'm beautiful? No one tells me that, well except my parents, but that doesn't count."

"Surely Colin does."

I shook my head. "No, never."

"Then he's an idiot."

I lowered my gaze, not sure what the protocol was for what I had to do next.

"Um, I think I am going to have to go soon." I bit my lip and looked apologetically at him. I felt a sharp pang of guilt but pushed it down. I would deal with that later when I was on my own. I was not going to spoil what had been one of the very best afternoons I could remember.

A raw emotion passed across Will's face, but when he looked at me again, his expression was guarded. "Okay," he said.

My phone chose that moment to beep with an incoming text. I had dropped my bag in the lounge when we arrived, so I rolled off the bed and padded along the hallway to retrieve my mobile. Tapping the screen as I walked back to the bedroom, I saw the message was from Colin.

'Dinner cancelled. Eating at golf club instead. Don't wait up. C'

I glanced up from the doorway of Will's bedroom. He was lying in bed with just a sheet covering his modesty, clearly enjoying the view I was providing.

"See something you like?" I teased.

"Oh, yeah, come here," he said in a husky voice, crooking

his finger at me.

"Hang on," I replied, tapping a reply to Colin.

"You don't want me to have to come and get you." Will's voice had taken on a teasing, challenging tone.

"I don't?" I replied, then shrieked as he leapt up, grabbed me around the waist and gently threw me on the bed.

"Okay, so maybe I do," I said as he braced himself over me.

Chapter 14

December 22

I woke with a start and glanced at the bedside clock. Its bright red digits told me that it was three am. I could hear Colin talking in the next room.

I sat up and rubbed at my eyes, my bladder urging me to get up and use the bathroom. Half-asleep, I obliged.

A line of light cut across the hall carpet from the half-opened study door as I stumbled to the bathroom. I could hear Colin talking in a harsh whisper.

"Yes, I understand, but the timing's not right. If we wait a little longer…"

I groaned. Didn't he ever switch off?

"I can't risk another security breach right now. Especially when I'm not certain that we really found out who was behind the last one. We don't need the cops sniffing around."

It was as though a bucket of cold water had been tossed over me. I was wide awake now. I paused at the study door and listened. Almost immediately the door was flung open and Colin stood towering over me, his eyes blazing with anger and suspicion.

"What are you doing?"

I jumped backwards. "Just going to the bathroom," I mumbled, trying to sound half asleep. "I heard voices."

As I padded down the hall to the bathroom, I could feel his eyes boring into me. I closed the door behind me and leaned against it, my heart beating fast. The shine from the streetlight outside illuminated the bathroom with an eerie glow. I took my time, trying to compose myself. What the hell was going on? In that moment, I was actually frightened of Colin, frightened of my own husband.

Chapter 15

December 26

Mum leaned across the kitchen table and switched off the news report on the radio. "I worry so much with you two living in London. I would feel so much happier if those awful terrorists were caught."

"It's fine, Mum. There's a lot more police on the streets now. In fact, it's probably safer than it's ever been," I replied. "Don't you think, Col?"

Colin was working his way through a large plate of bacon, eggs, black pudding and toast that my mother had cooked for him. He glanced up and grunted.

"At least you've both been here for Christmas and not there," Mum continued. "Although it was not the same without…"

"I know, Mum." I reached across the table and gave her hand a squeeze.

Colin scraped his chair back across the wooden floor and stood up, draining the remains of his cup of tea as he did so.

"Thanks, Eileen. Jess, I'm going to make a move," he said.

"Already?" I looked up, surprised. "I thought you weren't going over to the coast until tomorrow," I said. "We've only been in Edinburgh for a day."

"Everyone is gathering in Strathgarvan today, so I need to be there too."

"Oh. I'd hoped we could spend today doing something together, here," I replied.

He looked at me in surprise. "Maybe next time, Jess." He left the room and a few seconds later we heard him bounding up the stairs.

"Well, we'll just have to do something together instead, love," Mum said in a breezy voice, clearing Colin's discarded plate from the table. "The Boxing Day sales start today."

"How anyone wants to shop again after the madness of Christmas is beyond me," I muttered, resigning myself to a day trailing around after my shopaholic mother.

Colin ran back down the stairs a few minutes later carrying his bag. He dropped it at the foot of the stairs and reached for his coat, which was hanging on a hook on the wall by the front door.

"I'll see you back in London, Jess," he said, walking back into the kitchen and kissing the top of my head.

"Okay," I said in a resigned voice. I'd learned long ago that once Colin had made up his mind to do something, there was no dissuading him.

"What are you two doing for New Year?" Mum asked.

"I always have Hogmanay with the lads. We don't get to see each other very often now, so we've made a pact to always see in the New Year together," Colin said.

"You should take Jessica one of these days. You've got a cottage there, haven't you, Colin? Have you even seen it, love?" Mum asked turning to me.

"No," I replied, not wanting to get into the usual argument

with Colin. It was his place, bought before he met me; his, not mine, and definitely not ours.

"It's pretty rustic, Eileen. Not much fun for a city girl like Jess. Anyway, I'll see ya." He leaned over and kissed her cheek. "Thanks again for Christmas."

* * *

Colin was back, when I arrived home from work on January 3rd. I tripped over an enormous pile of dirty smelly clothes on the floor in the kitchen in front of the washing machine.

"These won't wash themselves," I called.

"Jess, I'm really busy, can you do it?" he called from the study.

I shook my head. "Ah, no. I've just come home from a long day at work. It's not my bloody washing."

The sound of footsteps followed and Colin appeared in the doorway, a bottle of beer dangling from his fingers. He leaned against the frame and scowled at me.

I nodded towards the beer. "Really busy, then."

Colin pushed off the door frame and came towards me. "God, you can be such a bitch."

I gaped at him, not believing what I was hearing. "Yeah, that really makes me want to do your laundry." I tried to step past him, but he held his place in the small kitchen. "Excuse me."

Colin glared at me for several long seconds before stepping aside. Taking a deep breath, I continued to the bedroom and changed out of my work suit and into jeans and a jumper. When I returned to the kitchen, the washing was turning about in the machine and the study door was closed once again.

Chapter 16

January 4

My phone rang the following morning as I analyzed the test results from a proposed new hedging strategy. The results weren't what we'd expected, so further work was going to be required which was frustrating.

"Jess, are you free tonight? Do you want to come and see the new warehouse? Everything is finally up and running," Colin said.

I hesitated. Was this his way of apologizing? He hadn't spoken a word to me since the incident in the kitchen the previous evening. To date, every overture that I made to come and see progress on the new building had been met with obstacles, so this was unexpected.

"Yeah, okay," I said. "I could get there around six-thirty."

* * *

I grabbed an afternoon coffee with Marie in the lobby café. It was a miserable day outside with the rain lashing down, and it seemed that everyone had decided not to leave the building for their coffee break and as a result most of the tables were full. We took our cups to a two-seater couch in the far corner. Marie crossed one long leg over another and leaned towards me, concern etched into her features.

"Jess, sweetie, is everything okay?" she asked. "It's more than just missing your dad isn't it?"

I sighed as tears smarted in my eyes.

"Colin and I have a stupid argument last night about me not doing his washing when he got back from holiday."

"That sounds fair enough. It's not your washing."

"The trouble is it's not the first time we've had words by any stretch. We're both niggly with each other more and more these days. It feels like we're growing apart. He never wants to go out or socialize with any of my friends. I mean, even my mum has noticed that something isn't right between us."

"Aw, Jess, I'm sorry," Marie said reaching out and giving my hand a squeeze. "I have to say, it was a little awkward when he arrived at your flat that night after we helped you move in a couple of months back."

"I know and I'm sorry about that. Surely he must have realized that when he suddenly became unavailable due to some business emergency, that I would call on you, Jimmy and Dave to help me move," I said.

"I guess we were a bit merry sitting on the floor in your front room eating pizza and drinking wine out of coffee cups," she laughed at the memory.

"Yeah, I couldn't find any wine glasses for days," I said, smiling. But my smile turned to a grimace. "We argued after you left. The first night in our new home should have been magical, but it was marred by his nasty words and criticism of the flat. Things seemed to have been going downhill since then."

"Aw, Jess, I didn't know this was going on, you should have said something."

"I don't think I was ready to say out loud what I was thinking inside," I said.

She nodded, understanding.

"It sounds really awful to say, but sometimes I wonder if I jumped into marrying him too quickly after university, rather than taking the time to grow up and find out who I was and what I wanted out of my life," I continued.

"That's something you'll never know, but surely you can work those things out together."

"You would think so but we seem to only ever move to his tune. I'm beginning to feel like I'm no longer content to be a bit player in my life, I need to take charge and that includes sorting out where, if anywhere, my marriage is going."

"I figured that something wasn't right, but I didn't realize it was this bad," Marie said.

"I didn't either. I'm going to see his new warehouse tonight and after that I'm going to have a talk to him about us."

"Good luck. Call me after if you need to talk."

* * *

I left the office at a quarter to six. It was already dark and cold, so I was grateful that I'd put a warm hat in my bag that morning. I jumped into a taxi that was idling at the side entrance to my office.

"Limehouse please, Violet Road at the canal end."

I sat back as the taxi driver wove his way among the rush hour traffic. The deeper we drove into the East End, the less familiar the area became. The new apartment buildings and cool warehouse renovations gave way to dingier buildings, their sides sprayed with graffiti. We passed several tall council estate blocks lined up next to one another. A group of youths was hanging around the front entrance of one of the towers kicking a ball. We drove on a little further.

"I'm gonna have to drop you here, love. The road's closed up ahead with road works," the driver said pulling over.

"Okay," I hesitated. "I think I can find my way from here."

I paid him and climbed out. The taxi did a U-turn and roared away back in the direction that we'd come and I was left standing on a bridge overlooking the canal. While we'd been driving it had started to rain again. I put up my umbrella and pulled out my phone to call Colin whilst looking around trying to get my bearings.

I was near a small block of rundown shops including several takeaway food outlets, a bottle store and a 7-Eleven with heavy metal bars on its windows. The road up ahead was blocked with a large bulldozer and a heap of orange traffic cones. Flashing yellow lights illuminated a detour sign pointing to a side road. A couple of homeless men sat wrapped in blankets under an overhang at the end of the bridge. Apart from the odd car, the street was almost deserted with very few pedestrians. I shivered and wrapped my coat a little tighter around me and listened to the engaged signal on Colin's phone. I cursed under my breath and dialed again as one of the homeless men stood and approached me.

"Spare some change, love?" he asked, his beery, stale breath enveloping me.

I screwed up my nose and shook my head. "No, sorry."

He shuffled back to his position, but the intrusion unsettled me. Colin's mobile rang this time before going to voicemail. I left a message.

"Colin, I'm on the bridge over the canal on Violet Road. I know I'm close, but I don't know where to go from here. Can you come to meet me?"

I heard voices and glanced behind me. The homeless man was complaining to his companion that I wouldn't give him any money. They both glared at me and started to rise.

I looked about; there was nobody around and the little shops didn't look at all inviting.

I crossed over and began walking down the road in the general direction of Colin's warehouse. I knew it backed onto the canal, so it had to be down one of these side streets. I glanced over my shoulder. The two men were standing watching me. The rain had eased to a light mist and I felt uneasy as I stepped off the curb to cross the intersection. Damn it. Walking after dark in an area that I didn't know was just stupid. Where the hell was Colin? I speed-dialed his number as I walked the next block, continuing to glance over my shoulder to make sure that I wasn't being followed. The street was still deserted, but I had the creepy feeling of being watched. I told myself to stop being paranoid, as once again Colin's voice message came on. I pressed end without leaving a message, and I paused before turning down a side street. I checked the map function on my phone. If I was correct, his building was one block down and one block along, bordering the canal.

The side street was even quieter. Actually, it was more of a single lane alleyway than a street. There were only a few street lights and those that were working flickered on and off, like faulty neon signs casting menacing shadows across the lane. I was really beginning to feel scared now. There were no houses or shops along this street, just three- and four-story red-brick warehouses and factories. Metal walkways joining the building's upper levels crossed above my head. There were no cars either. Shit, shit, shit, this was stupid. I could see the canal up ahead, but just before I reached the end of the alleyway, I heard loud voices and running footsteps. The slap of shoes on the wet road echoed among the buildings. I collapsed my umbrella and flattened myself into the nearest doorway, away from the dull light pooling from the closest flickering streetlamp.

The voices were incoherent but getting louder and sounded angry. A man went racing past the corner as though the hounds of hell were on his tail. A few seconds later, I realized with a sick feeling that they were. Three large men were chasing him, shouting insults. One of the men launched himself forward and tackled the fleeing man and brought him down. His head hit the wet road with a sickening crack. I gasped and covered my mouth as I watched the other men lay into the man now lying prone on the ground, with feet and fists. He curled himself into the fetal position and covered his head with his arms, unable to defend himself.

I fumbled in my pocket for my phone to call the police, when strong hands clamped down on my arms. I opened my mouth to scream, but the sound caught in my throat when I saw it was Colin.

"What the hell are you doing here? I thought you were getting a cab," he demanded.

"The taxi had to drop me off because of the road works. We have to help that man," I whispered, turning to look.

Colin grabbed my chin and forced my face back around to him. "Don't look. There's nothing we can do. Shit, Jess, you can't walk around here alone after dark."

"But shouldn't we call the police?" I asked in a shaky voice.

Colin shook his head and pulled me out of the doorway leading me back along the street in the direction that I had come. I could hear the man groaning behind me and the nauseating smack of flesh on flesh. I glanced over my shoulder at the exact moment one of the attackers looked in our direction. He was a large man wearing dark clothes and a beanie. He briefly made eye contact with me before shifting his gaze to Colin. I froze, terrified. He nodded once in our direction and returned to beating the man, who had stopped moaning and now lay motionless. I glanced back at Colin, who returned the acknowledgment with the slightest incline of his head. I didn't think that my heart could beat any faster, but at that point it sped up.

I allowed Colin to lead me back up the alley to the main road, where his car was now parked. He released me as he pulled his keys from his pocket and pressed a button to unlock the door. I wobbled before leaning over and vomiting in the gutter.

"Get in," Colin said in a rough voice.

I sucked in several deep breaths and wiped the back of my hand across my mouth before allowing him to help me into the passenger seat. I stared straight ahead as we sped away down the road, away from the scene.

"Your building....?" I began.

"Another time."

Chapter 17

January 5

I scanned the news online the next day for any report on the beaten man, but found nothing. What had become of him? I felt guilty for having done nothing to stop the beating. But what could I have done? Colin refused to discuss it when we got home. To ease my guilt, I called the anonymous police crime watch line from a pay phone in the station near work during the morning and reported what I had seen, without mentioning Colin in any way.

I bumped into Marie as I returned to the office.

"How did last night go?"

I shook my head. "The timing wasn't right."

"Listen, I'm late for a meeting, but do you want to meet up after work?" she asked.

"I can't tonight," I hedged.

"Okay," Marie said. "I'm here whenever you need me."

* * *

I was jumpy and distracted when Will and I had lunch together that day. He knew something was up, but didn't press me to explain.

"What was Colin's new warehouse like?" he asked between mouthfuls of sushi.

I had no appetite and moved the tuna rolls around on my plate with chopsticks. "I didn't make it."

"Oh?"

"Bad timing. I'll go another day. I don't want to talk about it."

"Well, what do you want to talk about?"

I heard the slight edge in his voice and knew that I had to pull myself out of my mood.

"Tell me something I don't know about you."

"Such as…?"

"Why do you not have a girlfriend?" I asked giving him a sly little smile.

"I have you."

"Before me? I've known you for months and there hasn't been anyone," I replied.

Will shrugged. "I've had trouble committing to anyone in the past for longer than a few months and I guess I never really found anyone that I wanted to commit to." He leaned over and helped himself to a piece of sushi from my plate. "Now, if you're just going to play with your food and not eat it, I will."

I pushed the plate towards him. "All yours."

I went back to work and sat at my desk deep in thought.

Will and I didn't talk about the future, but our attraction was all encompassing. I enjoyed being with a man who saw me for who I really was and although I knew it was wrong, at the same time it felt so right. We talked and talked about everything and anything; politics, travel, books, movies, music. He seemed to value my opinion which was novel for me, and we had some heated discussions at times. For the first time in my life, I felt truly happy. I tried not to allow the little niggle of guilt that plagued me most days to ruin how I was feeling. The irony that I was doing what I wanted and not what everyone else expected, was not lost on me. However, with a husband such as Colin, I shouldn't have even considered stepping out of line.

I was still so angry at him for abandoning me when Dad died. I also now knew that there were many things that he kept from me. I was a little wary of him. I guess if I was honest, I'd always known that he was secretive and manipulative, but he was becoming openly hostile towards me and that change worried me. I should have brought matters to a head sooner, but I kept telling myself that I was waiting for the right moment to talk to him. The trouble was that right moment didn't seem in any hurry to present itself.

While it had been a relief to voice my concerns to Marie, the other thing holding me in check was my mother. After everything she had been through over the past few months, I didn't want to add to her burden either. She was so proud that I was married and settled, as she saw it. I knew she would be disappointed in me if I left Colin. I felt the pressure of being the good daughter and not letting her down.

Sometimes, I nearly just blurted out to Colin that I'd met someone else, but I knew that he would turn it into something tawdry and disgusting and make me out to be a whore. In hindsight, I should have just left, but I didn't have the energy for the fight that would ensue. I knew that he would make it all my fault and everyone would end up hating me. And on top of it all, after last night, I was a little scared of him and the people he knew.

* * *

The following afternoon at work, I shut myself in a meeting room and spread out the information that I'd taken from Dad's safety deposit box.

The first step was to look into the companies on Dad's handwritten chart. The three companies in the center of the page all had Scottish names: Tartan Warriors Ltd, Scottish Wanderer Ltd and Highland Avengers Ltd. Each company's name had a box drawn around it with a solid line linking it to its owner, whose names were written in three smaller boxes above; three companies in different offshore jurisdictions. Each of these had a dotted line to a box at the top of the page where Dad had written 'Ultimate owner, Offshore Trust'.

The names of Colin's two businesses, Loch Freight Logistics International Limited, known by its acronym L-FLI and Labour for Hire Limited, were written in boxes further down the page. L-FLI was linked with a solid line to a company called CMEC Ltd. I recalled that Colin had originally bought the courier firm through a company structure that he'd set up, rather than in his own name, so this made sense. However, both businesses had dotted lines connecting them to the Offshore Trust at the very top of the page. Beside each dotted line on the chart was a £ sign.

I looked up the UK Companies Office on my laptop and

typed Scottish Wanderer into the search bar. I wasn't sure what I was looking for but saw that it was wholly owned by a foreign company with an unpronounceable name domiciled in Liechtenstein, matching what Dad had noted on the chart. Scottish Wanderer's sole director was someone I had never heard of, a John Smith of London. His contact details were a PO Box which was not helpful. How many John Smiths would there be in London? The company's physical address was listed as being on Fulham Palace Road in south-west London. I made a note of it and moved on to Tartan Warriors. Its single shareholder was a company registered in the Cayman Islands. Joe Brown was its only director, again very common, but I noted down the address of the company, this time on London's Wandsworth Bridge Road. It was a similar story with Highland Avengers, offshore ownership and a director named Ian Clark and an address in Swiss Cottage.

I put the company chart to one side and moved on to the other document. It appeared to contain pages from a contract between Her Majesty's Government and a company called Mendelson. I flicked through the pages of legal speak, relevant dates, termination clauses, contract law conditions until I came to a schedule detailing delivery of 1,000 units of SA80a2 each month for a year to an army base in Scotland.

I reached over for my laptop and Googled Mendelson. After scrolling past web pages related to the composer, I came across one for Mendelsonuk. I clicked on it and was taken to a home page with a beautiful scenic photo of Loch Lomond in Scotland. Mendelson, it transpired, was a manufacturing business near Glasgow. I typed SA80a2 into the search bar and a photo of an assault rifle filled the screen. Resting my elbows on the desk, I leaned my chin into my palm and scrolled through the webpage. So, Mendelson was a weapons manufacturer, who was a major supplier to the British Army, but what, if anything, did that have to do with Colin?

I returned to the company's office tab and ran a search. Mendelson had an extensive shareholding including a number of UK based investment funds. I scrolled through the list and three companies jumped out at me. Highland Avengers Limited, Scottish Wanderer Limited and Tartan Warriors Limited who each had a seven percent shareholding.

I sat back and frowned. I was none the wiser.

I checked my watch. 4pm. It was Friday and I was pretty much done for the week. I could finish early and go and check out the two companies on Dad's chart with addresses in south-west London on my way home. I gathered all the information together, took it to the scanner and fed the pages through. I returned to my desk, located the scanned file and emailed it to my personal email account. I locked the documents in amongst a number of other files in my desk drawer.

I bade farewell to my colleagues and caught the tube. After changing trains at Earl's Court, I alighted at Fulham Broadway station just after 4:30 pm. I walked through the small shopping mall past the billboards advertising the latest movies playing at the large cinema complex upstairs. Out on the street, I checked the map on my phone and crossed over as the lights changed and walked down Harwood Road. The sun was setting and the temperature dropping, so I buttoned up my overcoat and turned up the collar.

The walk to the address on Wandsworth Bridge Road took around ten minutes. It was three blocks down, a doorway nestled in a block of shops, between a pizza restaurant and a hardware store. The blue wooden door had a gold letterbox flap and around ten name plaques, including one for Tartan Warriors. I tried the handle, but the door was locked, so I pressed the button on an intercom set into the wall at one side of the door.

"Can I help you?" a pleasant disjointed female voice answered.

I leaned closer to the intercom. "I'm looking for Tartan Warriors."

The door buzzed as the woman replied, "Come on up."

I took a deep breath and pushed the now unlocked door. It opened onto a carpeted stairway. Square wall lights glowed at regular intervals at ankle level all the way up. I started climbing as the heavy front door clicked shut again behind me. I glanced back at it, wondering what I was about to find. The stairs turned ninety degrees onto a landing with two doors leading off. One was ajar and I could hear the chatter of several women's voices. I knocked and entered.

The office was plain, with six wooden desks, each with a computer terminal, telephone and overflowing trays of paper. A smartly dressed young woman sat behind each desk. The talking stopped and they turned to look at me.

"Over here." An Asian woman in her mid-twenties with short dark hair and bright red lips beckoned. "I deal with Tartan."

I smiled at the other women, who returned to their conversation, a discussion of Friday night and weekend plans, as I walked over to the desk in one corner.

"What do you have for me?" the woman asked.

"Just some papers," I replied, digging into my bag. "What does Tartan do?" I asked looking around.

"Beats me," the woman replied. "We're just their mailbox.

Although I like to picture hunky Scotsmen wearing kilts whenever I deal with their stuff."

The other women in the office laughed, but I must have looked blank because she continued. "A number of companies pay us to be their postal address and address of record with the Companies Office."

"Oh," I replied. "So you're not involved in running the businesses?"

She shook her head, large gold earrings swinging from side to side as she did so, and held out her hand for the white envelope that I pulled from my bag.

"So where do you send the mail?"

"Each company has different instructions. Some have forwarding addresses and others have people who come by weekly to collect anything," she explained.

"Does someone come and collect the mail for Tartan?" I asked.

"We forward everything to a PO Box in Scotland."

"Can you give me that and I'll just post this, save you a job?" I suggested with a winning smile, pulling the envelope back towards me as she reached for it.

"Sorry, that's confidential information." She leaned over and took the envelope from me.

"Okay, thank you," I said, turning to go.

"Wait," the woman called as I reached the door. "This isn't for Tartan Warriors. This is addressed to Tartan Wools Ltd. Not the same."

I let out a loud sigh. "Oh, you're kidding me? My boss has sent me all this way for nothing?" I walked back over to her desk. "I'm sure he said Tartan Warriors." I read the label on the envelope she gave back to me. "Sorry, I've wasted your time."

"No problem. Have a good weekend." She turned to rejoin the conversation with the other women.

I raced down the stairs, through the blue door and back onto the street. I hailed a passing black cab with its yellow light illuminated and gave the driver the address of the second company on Fulham Palace Road. The Friday night traffic was getting heavier as he drove past Parsons Green Station and turned onto Fulham Road. We were stuck behind several red double-decker buses before merging into Fulham Palace Road. The driver asked me to confirm the address. Several minutes later we pulled up outside a small square white two-story building sandwiched in the middle of a row of red-brick terraced houses.

"Can you wait for me?" I asked. "I'm only dropping something off."

"Sure, love," he replied.

I walked up to the front double glass door entrance. I could see a long unattended reception desk in the center of the lobby. I tried the door. Locked. I looked at my watch; five minutes past five. They were most likely closed for the day. Damn. An opaque panel attached to the wall drew my attention. It contained the names of no less than fifty businesses. I looked back up at the building. There was no way that fifty companies operated out of a building that size. It was safe to assume that this was another corporate mailbox. I ran my eye down the list. About two thirds of the way down the second column the name Scottish Wanderer Ltd jumped out at me. I pulled my mobile phone out and snapped a quick photo, before walking back to the taxi.

Chapter 18

The trading floor was due its annual winter party. This year it was to be held in a series of marquees at Greenwich Park. A select number of middle office staff were invited, including Jimmy, Dave, Andrew, Marie and me. I was really looking forward to it and had bought a gorgeous new dress to wear, when Colin announced that he needed me at a dinner with his new Middle Eastern contacts, the same night.

"Sorry, I have a work function," I replied.

"You have so many of them that you can miss one," he grumbled. "This is really important to me. The Arabs like to see a pretty face at dinner."

"I'd much rather go to my work party," I replied.

"Please, Jessie, I need you there," Colin wheedled.

I acquiesced; perhaps it would be an opportunity to find out some more about Colin's businesses and the three companies that I'd drawn a dead end on.

"Where is the dinner?" I asked Colin as I began to get ready on Friday night.

"It's at La Marx," he said, naming an exclusive restaurant overlooking the Thames near London Bridge.

My eyes widened. "Can we afford to eat somewhere like that?"

"For these clients we can. They have almost signed on the dotted line for me to manage their freight requirements to and from the UK, as well as supply labor teams to their construction sites in Dubai and Qatar," Colin explained as he stood in front of the bedroom mirror straightening his tie. He was dressed in a smart dark navy suit, one of the few times I'd seen him really dressed up in ages. I walked out of the bathroom in a black figure-hugging knee length dress and very high heeled shoes. I had pulled my hair up into a messy bun, with several tendrils hanging down around my face. I checked myself in the mirror and was pleased with the sophisticated woman who looked back at me.

"No, no. What are you wearing?" Colin looked aghast.

I glanced sideways at him. "Ah, business dinner attire."

"No. That won't work." He slid open my wardrobe door and rummaged around, pulling a skimpy red silk dress with tiny shoestring straps from the recesses. "This," he said thrusting it towards me. "And lose the tights."

I looked at him as though he'd stepped in from another planet. "Colin, you do realize that it's winter? That's a summer dress and besides I haven't worn it since I was a teenager on holiday in Spain. It's trashy. I don't know why I even still have it."

"Trashy will work with the Arabs. Now hurry up and get changed. We cannot be late."

"No way. I'm not wearing that." I took a step backwards.

A look of fury took residence on Colin's face. He covered

the distance between us in two strides and gripped my upper arm tightly. "You agreed to do this for me."

"Colin, you're hurting me." I struggled in his grip.

He let go and gave me a little push as he thrust the dress into my arms. "Get changed."

"No," I said.

The crack of his palm across my face sent me sprawling against the bed. The sting that spread across my cheek was like fire and brought unwanted tears to my eyes.

"You bastard."

"Yes. Now get changed or there will be more of that."

I pulled on the little dress with its plunging neckline and short skirt. The tiny straps meant that wearing a bra was impossible and I felt practically naked standing there as he handed me a pair of stiletto-heeled strappy sandals. I glanced in the mirror at the miserable looking girl with the red mark across her right cheek. Colin came to stand behind me and I flinched as he reached up and pulled the clips from my hair, letting it fall in loose curls around my shoulders. He tucked a strand behind my left ear and pushed some of the curls over the red mark.

"There," he said. "Much better. Now go and redo your makeup."

"You should have just hired a prostitute," I spat at him.

"Next time I will."

The dinner was excruciating, and I learned nothing useful. I wasn't included in any conversation and several times Colin leaned over and hissed, 'smile' in my ear. The two middle-aged Arab gentlemen quite openly leered at me throughout the meal. The waitresses gave me filthy looks and I felt dirty and embarrassed. I hoped that no one from Dobson Stone was there to see me looking so cheap and wretched. At the end of the dinner Colin announced that they were off to a gentlemen's club down the road and that I could go home.

"Great night, so glad I came," I muttered to him as I got in the cab.

He arrived home very late and crawled into bed stinking of whiskey and cheap perfume. I wondered how many lap dances he'd had at the club and felt even dirtier. I feigned sleep when he rested a hand on my hip and whispered my name several times. Did he really think that was an option after hitting me? He finally fell asleep, snoring.

* * *

I left the house early and met Marie for lunch at a café just off the King's Road. It was bustling, but we managed to secure the last spot on their winter garden terrace. We followed the maître d' to a small table nestled among planters filled with colorful cyclamens and pansies. Marie looked amazing in tight blue jeans and a red overcoat, her glossy locks loose around her shoulders.

"I don't know how you can look so good after the night you must have had," I said.

She hugged me and pulled back looking at my cheek frowning. I'd mostly covered the red mark with makeup.

"What's wrong with your cheek, Jess?"

"Just a rash," I replied. "Now tell me about your night."

She seemed to accept that explanation and launched into a long description of the winter party venue, the food and the band.

"Both Jimmy and Dave got lucky," she added with a wicked grin, between morsels from our shared platter.

"Really? Details?" I grinned. Those two boys were incorrigible and quite a force to be reckoned with at the best of times.

"Well, they hooked up with a couple of girls who work on the swaps desk who share a flat and the last I saw, they were all piling into a cab together," Marie said.

"Those poor girls. Didn't anyone warn them?" I asked.

"Oh I think the boys may have met their match," she replied, tapping a text into her phone as she spoke.

Her phone pinged a few seconds later. She read the message and shrieked with laughter. She passed it to me.

'I don't think I will ever be able to walk again. Jim'
I smiled.

"Will looked like he was doing well too. Actually, it was nice to see him with someone," Marie said. "I was beginning to wonder if he was asexual."

I suddenly found the food in my mouth hard to swallow. I grabbed a quick mouthful of water and forced it down.

"Who?" I asked. The room had begun to tilt. I felt as if I'd been thrown off balance.

"You know your friend Frankie, from the New York office?" Marie answered. I nodded. "Her," Marie said.

"What were they doing?" I asked feeling like I was staring into the headlights of an oncoming car with no chance of getting out of the way.

"Dirty dancing, the last I saw. I left before him, so I don't know how it ended," she added, oblivious to my discomfort. "We should text him–you must have his number. Frankie would eat a guy like Will for breakfast."

"Yeah," I answered, head down, fishing around in my bag to hide the tears that were pooling in my eyes.

I pulled out my phone and Marie frowned. "You okay, Jess? You've gone a funny color."

"I think I'm going to be sick," I said, jumping up from the table and running to the bathroom. I lost the contents of my stomach and stood leaning against the cubicle door shaking, with tears rolling down my cheeks. There was a gentle knock against the door a minute or so later.

"Jess, are you alright?" Marie called.

"Yeah, I'll be out shortly," I said, trying to pull myself together. I splashed water on my face and squeezed my hands into fists and forced myself to stop crying. Bastard.

I sat back down at the table a few minutes later. Our plates had been cleared away and Marie was paying the bill. She looked concerned.

"Sorry, something didn't agree with me," I mumbled as my phone chimed again with a message that broke my already bruised heart.

'OMG Jess, I met Will last night. Call me! Frankie'

I gasped, my hand flying to my mouth.

"Oh poor you," Marie said misinterpreting my reaction, concerned that I would hurl again. "Do you want to go home?"

I nodded and we gathered our things and headed out onto the street to hail a black cab. I apologized again, but Marie brushed it off telling me to go home and rest.

I pulled out my phone and sent Will a text from the cab.

'Do you have something to tell me?'

He replied straightaway.

'It's not what you think.'

120

'What do I think?'

'Can you come over?'

'Are you sure you're alone?'

My phone rang. It was Will.

"Jess…" he began.

"Don't 'Jess' me. Frankie? Really?" I replied, unable to keep the hurt from my voice.

"Let's not do this over the phone. Come over, please," he said.

I sighed and leaned forward giving the driver the change of address. I rooted around in my bag for breath mints and spent the rest of the journey fixing my makeup.

Will buzzed me in the front door of his building and was standing holding the door to his flat open by the time I'd climbed the stairs to his floor. He ushered me along the hallway and into the lounge. He had the sense not to hug or kiss me and sat down on the sofa beside me with a wary expression on his face.

"I don't know what you've heard, but nothing happened," he began, staring at his hands. He was unshaven and his hair was flat on one side, sticking up on the other. He looked like he'd just crawled out of bed and pulled some random clothes on. Not his usual well put together self.

"Except for a major public display on the dance floor," I spat back.

"Yes, but that was all." He lifted his head and his eyes roamed my face. "What's happened to your cheek?"

"Nothing."

Will's expression turned stony. "Don't tell me that he hit you? I'll kill him."

I shook my head letting my hair fall over the bruise on the

121

side of my face. "I've been crying. My face goes blotchy."

"Jess, I'm sorry."

I looked away. The thought of him with someone else was like a dagger to my heart, and even worse the thought of him and Frankie, who was a gorgeous Italian-American New Yorker, with lustrous dark locks and sultry come-to-bed eyes. When Frankie set her sights on someone, he didn't stand a chance and now she had Will in her cross-hairs. I was the country cousin to her city chic. There was no way that I could compete.

I looked back at Will. How could he? Not when he knew how I felt about him and how he felt about me. That thought ground my pity party to an immediate stop. I didn't know how he felt about me, not really, apart from the obvious attraction. And I hadn't admitted the depth of my feelings for him, to myself even. It seemed wrong to do so when I was married to someone else. We had carefully avoided all discussion on the subject and the 'L' word had certainly never been uttered by either of us.

Oh, shit. I realized there and then that I had absolutely no right to be reacting to this the way I was, as the wounded party. I had no claim to him. I was still married to Colin. This was just an affair. He was single and could date who he liked.

I stared at him and nodded.

"Okay," I said. "Thanks for telling me. I have to go."

I grabbed my bag and bolted for the door before he had a chance to react. I heard him call my name, but I ran down the stairs and out of his building without pausing to answer.

I spent the rest of the day mulling over what to do. I ignored all of Will's texts and calls. After a long walk through Hyde Park, I checked into a little spa just off the King's Road near the flat and had a massage. It had been a hell of a weekend, first Colin, then Will. As I lay being pampered, I came to a decision. It was right that things had ended with Will. I had fallen into his arms following Dad's death and maybe my need for comfort and his desire to provide it had gotten all mixed up. What I really needed to do was sort out what I was doing with Colin. This kind of deceit wasn't me. I was clearly in much deeper with Will than I had realized. I needed to end things with Colin if Will and I were to have any future. Although I was not certain that was an option any longer. Colin hitting me had also strengthened my resolve. I was done. I was leaving him.

I arrived home to find the flat resembling a florist's shop; every available surface seemed to contain a vase or basket of flowers, and the floral scent was overpowering.

"Jess, I'm so sorry. I don't know what came over me. I've been so anxious about this contract, that I wasn't thinking straight," Colin said, meeting me at the door and taking my coat.

I looked around the lounge at the bouquets. I didn't know what to say.

"Colin, I don't think we're working anymore," I began.

"Don't say that, I will make it up to you, I promise. Starting now." He took my hand and led me into the kitchen where the tiny table was set for two with candles, red roses and wine. "I've made dinner," he said.

Stunned, I sat down as he held out a chair for me.

He sat down opposite and took my hand. "Can you forgive me? I know I've been distracted and neglecting you lately. I've just been so busy expanding the business, setting up our future," he said. "I love you; I never meant to hurt you."

Chapter 19

Colin's mobile buzzed just after 9am, waking me from a deep sleep.

"What?" He sat up in bed taking most of the duvet with him, leaving me shivering from the sudden hit of cool morning air. Phone tucked between his shoulder and his ear, he leapt out of bed and grabbed the jeans he'd discarded on a chair in the corner of the room the previous evening and pulled them on. "I'll be there as soon as I can." He disconnected the call and threw the phone on the bed, rummaging under it to find shoes. He stood and pulled the t-shirt that he'd slept in over his head and dumped it on the floor. As he turned and opened his chest of drawers, I sat up and watched him.

"What's going on?"

He pulled a clean shirt over his head and down over his torso, giving me a glimpse of the shrapnel scars that ran down his left shoulder and side. Even though I'd seen them hundreds of times, they still gave me cause to pause. A hunting accident as a teenager had nearly cost him his life.

"There's been an explosion at a building site near Canary Wharf," he said. I must have looked blank. "I have men working on that job. I want to check that no one has been injured," he continued.

"But isn't it Sunday? No one will be working," I asked.

"Yes, but I need to make sure."

"God, Col, it's not another terrorist attack?" I asked sitting up. My mind took me straight back to that dreadful evening on Cheapside with the chaos and horrific injuries I'd witnessed.

"No," he said. "Something in a shed at the site caught fire, that's all."

"What kind of something?"

"The police and fire appliances found the burning remains of a van. It was probably an LPG cylinder or something. But it made a loud noise and with everyone being jumpy, y'know, I need to be seen to check it out." He finished dressing and pushed his wallet and phone into his pocket. "I'll be back later."

I lay back down, as the previous day's conversation with Will came flooding back, followed by the strange evening with Colin acting like he used to when we were first together. A dull pain formed in my chest and a few tears slipped from my eyes. Annoyed at myself, I wiped them away.

"Come on, Jessica, you're awake now. Might as well get your lazy butt out of bed and stop wallowing," I told myself as I forced my legs over the side. "You've got some decisions to make."

After a shower, I started sorting through my belongings and before long I had set aside those that I would take with me when I left and those, including the red dress, that were going straight to the nearest charity shop.

* * *

I stepped into a lift at work on Friday afternoon, to find Will following the bank's dress-down Friday policy, wearing snug black jeans and my favorite blue button-down shirt, leaning against the back rail, chatting to a short, bespectacled guy whom I didn't recognize.

"Hi, Jess," Will said, flashing me a wary smile that didn't quite reach his eyes.

"Hey, Will," I replied. I had the presence of mind to press the button for the next floor, so that I wouldn't have to be in the lift with him any longer than necessary, even though I was actually going up five floors.

I stood with my back to him as his companion continued talking. Will said nothing, but I could feel his eyes boring into my back. The lift car jerked to a stop and the doors opened. I jumped out relieved, only to hear Will say goodbye to his colleague and step out after me. I hesitated, wondering if I could bluff it. I wasn't even sure what was on this floor. Will, of course, knew what I was doing.

"Since when did you work with the private bankers?" He indicated with a nod of his head towards the plaque on the wall, which listed the business units on this level. He smirked.

"Since I had to evacuate the lift quickly to avoid someone." I decided that honesty was the best policy. I leaned over and pressed the up arrow, calling the lift back.

"Ouch," he said, feigning injury. "Don't sugar coat it, Jess."

I shrugged. "You got me."

The lift arrived and we both got in.

"How have you been?" he asked as we began to ride up. "Will you be at The Tower tonight?"

"No," I shook my head. "I don't think that's a good idea." The lift arrived at my floor. I stepped out straightaway and hurried to my desk, where I sat with my head in my hands, breathing deeply to regain my composure.

God, I missed him.

* * *

On Monday, an email arrived in my inbox from Dave inviting me for drinks on Friday at a nearby Mexican restaurant to celebrate his birthday. I checked the email list and saw Will's name. I hit reply and was typing my excuse when Dave leaned over the wall of my cubicle.

"I am not taking no for an answer, Jess. We haven't seen you for a couple of weeks. What's up?" he asked.

"I was just replying to say I'd love to come," I said, smiling at him.

"Good. I will pick you up here at seven," he said, wandering off again, my nice new red pen tucked in his back pocket.

I sighed. Well, everyone would be there. I couldn't keep avoiding my friends because of Will.

Chapter 20

January 23

Colin was preparing to leave for the airport to fly to New York for a week, on Thursday evening. He mentioned something about expanding further into the US market, but as usual the details he provided me with were sketchy. I no longer cared. The timing couldn't have been better for me. I was going to move out while he was away, coward that I was. I curled up on the sofa in the lounge to read, when my mobile rang. I didn't recognize the number.

"Jessica, it's Dr. Sorrenson," the warm, friendly voice said.

"Hi, Dr. Sorrenson, how are you?" I immediately sat up.

"Good thanks. I thought you'd like to know that I finally met with the doctor who attended your father," he said.

"What did he say?"

"There was nothing to suggest that it wasn't simply a massive heart attack. He wouldn't have suffered, Jess," he said. "He did say there was one thing that was unusual, your father's eyes had broken capillaries, petechial hemorrhaging, consistent with asphyxia but there was no evidence of strangulation. He remembers that your father's secretary was rambling about the two men whom he'd met with earlier in the day, but everyone assumed that she was in shock. You may want to talk with her."

"Okay. I will. Thanks," I replied.

"Just don't go looking for answers that aren't there, Jess. Sometimes in life these things just happen," he advised.

"I know. Thanks for your help."

I stared at the phone for a long time after I disconnected the call. Was I looking for something that wasn't there? Dad clearly thought he had found something or he wouldn't have gone to the elaborate ruse of leaving me the safety deposit box. I tried to think back to the last time that Dad had been in London, about a fortnight before he died. He, Colin and I had dinner at the restaurant in the Oxo Tower. Colin had been in one of his moods and had gotten worse during dinner. Actually, now that I recalled the evening, I could have sworn that he and Dad appeared to have had words while I was in the bathroom at one stage. The atmosphere at the table had been tense when I had taken my seat again, and I remember noticing the diners at a couple of adjacent tables giving us odd looks.

Colin breezed into the lounge interrupting my reverie. "Right. I'm off," he said.

"Sure. Safe travels," I replied. "Ah, Colin, do you remember the last time we had dinner with Dad? At the Oxo Tower?"

Colin paused in the doorway, his posture immediately tense, alert. There, I wasn't making it up. "Yeah," he replied.

"Did you two argue when I was in the bathroom?" I asked.

Colin laughed. "Yeah, but just about who was getting the bill. Jess, you've got to stop this. It's time to move on. He'd want you to."

129

I watched from the front window until Colin's taxi had pulled away, before grabbing my iPad and looking up the website for Dad's firm. I tapped into the About Us page and let out a long breath as Dad smiled back at me from the group photo of the firm taken before their Christmas function the previous year, where everyone was all smiles and laughter. Below the photo was a list of the firm's partners. I tapped the link on my father's name. His obituary came up on the screen along with a photo of him sitting behind his desk.

"Oh, Dad," I murmured reaching out to stroke his face on the screen. After a few moments I scrolled to the bottom of the article where the names of his old team were noted, including his assistant, Emily MacIntyre. I had known her name was Emily, just not her surname. I opened up a new tab and searched the online telephone directory for her number. There were several E. MacIntyres in Edinburgh, but I whittled the list down to three. Nothing for it but to telephone each one and I lucked out first time.

"Hi, Emily speaking."

"Emily, it's Jessica McDonald, Don's daughter."

"Jess, how nice to hear from you. How are you doing? We miss your father so, so much," she replied.

"Me too, Emily. I'm not sure how to ask this without it sounding odd…" I began.

"Just ask away, Jess."

"Can you remember the clients Dad met with immediately before his heart attack?" I asked.

There was a moment of silence on the other end of the phone, although I heard Emily's sharp intake of breath.

"Why are you asking, Jess?" Emily asked in a whisper.

"I'm not entirely sure, but some things don't add up for me."

"I do remember, Jess. They just turned up. The meeting wasn't scheduled. Your father was a little rattled when he saw them. He asked that I hold his calls and that they not be disturbed."

"Was that unusual?"

"No, but the men were. We normally have business clients. These guys were dressed like workmen, dirty jeans and heavy boots," Emily said. "In fact, one was carrying kind of a toolbox."

"Huh? Do you know what the meeting was about?"

"No, but there were raised voices at one stage and they didn't stay more than fifteen minutes."

"What did Dad say after they left?" Jess asked.

Emily sighed. "Well, that's just the thing. He kept the door closed, so I finished the report that I was editing and went for a late lunch. It wasn't until I got back that I knocked and went in and found that he was dead. The doctor said it was a massive heart attack. Do you think those men did something to him?" she added in a whisper.

"Yeah, I'm beginning to," I replied. "Would you recognize them again?"

"Honestly, I'm not sure. I tried to tell the police when they came, but the doctor was adamant that it was a heart attack, so they didn't want to know. I'm so sorry, Jess."

"It's not your fault, Emily. Thanks for your help."

"Of course. Let me know if you need anything else."

"Actually, there might be one thing. Your building has security cameras in the lobby right?"

"Yes."

"I'd like to know who those guys were. Do you think you can find the one from the day he died?" I asked.

"I honestly don't know, but I'll try in the morning," she said.

Chapter 21

January 24

"Come on, Jess, time to go," Dave said leaning against the wall of my cubicle. He had risen to the occasion and was well dressed in smart dark navy jeans with a blue and green button-down shirt topped by a tailored black jacket. He'd had his hair cut and was clean shaven, although he still reminded me of the clichéd Aussie surfer.

I reached into my desk drawer and extracted the gift that I'd picked up for him at lunchtime. I knew that he liked to read, so I'd bought him a new release paperback.

"Happy birthday, Dave," I said handing it to him.

He looked delighted as he tore the gift wrapping off. "Awesome, mate, I haven't read this one," he said. "Can I leave it here so that it doesn't get lost tonight?"

We met Jimmy and Marie in the lobby. Jimmy was lounging against the wall, his muscular frame dwarfing Marie whose shrieks of laughter could be heard as soon as the lift doors opened, and we filed out to meet them.

She and Jimmy would actually make a great couple, I thought, looking at them, bantering with each other. I made a mental note to mention that to her. I wasn't sure how she would take such a suggestion, but it made perfect sense all of a sudden. Maybe my messed up situation had turned me into the last of the romantics. She looped her arm through mine as we walked up the road to the restaurant.

"You're looking a lot better," she said.

"Yeah, it must have been food poisoning," I agreed. "I'm over it now though," I added with determination. She gave me an odd look.

A crowd of Dave's friends were already assembled and with the arrival of the birthday boy, the party got underway. He had one side of the restaurant sectioned off and people just kept turning up.

"So this is London's vast Kiwi and Aussie network in action," I said to Marie.

We pushed through the crowd and found Will seated at a table with Andrew and Rachel, who were munching their way through a bowl of corn chips and salsa.

My heart sank. Well actually, that's not true. My head sank and my heart went woo-hoo. Rachel jumped up and hugged me. The peroxide blonde was gone and in its place she was sporting a sleek black bob. Will and I exchanged easy smiles. So maybe this wouldn't be so hard after all. Then Frankie came sashaying back to the table carrying a jug of margaritas and slipped onto Will's lap instead of onto the empty seat next to him. There suddenly wasn't enough air in the room. I looked away. Okay, so maybe it would be hard after all. I pulled Marie to the bar with me and motioned to the barman ordering a skinny gin and tonic each.

"I didn't know Frankie was back in town," I said to her.

"Me neither. I haven't seen her at the bank this week.

Perhaps she's here to see Will," Marie replied, looking over her shoulder at the table.

"Obviously," I muttered, handing some money over to the barman. "Same again please." I added a splash of tonic from the little bottle he'd delivered with the nips of gin and knocked the drink back in one go, feeling the heat of the liquor travel through my system.

"Whoa, go you." Marie looked at me sideways. "I hope you don't mind if I don't follow suit. I'm going to pace myself tonight. I have to catch an early train up to my parents' place in the morning."

"All good," I said and knocked back the second drink. The only way to get through tonight was going to be to drink through the pain. I didn't care if no one else joined me. "Just stay here and talk to me for a bit."

"Sure. What's up? Did you get a chance to talk things over with Colin?"

"He's gone to New York for a week and I'm moving out while he's gone."

Marie's eyes widened. "Have you told him?"

I shook my head. "I will when he gets back. It's easier this way, believe me. He's playing the loving husband at the moment, but I'm not sure how long that will last. I've seen him turn quite nasty at times, so I need to have everything planned because I've no doubt that he will make things difficult."

"Aw, Jess. Where are you going? Do you need a place to stay?"

"Actually, that would be great, just for a few nights. I'm viewing a flat on Monday night that sounds perfect, but it's not available for ten days."

"Give me a couple of days to tidy up when I get back from

Mum and Dad's, and then come, say, Tuesday after work?"

I leaned over and hugged her. "Thank you."

"Of course, what are friends for?"

"Anyway, enough about me, what's new with you?"

Marie launched into a long story about how her mother and sister were annoying the hell out of her. I leaned against the bar and listened, nodding and making the appropriate noises of agreement or shock. After ten minutes, Jimmy joined us and the two of them fell into their usual pattern of flirting with one another. I smiled and took a deep breath, preparing myself to approach the table where the rest of my friends were seated, when a voice beside me spoke. I spun around.

"Hey, Jess, it's good to see you," Will said, holding my gaze.

"Sure. How are things? I have to say, Frankie's looking hot tonight," I said, the alcohol loosening my tongue.

Frankie had gone all out and was wearing sexy low-slung black leather pants, high spiked heel boots and a blue sequined crop top which showed off both her ample breasts and toned midriff complete with belly button piercing and tattoo peeking out of the top of her waistband. I, on the other hand, had come straight from work and wore tailored black trousers, high block-heeled pumps, and a purple silk t-shirt cut in a V-neck giving just a glimpse of cleavage, topped with a black jacket pinched in at the waist, accentuating my curves. My hair was loosely pinned up with curls falling around my face. Although I looked sophisticated, next to Frankie I felt old, fat and frumpy.

"No," Will said shaking his head. "She looks like a stripper, *you* look hot."

"And yet, you'll still go home with her." I couldn't help sounding bitter.

"Well, I can hardly go home with you to the Businessman of the Year, can I? Is he still treating you well, then?" he added, sarcasm heavy in his voice.

We glared at each other for a long moment before Frankie came up, hooked her arm through Will's and looked from Will to me and back again.

"How are ya, Jess? You haven't returned my calls," she said, pouting.

I shrugged. "Sorry, been crazy busy."

"Are you ready to go?" she asked Will, husky and suggestive, before shooting a slight frown in my direction.

"No, not yet," Will replied.

Disgusted, I turned and looked around for Jimmy and Dave. "Where are those Antipodeans? Didn't they say something about shots?"

Jimmy and Dave needed no encouragement and were beside me within seconds, along with several mates, ordering tequila shots, salt shakers and lime wedges, to be lined up along the bar. I turned my back on Will and Frankie and started chatting with two of the guys, who turned out to be Australian rugby players on contract to a London Club. Will's eyes narrowed but he allowed Frankie to drag him back to the table, where he sat looking uncomfortable as she draped herself over him while she talked to Rachel.

"Okay, everyone ready," Jimmy called. Ten shots of tequila were lined up on the bar each with a salt shaker and a lime wedge. "Three, two, one."

We all knocked back the shot, licked the salt off the back of our hands and sucked the juice from the lime.

"Whoa." I blew out a breath. The tequila burned harder than gin.

"Same again," Dave called.

I caught Will watching me with a concerned expression but by that stage I was drunk enough that I decided that he could just sod off. I excused myself and wandered towards the bathroom after the second round, swaying my hips a little more than usual. In the big mirror behind the bar, I could see the eyes of the two rugby players following me. As I passed Will, I saw his expression change and he scowled.

Frankie was at the hand basin retouching her makeup and sulking that Will wasn't in a hurry to leave with her.

"You'd think he want a bit of this," she said adjusting her top in the mirror, so that her breasts were even more prominently displayed.

I giggled. I so did not need that image in my head. I felt my giggle begin to turn slightly hysterical, so I left the bathroom and headed back into the restaurant.

Jimmy had commandeered the jukebox in my absence and Dave took my hand and pulled me up onto a table to dance with him when I returned to the bar. I was at the point of no return and needed no encouragement. I looked down into Will's furious face and smirked. Jimmy, of course, picked up on the tension as he jumped up to join Dave and me.

"Hey, English, we call this an Antipodean sandwich," he called down to Will, as he and Dave began to bump and grind suggestively either side of me. Will helped me down after the song finished and tried to talk to me.

"Don't do this on my account. I'm not worth it," he hissed.

"Oh, you don't need to tell me, I already know that," I retorted.

"Jess..." he started.

"You might as well make someone happy tonight, why don't

you just piss off back to Frankie's hotel," I snarled.

Will shook his head and dragged his fingers through his hair in frustration. Jimmy stepped in and pulled me to the dance floor, but having heard the last part, drunkenly agreed. "Yeah, if you are going to stand there with that sour look on your face, you should just go, Will."

* * *

I woke the next morning horribly hungover. That was the last time I was going out anywhere with Jimmy and Dave. I leaned out of bed and grabbed my mobile to check the time. There was a text from Will.

'Let's meet. We need to talk. W'

I groaned and flopped back against the pillow as a few hazy images of the previous night swam through my fuzzy brain. I knew that I had argued with Will at the Mexican restaurant and that after he and Frankie had left together, I had gone on partying with Jimmy, Dave and several others.

Shit. I had done such a good job of keeping my feelings for Will under control. What on earth had caused me to slip last night? I really didn't want to *meet and talk*. I knew that I wouldn't come out on top in the state I was in and it was very important that I didn't let him get under my skin again. I was determined not to let him know that I still had feelings for him, although my lapse the previous night probably told him that anyway.

Taking a deep breath I made my way to the bathroom and had a long hot shower, and downed a couple of paracetamol to help ease my thumping head. Feeling a little more human, I made coffee and sat down to text Will back.

'Ok. Where?'

'How about a walk in Hyde Park? Meet you at the Kensington High Street gate.'

I was late arriving, of course. I almost sent him a text to cancel several times, but it was one of those cases of, let's just get this over with. Will was standing by the gate waiting for me with takeout skinny lattes and a paper bag containing two toasted bagels.

"Thought you might need caffeine and carbs," he said.

"Mmm… thanks. I'm feeling a little rough," I acknowledged, taking the coffee from his hand and having a grateful sip as we wandered into the park to find a spot to sit, among the lunchtime crowds and tourists. A grey squirrel bounded across the path in front of us with a nut held in his mouth and ran straight up the nearest tree without pausing.

"We need to talk about last night," Will began as we walked.

"I'm a little vague, which particular part of last night, cos I don't remember much past the tattoo parlor." I frowned, trying to dredge up the rest of the evening from the recesses of my memory.

"What?"

"No, not me, bloody Jimmy. Although he would have had a kiwi tattooed on my butt if he'd had his way."

"I'm not sure that's the only thing he had in mind for your butt," Will muttered.

I rolled my eyes. Will was way off. The only thing Jimmy wanted to talk about last night was Marie, who'd had the sense to leave early.

We settled in the sun on a gently sloping grassy bank with

the red-brick splendor of Kensington Palace behind us. I leaned back and turned my face to the sky, letting the warmth of the winter sunshine soak into me. Vapor trails crisscrossed overhead and the odd fluffy cloud curled around. I watched as a mother rushed to pick up a toddler who'd taken a tumble at the edge of a pond.

"I'm sorry Frankie turned up like that," Will began. "I didn't even know she was in town until just before you arrived at the restaurant last night."

I shrugged as if I didn't care. "It's nothing to do with me, Will, remember?"

"Jess, I know I hurt you. I was stupid and feeling a little scared about how close we were getting, and I didn't handle it at all well. I was pissed that you'd gone out with Colin instead of me and I got drunk and the next thing I was dancing with Frankie at the Greenwich thing. I'm sorry," Will said.

I shifted my gaze down to my coffee cup and took a long swallow. "Yeah, you did hurt me, but I'm over it," I replied, hoping to convince myself as much as him. I thought he perhaps saw through me. "Maybe we should just try being friends for a while."

"Let me get this straight. You have moved on and let this go already. Yeah, right," he concluded.

I shook my head. "Don't do this."

"Why not, Jess? We still have strong feelings for each other. Don't tell me Colin has finally stepped up to the plate?" he asked, his lip curled.

"That's none of your business," I spat back.

"So he hasn't, then," Will retorted, his eyes flashing. "And we both know that even if he did, it wouldn't come close to what you and I had."

"So how was your night with Frankie?" I changed the subject.

"We argued about you, if you must know," he said.

"Why?"

"Because I dropped her at her hotel and then came back to the restaurant to get you, but you'd already gone. She wasn't best pleased. Told me not to bother coming back," he explained.

"Okay. That explains why she hasn't been in touch with me this morning. I expect she had big plans for you last night."

"Yeah, well, we're on different pages. My interest lies elsewhere." He paused, tilting his head to gauge my reaction.

"Will, this can't go anywhere. We'll only end up hurting each other again," I said, my voice catching and a big fat tear rolling unbidden down my cheek. The realization hit me like a blow. I was in love with him. Oh shit. Avoiding his gaze, I gathered my bag and started to get up. "Thanks for the coffee. I should go."

Chapter 22

January 25

I cleared my schedule for the morning on Monday. Things were a little slow at the office at the moment, so I decided that I would go in late. I wanted to check out the address of the third company on Dad's schedule, although I suspected that it would be a similar story to the other two. I scrolled through my email while eating breakfast. There was a message from Dad's assistant Emily in my inbox.

'Jess, I've had no luck on the cameras at the front of the building or the ones in the lobby. The ones out front have been sprayed over by vandals and the lobby ones are blank for that day, which is strange. The technician said there appears to have been a glitch or something.'

I grabbed my mobile and called her.

"Hi, Jess. Did you get my message?" she answered.

"Yeah, that's too bad."

"It's not all bad. I've just checked with the buildings either side in case their street cams picked up the men arriving and one of them has something. I'm just getting some stills copied for you."

"Great," I said. "Can you see who they are?"

"No, the camera was tilted down so you can only see their legs. Probably the same vandals damaged their camera as did ours. What you can see though, is their car and a partial license plate."

I gave a sharp intake of breath. "That's brilliant, Emily. Thank you. Can you send them to my email?"

I stood up to make another coffee, when the intercom buzzed.

"Delivery for Colin McDonald," a muffled voice announced when I answered.

I pressed the door release to let the courier in the main door downstairs.

I had just unlocked the front door of the flat, when it was thrust hard into me knocking me off balance. A man wearing a motor cycle helmet and dark clothes stood on the threshold.

"Colin. Where is he?" he demanded.

"The States," I replied, holding on to the door and trying to push it closed. "Who the hell are you?"

He grabbed me by the throat and shoved me up against the inside wall by the door. I clawed at his hand as I struggled for breath. "You tell him that he owes us," he said in a nasty voice. I couldn't place the accent, but it wasn't English. He released me and threw me to the ground. I caught the side of my face on the hall table as I fell, hitting the floor and seeing stars. The man reached for me, pulling me to my feet and ripped my shirt down the front. His hand snaked underneath, roughly fondling my breast, as a door slammed somewhere in the stairwell. He hesitated and swore, before pushing me to the ground again and kicking me hard in the ribs, twice. He rushed through the doorway and down the stairs. I lay there for a few moments trying to get my breath back and get control of the pain coursing through my body. Once I had managed to suck in a good deep breath, I crawled to the door and pushed it closed, hearing the deadbolt lock into place. I leaned back against it as tears started running down my cheeks.

After a minute and several uneasy breaths that made my chest feel like it was on fire, I fished my mobile phone from the pocket of my skirt and speed-dialed Will.

"Jess," he answered on the second ring, sounding delighted. "I was just thinking about you."

"Will. Can you come? I've had an intruder. I'm hurt," I sobbed.

"God, Jess. Has he gone?"

"Yeah."

"I'm on my way. I'm on late starts this week, so I'm still home. I'll be there shortly." I could hear him running down stairs and a door closing. "How badly hurt are you? Do you need me to call an ambulance?"

"I don't think so," I answered, although there was blackness at the edge of my vision and I'd begun shaking.

"Stay talking to me, Jess," he instructed, sounding concerned. I heard him give my address to a taxi driver. I felt very dizzy but continued holding the phone to my ear. "Where are you in the house?"

"Sitting by the door."

"Do you know who it was?"

"No but, Will, I'm scared that he is still downstairs. Be careful. He was wearing a motor bike helmet," I said.

"Okay, Jess. Keep your door locked until I get there."

"Mm…" I mumbled, blinking to try and clear my cloudy

vision.

"Jess, stay on the line," he said. "Can you go any faster?" I heard him ask the taxi driver.

"You still there, Jess?"

"Yeah, not going anywhere."

He gave a soft laugh. "Good, I'm nearly there. Have you called the police?" he asked.

"No. I just called you."

"Oh, Jess. I'm almost there. Stay on the phone."

I could hear him talking to the taxi driver and a door slamming.

"Okay. I'm outside your building. There's no one hanging around here. Let me up," he said.

I pulled myself up using the door handle. The pain was sharp and immediate. I dropped the phone and swore, but managed to push the intercom button, which released the front door. I could hear footsteps thundering up the stairs, but I still jumped at the knock on my door.

"Jess, it's me. Open up," Will called.

I used the peephole to check before opening the door with one hand and holding the front of my shirt together with the other. The shocked expression on Will's face showed how I must have looked. He closed the door and pulled me into his arms. I whimpered and he released me, with a concerned expression.

"Ribs," I muttered by way of explanation.

"God, sorry. Here come and sit down." He helped me into the lounge and onto the sofa before disappearing and returning with a towel from the bathroom. It was only then that I felt the blood running down the side of my face. I lifted my hand to touch my temple.

"No, don't touch, Jess. Here." Will pressed the towel to the contusion. "Can you tell me what happened?" He crouched down in front of me, continuing to hold the towel against my head, his other hand on my leg, which had an uncontrollable shake.

"Will, I think if there hadn't been a noise on the stairs, which scared him off, that he might have done worse to me," I said, the realization that I had probably come off lightly, dawning on me.

Will's expression darkened as he took in the ripped shirt. "Okay. I'm calling the police."

The next couple of hours were spent answering questions and drinking tea. The police officers that came, a man and women, were both professional and kind. The man door-knocked around the neighbors, but of those who were home, none had seen the assailant, and all were shocked that I had been attacked and they hadn't heard anything.

"I think you should see your GP," the WPC advised. "You may need stitches on that eyebrow, and it would be good to have a doctor's report of your injuries, in case we manage to catch him."

I tried calling Colin several times, but his phone was switched off and went straight to voicemail. I eventually left him a message to call me urgently.

The police officers left their cards with instructions to call if I thought of anything further and for Colin to get in touch when he returned from the United States.

Will booked an Uber to take us to my doctor's surgery, after he managed to sweet-talk the receptionist into squeezing me into their already overbooked clinic. By 4 pm, we were back at the flat. My injuries had been tended to and I was feeling exhausted. I tried calling Colin again. His phone was still switched off.

"Would you like another tea?" Will asked.

I grimaced. "I've had way too much tea. I'm tea-logged. Why don't you open a bottle of wine instead? Medicinal purposes only, of course." A sudden thought entered my head. "Sorry, Will, I've taken up your whole day. I hope work was okay with you taking the day off at such short notice. Don't feel you have to stay, if you have somewhere to be. I really appreciate everything that you've done." What I didn't say was that the thought of staying in the flat on my own after dark frightened the hell out of me. What happened if the guy came back? He knew Colin was away, because I had told him, but I didn't feel that I could ask Will to stay any longer.

Will came and sat down beside me, taking my hand and tilting my chin up gently to look at him.

"Listen to me. There is nothing that will take me away from here tonight or tomorrow, for that matter. I'm so glad that it was me you called," he said.

I let out a deep sigh and closed my eyes. He was watching me with such intensity when I opened them again, that I blushed. "Thank you. If I'm honest, the thought of being here alone tonight is a bit scary," I admitted.

"I'll take the sofa, Jess. No one is getting through that front door, without me knowing it," he said. "Now, food as well as wine, I think."

"There's not much here, we'll need to order in," I said. I didn't add that the reason there was very little food was that I was due to move out the following day.

I was in the bathroom trying to fix my hair and makeup, so that I didn't look quite so hideous, when my mobile rang a little while later. The bruising was coming out around my eye, which was almost swollen shut. The split on my right eyebrow, which had bled so profusely, was held together by five little pieces of surgical tape and my lip was fat and swollen on the same side. I had red marks on either side of my neck. In fact, if I turned my head, I could see the outline of three fingers, no wonder my throat was sore. I didn't look at all attractive. I styled my hair so that it hung over the right side of my face covering some of the damage and tucked it behind my left ear, letting it fall over the finger marks. A little better. I could hear Will talking, as I walked back into the lounge.

"Here she is." He handed my mobile to me, his expression was neutral.

"What the hell is he doing there?" Colin demanded.

"I called him, after someone looking for you beat me up," I snapped. Unbelievable, did he even care how I was? Surely Will had told him.

There was a pause. "What happened, Jess?"

I explained the events of the morning.

"Are you hurt?" he asked when I had finished.

"Cuts and bruises."

Will placed a glass of red wine on the coffee table in front of me and went to stand by the window across the room with his back to me, drinking his. I noticed his free hand kept clenching and unclenching as I spoke.

"When are you back?" I asked Colin.

"Not until Thursday night," he replied. I noticed that there was no offer to come sooner.

"Just so you know, Will is going to stay here tonight," I told him.

"What the hell for?" Colin's voice was raised. Across the

room I saw Will's shoulders stiffen. He had heard. I stood and walked into the kitchen to continue the conversation.

"Colin, I have a black eye, split lip, choke marks around my throat, not to mention two cracked ribs and I'm as frightened as hell that the guy will come back. If he hadn't been disturbed this morning, he may well have raped me, if ripping my shirt open and grabbing my breast was any indication. So, yes, Will is staying and no, I won't be screwing him in our bed."

"Jessica. There is no need to take that attitude," Colin said, sounding more like a parent than a spouse. I said nothing. "Fine," he conceded after a long silence.

"Oh, and the police want to talk to you. They want to know who you owe something to. Actually, I'd like to know that too," I added.

"I'll talk to them when I get back," he said. "Now you go and rest. Put William back on."

"Is that really necessary?" I asked.

Colin sighed as though I was being a petulant teenager. "Just do it, Jess."

I walked back into the lounge to find Will still leaning against the window, with a furious expression on his face. I handed him my mobile shrugging my shoulders and mouthing 'sorry'.

"Colin," he said, listening. "Sure, no problem, will do." He ended the call without saying goodbye.

We looked at each other for a long minute, until I broke the silence.

"I'm sorry that you had to hear that. When he stops to think, he will be appreciative that you came to my aid," I said.

"Don't make excuses for him. I don't want to hear them," Will said, curling his lip in disgust.

I sighed and sat down again, wincing as pain shot up my right side. Will was beside me in an instant.

"You okay?"

"Yeah, I will be. It just hurts when I move suddenly."

We sat on opposite ends of the couch sipping our wine. Will switched the TV on and we watched one of the news channels. After a while, he helped me put my feet up and slipped my sandals off, settling my feet in his lap and began to massage them. I closed my eyes and relaxed. Will gave the best foot massages. I could feel the tension and pain in my body retreating to a dull ache and I let out a big sigh. My eyes suddenly shot open. The thing with Will's foot massages was that they had always started out innocently enough, but usually ended up with me naked on top of him. My thighs clenched at the thought. Will stopped circling the balls of my feet with his thumbs and quirked an eyebrow at me. *Shit.* He knew my body too well. I pulled my feet away, muttering thanks and retreated to the kitchen to gather plates and cutlery for our delivery.

He appeared beside me a moment or two later. "Here, let me get those," he said leaning over me to pull down two plates from a cupboard above the bench. "You don't want to stretch with those ribs." His chest brushed my arm and I inhaled the clean, fresh peppery scent that was all Will. Despite everything that had happened that day, I was still feeling attracted to him. Oh God, I was in trouble.

Will carried the plates and cutlery into the lounge and set them down on the coffee table. I followed and gave a little shriek as the intercom buzzed.

"It's okay," Will reassured me, putting his hand on my shoulder. "It'll just be the pizza." He spoke through the intercom and let the pizza delivery guy up the stairs and paid him in the hallway. I only relaxed once the door was double locked again with the chain in place.

I was still standing when he carried the pizza and salad back into the room. He put them down on the table and coaxed me into his arms.

"It's okay to be frightened, but I won't let anyone hurt you," he murmured, kissing the top of my head. I swallowed a painful lump in my throat. I was not going to cry again. He released me.

"I don't know about you, but I am starving," he said.

Between us we demolished the food; well he did really, I didn't have much of an appetite and it hurt to swallow.

"Jess, can I ask you something?" Will said, pausing between slices.

"Sure," I replied, picking at my salad.

"Who does Colin owe money to?" he asked. "How is he financing his business expansion?"

"I've been wondering that too. He keeps me out of all his business decisions," I replied.

"You may want to be careful with that," Will replied. "I mean, as his wife, his personal liabilities will affect your assets too."

"Dad set things up for me before we married, trusts and the like, so legally I shouldn't be compromised," I replied.

But that sparked a thought. I had run into a brick wall working through the company structure because there were a number of trusts involved, and trusts had no easily accessible public records. However, there had to be lawyers involved in the set-up and administration of the trusts and someone had to be doing the accounts and taking care of any tax obligations. That was the next avenue to follow.

Chapter 23

January 25

"Will, I'm just going to check something, okay?"

"Do you need a hand?" he said as he devoured his sixth slice of pizza.

I shook my head and eased myself up off the sofa, wandered into the small study and sat down in the swivel office chair at the desk. It was an odd-shaped little room, tucked away under the eaves with only enough room for a desk, a small bookshelf and a comfortable armchair. The pine desk was from IKEA and sat beneath the only window in the room. It was dark outside, however, so I switched on the desk lamp. Colin used this room more than I did. I was only ever in here to check my email at the weekend or to pay bills. I sat for a few moments contemplating what I was about to do, justifying it to myself.

I pulled open the file drawer on the desk and flicked through the hanging files until I found one labeled 'Colin'. Bending over hurt, so I removed the file from the drawer and laid it on the desk. It was full of statements for his personal bank account, receipts and insurance forms from the last two and a bit years. I sorted through until I found his most recent bank statement. It had a closing balance of £500. Glancing at it, I saw no unusual transactions. The monthly salary that he drew from one of his businesses, and a regular outgoing into our joint account, which covered his share of the mortgage, utilities and food.

I reviewed each statement going back two years. There were no unusual amounts deposited or withdrawn. I closed the file and returned it to the drawer and flicked through the rest of the file dividers. There were no company or trust documents here, though. And no detail on which law firm he might be using. It must all be kept on site at the warehouse. Movement in the doorway attracted my attention. Will stood there watching me. I must have looked guilty, because he raised an eyebrow and said, "Everything okay?"

I nodded. "Yeah, just looking to see if I could find out who Colin owes money to."

"Any luck? Can I help?"

"No, there's nothing here other than our personal stuff," I replied, switching off the desk lamp and returning to the lounge, curling up on the sofa, my brain whirring, trying to process. "What would he owe if it weren't money? Perhaps he owed someone a favor?"

Will shrugged.

I wasn't ready to confide my father's investigation into Colin or my suspicions about his death to anyone, even Will, just yet. I didn't have any real proof, just a series of unrelated events which now included this morning's assault. Saying anything after that would only make me look paranoid or worse, nasty.

I woke with a start a while later. I was curled up against

Will on the sofa. Only the side lights were burning and dinner had been cleared away. The TV was on in the background.

"Hey, sleepyhead, I didn't like to wake you. Would you like me to carry you to bed? I wasn't sure how to lift you without hurting you," Will said.

I snuggled against him as the events of the day came crashing back. He had his arm around me, holding me, and I felt safe. "Can I stay here a little longer?"

"Of course. Whatever you want," he replied.

I shuffled around so that I was lying on my side with my head on his lap and my legs curled up on the sofa. I draped my arm over my ribs and felt tears pouring down my face. I guess it was delayed shock from the attack coming out. I pretended to watch the TV for a little while as he stroked my hair. If Will knew I was crying, he didn't say, he just let me lie there.

After a while I spoke again. "You know I had no chance to defend myself. He knocked me off balance when he forced his way in the door," I said.

"No one is suggesting that you should or could have, Jess," Will said. He tensed. "Or is that what Colin said?"

"No. I just always thought I would be able to protect myself in that kind of situation. Now I know I can't necessarily and that's very disempowering," I explained.

"You can't dwell on that," he said. "You could always install a panic button by the door that would sound an alarm, if that would make you feel better."

"I was thinking I should take self-defense classes." I sat up. "I think I will go to bed." I wandered into my bedroom and pulled my top and skirt off, dropping them in the washing hamper and pulled on my favorite tank top and PJ bottoms.

I brushed my teeth and started washing my face in the bathroom. My swollen reflection looked back at me from the mirror and I began to shake. I didn't really consider myself a vain person. Sure, I always liked to look my best, but this was hideous. I began to cry again.

There was a soft knock on the bathroom door a minute or two later. "Jess?" Will called. "Are you okay in there? Can you let me in?"

When I didn't answer, he cracked the door open and spoke again. "Jess? I'm coming in, okay." When he saw my shaking body and tear-streaked face in the mirror, he gathered me into his arms and held me. "Sweetheart, it's alright."

"Sorry," I mumbled, trying to pull away, but this time he held firm. "I can't seem to stop crying and I look hideous."

"Well, I have seen you looking better," he replied, smiling at me in the mirror. I let out a slightly hysterical laugh.

"Maybe this will stop your pursuit of me. I should have thought of it sooner."

"Or not, actually this just makes it worse. I would happily kill that bastard for doing this to you," he said, becoming serious all of a sudden. "And I don't care what you want to pretend, when it came down to it today, it was me that you called."

I looked up into his face. He held my gaze for a few seconds before leaning down and very lightly brushing my lips with his. "The cuts and bruising are temporary, you are still beautiful to me. Come on, let's get you into bed."

If I was in trouble before, I was on my way to hell now. Who wouldn't want to be told they were still beautiful, even when they looked like they'd been the victim of a car accident?

"Stay with me?" I asked as I slid under the duvet.

He nodded. "Let me just turn everything off." He disappeared and I could hear him moving around. He returned to the bedroom a few minutes later and sat down on the edge of the bed and removed his shoes.

"You sure? I can just sleep on the couch tonight," he offered.

"No," I replied, shaking my head. I watched him remove his jeans and shirt, folding them on top of his neatly placed shoes. Wearing boxers and a white t-shirt, he climbed in behind me and eased me into his arms. I closed my eyes and slept.

Sometime before dawn, I woke with a start and bolted upright, almost passing out from the pain in my side. Memories of the day before came crashing back in.

"Hey," Will said, his voice deep and husky with sleep.

"Mmm…" I wasn't the most coherent person in the morning, at the best of times. I eased myself out of bed and used the bathroom. I crawled back into his waiting arms and lay with my head on his chest. "Thank you for staying."

"My pleasure," he murmured, running his hand up and down my back and then over my hip. I arched into his touch and pushed a hand under his t-shirt and began stroking his chest.

"Careful, Jess," he cautioned. I tipped my head back to look at him and was met with his mouth on mine. Gentle brushes of his lips at first, but when I opened mine beneath his, he took control, sweeping his tongue into my mouth. I couldn't help but respond. God, I had so missed his kisses. Then *ouch*, I pulled away as his teeth bumped the swelling on the side of my lip.

"Sorry, Jess. I got a little carried away," he apologized as he flopped onto his back.

"Yeah, this isn't the time or the place," I agreed, climbing

157

out of bed. "Coffee?"

"Yeah, that'd be good," he said.

I padded out to the kitchen, needing to put some distance between us and got busy making the coffee. I had just finished frothing the milk when Will walked into the kitchen, fully dressed in his clothes from the previous day. He sat at the little table by the window and watched me pour the milk onto the espresso shots. I handed him a cup and sat down opposite with mine.

"Come and stay with me for the rest of the week," he offered.

I shook my head. "No, I'll be fine here."

"You didn't sound fine last night."

"I know, but in the cold light of day, I feel much better."

Will nodded. "Are we going to talk about us or are you going to ignore what just happened?"

I looked down at my coffee. "Will, I need you to give me some time. I'm going to leave him. I just need to sort a couple of things out first."

Will reached across the table and grabbed my hand. "Let me help."

"No, I have to do this on my own."

He sighed, resigned. "Okay, but you must promise me that you will call if you need anything. I mean it, anything."

"I will."

Chapter 24

January 28

I laid low for the rest of the week, while the bruising on my face went from black to purple to green and my ribs and the cut on my forehead stopped throbbing. I cancelled the appointments that I'd made to view flats as I figured it wouldn't be a good look to potential landlords to turn up looking as I did. Rachel and Marie dropped by on Wednesday night for a couple of hours with Jimmy and Dave in tow. Not such a great idea as it turned out. I laughed so hard at their attempts to cheer me up, that my ribs hurt more than they had all week, but I appreciated their efforts. By Thursday night, I was pacing backwards and forwards across the lounge waiting for Colin to arrive home from the States.

He let himself in, dropping his bags in the hall. Hearing the keys in the door had put me on alert and I stood waiting with the phone in my hand, ready to call the police if it wasn't him. He frowned at me and gave me an awkward hug.

"Ooh, careful. Cracked ribs, remember?" I said.

Colin pulled back, studied my face and grimaced. "You look awful, Jess."

I opened and closed my mouth, unsure that I had heard him correctly. "Ah thanks, good to see you too. So tell me, who do you owe something to?" I ground out the words.

He pulled a face and looked thoughtful. "No one that I can think of, maybe they had the wrong flat?" he suggested. It had taken him four days and 5,000 km to come up with that one?

"So it was just a coincidence that he was looking for someone named Colin," I spat back.

He shrugged and I knew he was hiding something. I was beginning to think that my father had been onto something after all. What, I didn't know, but I sure as hell intended finding out.

Chapter 25

Watery winter sunshine filtered through the lounge window as I sat down with my laptop and morning coffee, and pulled up the scan of the documents that I'd sent to my personal email account. I needed something to focus on other than myself and with everything that had happened over the last few weeks, I hadn't had a chance to look into the Mendelson government contract any further.

Sitting cross-legged on the sofa, I started reading the document. Mendelson were contracted to supply a number of weapons in varying quantities. The contract was slow going, full of legal jargon and I was about to put it down when an exclusivity clause caught my eye. I continued reading. Mendelson had agreed to produce the SA80a2 rifle exclusively for the British Army.

I continued reading through the rest of the contract, even the appendices. I was about to close the file when I realized that I'd scanned an additional page. A delivery docket from Mendelson's factory near Glasgow to the army base in the

Highlands filled the screen. Where had Dad found that? I sucked in a breath as I read the name of the delivery firm, Loch Freight Logistics International.

My phone rang just as I was closing down my laptop. It was Colin. "I'm going to be late tonight. A couple of the lads are down from Strathgarvan for the weekend, so I'm going out for a beer with them."

"Okay, I won't wait up."

"Gotta go, I have several meetings offsite with potential clients this afternoon."

As I hung up a plan formed in my mind.

I caught the tube to Monument and walked through the underground tunnels to connect with the DLR, alighting at Devon Road and jumping on a bus down to Limehouse Cut. It was daylight this time and I found Colin's new complex in no time. It was really just a glorified warehouse with a suite of offices on an upstairs mezzanine level. I announced myself using the intercom attached to the side of the main entrance and heard the buzz as the door lock released. Once inside I found myself in a cavernous space with a large number of pallets and boxes stacked in high towers all around. The whir of an engine getting closer caught my attention and a forklift came into view. Its driver, wearing earmuffs, figuratively tipped his hat to me before disappearing down a row of boxes.

"Jess, this way," Kathleen, Colin's office manager called from above. I made my way across the floor and climbed the stairs to meet her.

"Ooh, that looks sore," she said, peering at my face.

"You should see the other guy," I quipped.

She smirked at my lame attempt at humor. "Colin's not here." Kathleen was an attractive blonde in her late twenties, meticulously good at her job, according to Colin, with a sharp enough tongue to keep all of the mainly men around her in their place. I had met her on occasion and liked her.

"Oh," I said, trying to look disappointed. "I thought I would surprise him. He's been wanting to show me the new set-up. Is he due back soon?"

Kathleen looked at her watch. "Should be within the hour."

"Do you mind if I wait?" I asked.

"Be my guest," she said, leading me through a doorway into an open plan office with four workstations. A closed door at one end had a plaque with Colin's name stuck to it. "Sarah's off sick and Emma's on leave, so it's just me. Sit wherever you like."

I dropped my bag on the floor beside Sarah's desk. "Do you mind if I turn her computer on? There are a couple of things that I might as well Google while I'm waiting," I asked.

"Knock yourself out," Kathleen replied as she gathered up a stack of envelopes from her desk. "Right, I'm off to post these, shouldn't be long," she said, pulling her jacket on.

"Okay," I replied bringing up a food website on Sarah's computer. I also clicked open the icon for the L-FLI booking system. As soon as Kathleen closed the door, I opened Sarah's top drawer. Hopefully she kept her logons and passwords written down somewhere. Sure enough, a little notebook contained everything that I needed and within a few seconds I had logged in.

I took a deep steadying breath and tried to familiarize myself with the system. It seemed that customers made all of their bookings online, so I did a search on Mendelson. Within seconds, the factory address and contact details were displayed on the screen. A button took me to their orders. I searched for delivery dates for the previous month. Sure enough, there were two deliveries made in December. I opened the first. The delivery address was for an army base near Inverness and the schedules attached listed the items being delivered. I would need to check it against the contract. The second delivery docket was for two hundred units of SA800a2 semi-automatic rifles but didn't have a delivery address. I clicked print on each order. Across the room the printer whirred to life but it didn't print anything. I glanced at the clock on the wall. Kathleen had been gone ten minutes already. If this didn't print soon, I'd have to cancel it. I repeated the process for November, again there were two deliveries, one to the army and one to the L-FLI base here in London. Where were they going from here? A sudden thought hit me. If Mendelson had an exclusive contract with the British army then what was L-FLI doing with the surplus? Selling them? My breath stilled. That would be arms dealing. I shook my head in an attempt to dislodge the thought. No way. I had a few suspicions about Colin, but not that, surely?

I knew that I didn't have long until Kathleen returned, so I logged into my email account and sent myself a message, attaching a copy of each of the orders. I watched as the screen icon showed each file being transferred. *Come on.* It was taking too long.

The 'file attached successfully' message had just popped up on screen when I heard voices and the click of Kathleen's heels on the stairs. At the same time, the printer decided to come to life and started spitting out pages. *Shit, shit, shit.* I pressed send on my email and closed down the booking system. I clicked back into the cuisine site, maximizing it to full screen, opened the first recipe and clicked print. The door swung open and Kathleen walked back in.

"No queue for once," she said dropping her bag on her desk.

The printer continued to spew pages. We both glanced at it.

"Just printing a couple of recipes," I said, standing and walking over to the printer. I put myself between Kathleen and the printer and gathered the pages that had printed, just as the printer started beeping. I nearly jumped out of my skin.

"It needs paper," Kathleen said, starting to walk over. I spotted a ream of paper lying half open on the bench beside the printer. I almost pounced on it.

"It's okay, I can do it," I said. As I opened the printer drawer to add a stack of paper, I saw that my hands were shaking. I hoped that Kathleen hadn't noticed. The printer started printing again, page 7 of 12. *Come on, come on*. I glanced over my shoulder; she was sitting back at her desk, tapping away on her keyboard. I spied an A4 sized envelope on a shelf below the printer and slid my printouts inside.

The recipe finally printed and I added it to the envelope and hurried back to Sarah's desk. I slid the envelope into my bag.

"That's a few recipes," Kathleen commented.

"Yeah, well Colin's always complaining what a crap cook I am, so I thought I'd try to surprise him with something new," I said with a self-deprecating laugh.

I glanced at my watch. I just wanted to get away from the warehouse, but I couldn't exactly leave when I had said that I was there to see Colin. I sat back down at Sarah's computer, logged out of my email account and pretended to surf the Internet, my heart beat slowing, but my hands still shaking. I kept looking at my bag, which now felt like it had a bomb in it. How would I explain its contents to Colin if he looked? I hadn't thought that far ahead. Then again, why would he look in my bag?

There was a commotion in the hallway outside the office and Colin burst in. He looked surprised and, I could have sworn, a little unsettled to see me.

"What are you doing here?" he demanded.

"Well, I got bored at home and I thought since I didn't get the tour the other night, that I would come over and surprise you," I replied, smiling at him.

He continued to frown. "Okay then, let me just put this stuff down," he said. As a last thought I deleted the activity history from Sarah's computer and shut it down. If Kathleen thought I was acting strangely, she didn't show it.

Colin showed me through the office suite, meeting and staff rooms before taking me down into the warehouse, explaining that the boxes here were mainly items waiting to be transported around the country the next day in the fleet of vans and trucks that were parked in the large gated parking space adjacent to the building. Several vans were parked inside the warehouse and were being loaded as we watched. My gaze shifted towards movement through the open roller doors at the end of the warehouse leading into the adjacent parking area and the sea of white vans and trucks with their distinctive L-FLI red and black logos. A black SUV pulled up near the entrance. I did a double take as I registered its license plate. The last three digits were 692, the same as in the photo that Emily had sent from the security cameras of the building next to my father's law firm. That couldn't be a coincidence. I gulped.

"Whose vehicle is that?" I asked trying to sound casual. "It breaks the white van mold."

"Looks like the lads from Strathgarvan have arrived," Colin said, following my gaze.

I could scarcely breathe as the doors of the SUV opened and two men climbed out. Were these the same two people who visited my father before his death? One was tall and muscular, with a shaved head and a black goatee beard, the other was short and stocky with small round glasses. Colin strode towards them and embraced each man in turn, slapping them on the back.

"All set?" he asked them.

"Yeah," the taller of the two replied, glancing at me.

"This is my wife Jessica," Colin said.

Both men gave me a chin raise acknowledgement.

Colin turned to me. "Well, Kathleen will show you out and I need to show these boys some London hospitality. Don't wait up." Colin turned his back, threw an arm around each of the men's shoulders and walked away from me towards the SUV.

"Ya, ready then?" I jumped. I hadn't heard Kathleen approach.

"I guess I am," I said with a final glance at Colin and his friends.

Kathleen led me to a side door. She pressed a door release button and pushed the door open, stepping through and holding it for me.

"I'll see you again soon, Jess," she said as a gust of wind pulled the door from her hand and it slammed shut. "Damn it."

I watched as she keyed a six-digit code into the keypad beside the door, 200192. The door opened and Kathleen disappeared inside. I turned and walked away. Trust Colin to use his birth date.

Chapter 26

January 29

I called into work on my way home and transferred the emailed files to a flash drive, deleting all record of them from my email account.

Not for the first time, I wished Dad was around to talk to. I considered calling Will several times, but something stopped me. If my conclusions were correct, and Colin was using his freight business for illegal weapons trafficking, then I probably shouldn't voice that over a telephone line. Was that the conclusion that my father had arrived at? Was that why he was killed? I was due to have lunch with Will the next day, so I decided to wait until then to talk to him. This wasn't going anywhere, right?

I was just packing up, locking the printouts in my desk drawer and slipping the flash drive into my bag, when I heard the elevator ping. I looked up to see my head of department crossing the floor towards me with a big smile on his round face.

"Jess," he boomed. "I'm glad you're here, saves me a phone call. You're looking a lot better than I expected."

"Hi, Gregory, thankfully the bruising has faded quickly," I said, touching my face.

"Hope the police catch the guy."

"Me too," I said. "What can I do for you?"

"The opportunity to lead a technology project in the capital markets area out of the New York office has suddenly come up and your name was suggested," he said. I must have looked surprised because he continued. "Look, I know it's really short notice, but the project head has been in a car accident and is going to be in hospital for weeks and we can't delay the implementation any longer. What do you think? Are you up for a challenge?"

"Ah, yeah," I said. "How long is the placement?"

"Three months," Gregory said, stroking his beard and studying me. "Starting next week."

I gave a slow nod as my brain whirred. This was exactly what I needed to physically distance myself from both Colin, and Will, and to give me time to work out what, if anything, to do with the information I had on Colin. This was my opportunity to leave him, my opportunity to step out from his shadow and start again.

"We will need an answer fairly quickly," he continued.

"I'll take it," I said.

* * *

Despite a late night out with the lads from Strathgarvan, Colin was up working when I woke the following morning.

"It's the weekend, do you ever take a break?" I asked,

standing in the doorway of the study. The desk lamp was on and Colin was engrossed in whatever was on the computer screen.

"When you're growing your business, it's twenty-four-seven, Jess, you know that," he said continuing to type.

"I need to talk to you," I said. He looked up from the computer. "I'm going to be working out of the New York office for the next couple of months."

"What the hell for?" he snarled.

"Colin, it's a great opportunity for me to further my career."

"You won't need a career once we start a family," he said. "And that can't happen if we're in different countries."

I looked at him as if he'd grown two heads. A family? Where the hell had that come from? That so wasn't happening.

"Colin, things haven't been great between us lately. A break will do us good. And besides it's only for three months," I replied.

A look of fury took residence on his face. He pushed back his chair, stalked towards the door and slammed it in my face.

Chapter 27

January 30

I was waiting on the platform when Will's train pulled in. He called to me from a center carriage when the doors opened. I ran and jumped aboard.

"It's a gorgeous day. I thought we should go somewhere different," he said.

We travelled along the district line to Tower Bridge and walked to The Dickens Inn. The pub was in an old timber-framed warehouse. The balconies on each floor of the three-storied building were lined with window boxes and hanging baskets overflowing with colorful flowers. We were seated on the middle balcony at a small table overlooking the waterways. An outdoor heat lamp was attached to the wall to keep us warm.

"This is lovely, Will. I've never been here," I said. "What's the Dickens link?"

"Apparently, this is Charles Dickens' old stomping ground. It was his grandson who opened the modern version of this pub. Anyway, what's your news?"

"Firstly, I'm off to New York for three months," I said. "I'm project managing a capital markets tech implementation."

"Wow, that's great, Jess."

"Yeah it is for me. The person who was supposed to be leading it has had a car accident."

"Not so good for them, but a good opportunity for you. Congratulations."

"Thanks." I smiled at him.

"I will miss you though," he added.

"I will miss you too."

We gazed at each other for a long moment.

"Will, I want to run something past you," I said after a waiter handed us menus and took our drinks order. "I might be jumping to conclusions, but something isn't right and I don't know what to do."

Will reached across the old wooden table and gave my hand a squeeze. "Talk to me, Jess."

Unexpected tears pooled in my eyes and I took a deep breath before continuing, my gaze focused on our still linked fingers.

"My father was investigating Colin at the time of his death, unbeknown to me, and left me a secret safety deposit box full of information pertaining to his investigation," I said, raising my lashes to gauge his reaction.

Will's eyes narrowed and he leaned closer. "What do you mean?"

"There are several things and I haven't unraveled it all yet, but I suspect that Colin is using the freight business as a cover for arms dealing."

"Do you have some evidence of this?" Will asked, his eyes wide.

I nodded. "Dad somehow got a hold of a contract for a company called Mendelson, who provide weapons under an exclusive agreement to the British Army. He also found out that L-FLI had the contract to deliver the weapons from Mendelson's factory to an army base, however I've managed to download the shipping manifests from Colin's office which appear to show that there is surplus being produced which is transported from the factory by L-FLI to its London depot. I'd have to show you to explain fully." I took a deep breath. "You've no idea how good it is to tell someone about this."

"Jess, this is serious."

"I know, which is why I have been trying to gather as much information as I could before doing anything with it. If I get this wrong, I could end up like Dad."

Will released my hand and sat back, his face stony. "You don't think he was murdered over this?" he asked in a quiet voice.

"Possibly, I honestly don't know. There are a few things that don't add up."

Will swore under his breath.

"He thought his life was in danger," I said. "Dad's assistant told me that he had two visitors right before his death. I think that they either injected him with something that caused the heart attack or suffocated him in some way, as there was evidence of petechial hemorrhaging in his eyes that couldn't be explained. The cameras in their building were conveniently not working, but she managed to get some CCTV stills from a nearby office which showed the legs of these two visitors returning to a black vehicle and a partial license plate. The thing is, I saw a black SUV with the same three number plate digits at Colin's warehouse yesterday."

"What?!"

"I don't know what to do with this. I should probably do

nothing, but my instincts are telling me that something is about to happen," I said. "Colin is really volatile, more so than usual."

Will frowned. "I have a mate who's a detective at the Met–let's get him involved."

"I don't know. Will, I'm off to New York tomorrow for three months. I've been trying to leave Colin for a while, but I've been too scared. This is my opportunity to make a clean break. He knows who beat me up, Will, and he did nothing about it. And you were right, he has hit me and treated me poorly. I've been so stupid," I said, putting my head in my hands. "I'm better than this and I've let him control me for too long."

"I couldn't agree more," Will said. "But there's more going on here than Colin just being a crap husband. You need to tell the authorities, let them deal with things."

"There is more."

"Go on," Will said, a wary tone in his voice.

"I also think he knew the guys that beat and probably killed a man near his office a few weeks ago. I was there, I saw them beating him. Colin dragged me away. He has surrounded himself with some really nasty people." I sat back as the waiter delivered our drinks; beer for Will and red wine for me. I took a large gulp.

"Okay, why don't you give me what you've got and I'll send it on to my mate?" Will suggested.

I nodded. "Thank you. I've scanned most of it and saved it to a flash drive." I rummaged around in my bag before sliding the drive across the table to him.

"I'll pass it on. He may want to talk to you," he said. "Jess, I'm pleased you're going to be away from him for a few months," he added.

"Me too," I said. "I'm actually a little scared of what he might do if he thought I was leaving for good."

Will's knuckles were white as he gripped the edge of the table, but otherwise, he showed no reaction. "You need to do what's right for you, Jess. At best he's a bully and you know I think you'd be better off without him."

"I know. I feel like the scales have suddenly fallen from my eyes and I'm seeing him for who he really is. It's like he's a chameleon who adapts to the situation. At the start of our relationship he played the role of the caring, considerate boyfriend with ease, then the happily married newlywed. Now he's playing the part of successful young businessman with the skill of a Juilliard trained actor. I'm not sure what comes next. I guess in the beginning I was so under his spell that I didn't care if he seemed to be too good to be true. But now, it all feels off, wrong somehow."

"There is nothing in this that is your fault," Will said.

I nodded as it dawned on me that I was feeling hopeful for the first time in a long while. I hadn't realized that leaving for the right reasons, for me, not just to be with Will, was so important. The project in New York would give me the time I needed to move on from them both. I knew that I no longer loved Colin. Whatever had been there was gone. I also wasn't sure that I could allow myself to fall for Will again. My feelings for him were complicated and way stronger than I was willing to admit, even to myself. I knew deep down that what I really needed was time alone, to just be Jess again before I could commit to another relationship.

I didn't think I'd be able to eat after that conversation, but I felt an enormous weight lift off me after confiding in Will, and I managed to share one of the Inn's famous pizzas and a salad with him, before we wandered along the water ways admiring the boats and waiting for the pedestrian bridges to lower after boats passed through. The sun was shining and I felt as though I had a brighter future ahead of me.

We got the tube back to Earl's Court and walked to Will's apartment. I didn't intend on going in, but he insisted.

"Will Colin be home?" he asked.

I shrugged. "He said he was golfing, but I'm beginning to think that's a euphemism for something else."

"Stay out a little longer. I won't get to see you for a while after today," he said.

I followed him up the stairs. I stood at the window looking down at a group of children playing hide and seek among the trees and shrubs in the square across the road, while Will made coffee.

He came up behind me and slipped his arms around my waist and leaned down resting his chin on the top of my head. "Mmm... I'm going to have to come and visit you in New York," he said.

"I'd like that." I closed my eyes and leaned back into him. I tensed as he flexed his hands up and over my ribs and spun me around to face him. I tipped my head back to look at him. Those deep blue eyes roamed my face, before settling on my lips. I read his intent very clearly and began shaking my head trying to step back out of his embrace. All I succeeded in doing was backing myself up against the window ledge. Will moved with me, a smile dancing around his lips.

"Where are you going, Jess?" he asked, bracing his hands on the sill either side of me.

"Home, I think," I replied.

He looked at me for a long moment before stepping back and holding his hands up.

"As you wish," he said.

I stepped around him and walked across the room, picking up my bag from the chair where I had dropped it. At the door, I turned. Will was standing with his back to me looking out of the window. What the hell was I doing? I knew better than to spend time alone with him like this. It always led to one thing. I realized then that was another reason that I had agreed to see him today. I needed to say goodbye on my own terms, not because he decided it was time to move on, but because I had.

I dropped my bag and strode back across the room at the same time as he turned and stepped towards me. We met halfway. We held each other's eyes for several seconds before he lifted me up to kiss me. I wrapped my legs around his waist and my arms around his neck. Our kisses were gentle at first. I wound my hands through his hair and pulled his mouth harder onto mine. He made a small sound of surprise at my aggression and moving his hands beneath my butt to balance me, he began walking us towards his bedroom. He kicked the door open and we fell back on the bed, mouths still joined. I sat up straddling him and pulled my jumper off, followed by my t-shirt. Will propped himself up on his elbows and smirked, enjoying my performance. I turned my attention to the buttons on his shirt as his hands closed over my breasts gently squeezing and caressing. As I undid the last button on his shirt and ran my hands over his broad chest, I felt my bra give as he undid it, sliding the straps down my arms. I bent my head and kissed a very sensitive spot on his neck.

"Oh no you don't," he murmured and flipped me onto my

back. I arched into his touch, tugging his hair, and pulled his mouth down to meet mine.

Chapter 28

January 31

I closed my suitcases and took a final turn about the flat. Everything that was really important to me, but not going to New York, had been packed in several boxes and collected by a storage company earlier in the day. The rest was just the debris of married life and could easily be replaced–kitchen stuff, IKEA furniture, books and linen.

My flight was at 5 pm, so I had a few hours to kill before the car was picking me up to take me to Heathrow.

I gathered my courage and decided it was time to go and see Colin, who had left the flat early muttering something about going to the warehouse.

I spent the morning going over what I was going to say to him. After all it's not every day you leave your husband. Unfortunately, my conversation with Will the previous day had only served to have a number of my suspicions confirmed and I had decided when I woke this morning, that rather than just sneaking away, I needed to have a tough conversation with Colin, before leaving for New York tonight.

Walking to the tube, I typed a text to Will.

'Thank you again for listening yesterday and for passing the info on to your mate at the Met.'

My fingers hovered over the send icon considering whether I should say anything about what happened back at his flat, but I guess that kind of spoke for itself. It was our goodbye in a way. I tapped send. He replied as I reached the underground station.

'Anytime Jess. What time does your flight leave?'

'5pm. I'm on my way to confront Colin with some of my questions now, and to tell him that I'm leaving him.'

As the DLR train emerged from underground a little while later, my mobile chimed with notification of no less than ten missed calls from Will. I frowned as he rang again.

"Jess, I don't think it's a good idea to talk to him yet. Think it over for a few days, wait to see what my mate has to say and call him from New York if you have to." Will sounded out of breath.

"What? You've changed your tune." I was baffled by the sudden turnaround.

"I just don't think it's wise. You need to be careful. He could turn nasty."

"It'll be fine. There'll be other people around. Anyway, I'm almost there. I'll let you know how it goes."

I heard him swear as I disconnected the call and pocketed my phone. I needed to do this and not be dissuaded by him.

I alighted at Devon Road Station and hailed a passing cab to take me down from the station to Limehouse Cut.

The large roller doors on the L-FLI depot were all closed, which surprised me. There was no answer on the intercom, so I entered the building through the small side door using the passcode that I'd seen Kathleen entering a couple of days

181

earlier. The warehouse was silent and gloomy. I walked down the first row of stacked boxes towards the stairs to the offices on the mezzanine level.

"Hello?" I called. I had expected the warehouse to be a hive of activity during the day. The international freight business was 24/7 as Colin liked to keep reminding me, but perhaps all of the drivers had already picked up or dropped off their deliveries early since it was a Sunday. There was a solitary white van parked inside the warehouse.

The heels of my shoes were the only sound as I climbed the stairs. I peeked into the office not expecting to see Kathleen or Sarah, and sure enough, their desks were empty and computers switched off, but I heard a muffled noise coming from behind Colin's door. I crossed the room and pushed the door open. Lying bound and gagged on the floor was a man in a security guard's uniform. He was bleeding from his temple and struggling to sit up. I rushed over to him and helped him into a sitting position and undid the gag.

"Are you okay? What happened?" I asked the stranger as I moved behind him to untie his hands. "Where's Colin?"

"Right here." Colin's voice came from behind me as I loosened the knot around the man's wrists. I spun around to see my husband in the doorway, a gun dangling from his hand. I stared at it and then at Colin.

"What's going on? Who's this?"

"What the hell are you doing here?" Colin demanded as he entered the room pushing past me towards his desk.

I eyed the gun and started backing towards the door. "I thought I'd see if you had time for coffee before I go, but I can see you are busy," I said, taking the final couple of steps and turning to run.

Colin crossed the room in three large strides and pushed the door shut before I could leave, trapping me in the office with him and the security guard. I stood trembling, facing the door. Something was very wrong. It wasn't that my worst nightmares were coming true, it was beyond anything that I would have dreamed of. What could I do now?

"Turn around," he ordered.

I did as he asked.

There was movement as the security guard rose and launched himself at Colin. But Colin was ready and although I'd released the man's wrists, his feet were still tied and his balance was off. Colin wrestled with the man for a moment before punching him hard in the face. The security guard fell backwards, catching the side of his head on the edge of Colin's desk with a crack. I screamed as Colin raised his gun and brought the handle down hard on the back of the man's head. He slumped to the floor unconscious.

I took the opportunity of Colin's momentary distraction to escape. I pulled the door open and started running through the outer office. But Colin was too fast for me. He grabbed me around the waist with one arm, lifted me off the ground and carried me back into his office. I screamed again.

"Help me."

Colin threw me on the floor in front of his desk beside the unconscious security guard and closed the door with his foot. He stood over me. "Oh, Jess. Why couldn't you just stay being the little wife, playing at a career and having your little fling?" I must have looked shocked. "Oh come on," he continued. "You didn't think that I didn't know all about Will and how you pined like a lovesick teenager when he hooked up with Frankie," he laughed, bitterness lacing his words. "You and your bloody father couldn't help snooping, could you? What did you find, eh? Nothing, I bet. At least you turning up here rids me of one problem."

He turned and closed the wall safe, replacing a framed picture of a coastal island over it.

My mouth had gone dry and I struggled to speak. I wasn't aware that I was crying until I felt the tears drip off my chin onto my neck, warm and wet. I glanced at the man beside me on the floor.

"Who is he?" I asked in a small voice.

"No idea, Jess, but he stuck his nose in where it wasn't wanted."

Colin approached me and pulled me to my feet. He had some thick twine in his hands which he wrapped around my wrists. I tried to pull away as my phone rang in the back pocket of my jeans.

"Ooh, let's see who this is?" Colin said, reaching into my pocket and retrieving my phone. He held it up for both of us to see. Will was calling again.

"Still sniffing around," Colin said with disgust. He dropped the phone and crushed the screen under his boot. The ringing stopped.

"Oops," Colin said, laughing at the look of dismay on my face.

I gulped my tears and struggled harder.

"Don't make me use the gun, Jess," he murmured, his voice cold and devoid of emotion.

"Colin, what's going on? What are you doing?"

He laughed; a short, nasty sound. "You will see, darling wife."

He continued to wrap the rope around my wrists so that it

cut into my skin and I whimpered. I was really scared. It was beginning to dawn on me that perhaps he intended to kill me.

"Colin, this isn't you. What about all our plans, moving back to Scotland, having a family?"

He gave me a withering look as he opened his office door and peered into the corridor. "Were you thinking about those things when you were in his bed? I think not," he said as his lip curled. "Let's go."

He pulled me down the staircase so fast that I stumbled, falling to my knees before he hauled me up and pushed me towards the van parked in the center of the warehouse. The side door was ajar and Colin slid it open the whole way. A dark-skinned man in blue overalls was working on a piece of equipment inside the van. He replaced a small screwdriver in his tool box and closed the lid.

"Ready, Colin," he said in a thick Scottish accent as he climbed out.

"Get in," Colin said lifting me. "Pete here is going to take you for a little drive."

The piece of equipment looked like a bomb, wires wrapped around red cylinders, a timer and keypad, tubes. Pete reappeared in the doorway carrying a large cardboard box, which he slipped over the bomb. It now looked like any of the other boxes and packages stacked in the van. I screamed. Colin clamped a hand over my mouth, forcing my lips back into my teeth. I tasted blood. "For God's sake, shut up, Jess." He glared at me until I nodded. He released his hand.

"Colin. No. Let me go," I cried. I tried to climb back out of the van, but to little avail. Colin gave me a large shove and I sprawled on the dirty floor of the vehicle, coming face to face with a row of clear plastic containers full of nails and screws.

I scrabbled backwards away from the shrapnel.

Colin leaned into the van. "Bye, my love," he said as he raised the gun and brought it down on the side of my head.

I slumped forward, blackness flowing across my vision. I could see Colin's legs moving away from the van towards the stairs and back up to the offices. I struggled to stay conscious. Pete pulled the side door closed and I was encased in darkness. I could hear Pete's footsteps walking around the van, followed by the opening and closing of the driver's door. I forced myself upright and began tugging at the bonds on my wrists. I was so not ready to die.

A single gunshot echoed through the vast warehouse, followed by shouting. From the front of the van I heard Pete emit a muffled expletive and open his door again. The next shot sounded much closer. Who was shooting? I hoped it wasn't one of Colin's business rivals. I was in trouble either way, if that was the case.

I panicked. What would happen if someone shot the bomb? Would it go off? I started feeling my way along the inside of the van. The twine holding my wrists behind my back snagged on a rivet impeding any further movement. I pulled in frustration and felt the twine give.

I heard one of the forklifts start up. The muffled thud of bullets hitting wood and cardboard was intermingled with shouting voices. The van shook as Pete returned fire with what sounded like an automatic weapon. As panic threatened to overwhelm me, I pulled harder on the bonds around my wrists. A tearing noise sounded and I pulled one hand free. I pulled the twine off my other hand, rubbing the spot where it had cut into my wrist and felt along the side of the van for the door handle, as Pete gave a cry of pain and I heard the clatter of a gun falling onto the ground.

I located the latch and slid the door open a fraction. The noise of gunfire was deafening. I risked looking through the crack in the door to see what was going on. I could see several armed figures wearing dark combat fatigues creeping down the rows of stacked cartons, weapons drawn. From the left a forklift came out of nowhere and crashed into the first row, knocking it domino-like onto the next rows. There were shouts and cries as heavy boxes toppled onto the people edging further into the warehouse.

I moved so that I could see the top of the stairs. Several people were crouched clutching large black guns giving a continuous burst of fire onto the collapsed boxes. I gasped as I saw Kathleen come into my line of sight holding a weapon as though it was normal for her and begin firing towards the side of the building.

In my periphery I saw movement at the far end of the warehouse and more black-clad figures entered though a small door.

I started screaming. "Help me. There's a bomb in the van."

The firing ceased for moment and I jumped as a trail of bullets ran down the side of the van. Someone was trying to silence me. I crawled to the far side taking care not to bump the bomb. I tried to assess my rapidly diminishing options. If I left the van, I'd be shot, but if I stayed I'd be blown to pieces. The van shuddered as someone climbed into the driver's seat and started the engine.

I looked around for a weapon and in the pool of light provided by the open door I saw a square cover in the floor at the rear of the van. The spare tire well. I crawled over to it and pulled the plywood cover aside. A tire iron was nestled beside the spare tire. I gripped it in my hand and crawled back to the door, ready to move.

The van started moving forward. I leaned into the sliding door to keep my balance. At last I had a plan. As soon as we left the building I would jump out. A loud bang sounded, followed by another and the van shuddered to a stop and sunk down. The smell of smoldering rubber filled my nostrils. More shooting erupted as I cringed inside the van.

The door of the van slid open at speed. I raised the tire iron and swung it at the person who peered inside.

"Bloody hell, Jess. It's me," Will said, ducking as my swing missed its target and instead clattered into the door.

I lost my grip on the tire iron and it fell to the ground with a loud clatter. I stared at him. "What the hell are you doing here?"

Before he could answer two uniformed and heavily armed police officers arrived at his side.

"Get her out. We'll cover you," the taller of the two ordered Will. Will clicked the safety on his semi-automatic weapon, swung it over his shoulder by its strap and helped me climb out of the van.

"Careful, Colin's up on the mezzanine," I cautioned as I stepped down holding on to his arms. I looked up the stairs in fear. "And, Will, there's a bomb in here, under that box." I leaned back into the van and lifted the cardboard cover off.

"Shit." Will peered over my shoulder at the tangle of wires. "Come on, Jess, let's get you out of here." He signaled to a couple of other men.

"What about you?" I clung on to him, unsteady on my feet.

"I'll be right behind you," he said. "Now, one, two, three, go." He gave me a little push as the two officers put down a trail of covering fire towards the mezzanine.

I started running towards the front entrance, my blood pumping with each step, waiting to feel the thud of a bullet in my back. Where did Will get that gun and why wasn't he just coming with me? I heard further shouts and gunshots followed by footsteps pounding down after me. The trouble was I didn't know if it was Will or Colin and I was too scared to look, so I just kept running. As I reached the large corrugated iron roller door at the canal side of the building, a loud boom echoed throughout the warehouse and everything began to shake. I cowered as cardboard boxes, lights and sheets of roofing iron began falling. The whole building felt like it was swaying and I covered my face just as the side and front windows exploded with the pressure.

"Will," I screamed as darkness took me.

* * *

I dreamed that I was a child again playing hide and seek with Dad.

"Jessica?" he called. His voice sounded muffled, as though coming from a great distance.

"Dad?" I called and was racked by a bout of coughing as my lungs filled with dust.

"Jess," another voice said. This time a little closer and with an English accent, not Scottish.

The coughing subsided and I tried again.

"Dad." My voice came out husky and croaky.

"She's in here," the voice shouted.

I heard things being moved and forced my eyes open. I was in darkness, apart from a small chink of light in front of me.

"Jess," the voice called again. Definitely not Dad with that accent.

"Hello?" I tried.

"Hang on, Jess, we're coming." The voice sounded strained, but relieved.

The chink of light became bigger and there were several voices now. I struggled to hold on to what they were saying.

"There you are."

I opened my eyes. I was so tired. I just wanted to sleep. Yet someone kept talking to me. I wished that they'd shut up. I looked into a familiar face. Will. It all came flooding back. Colin. The explosion. A sudden pain tore through my chest.

"Colin?" I asked in a terrified whisper.

"It's okay, Jess. He's dead."

I just nodded. I didn't feel sad or relieved. In fact I didn't feel anything. That couldn't be right.

"Let's get you out of there," Will said, pulling more debris away. He crawled in towards me, reaching out and running his fingers across my cheek. "Hang in there, sweetheart," he said before turning his head and calling with urgency, "I need a medic here, now."

He turned back and held my flittering gaze. "Stay with me, Jess."

I frowned at his concern and tried to crawl forward to him, but my right side wouldn't obey. I glanced down and saw a huge gash in my upper arm and thigh. There was blood everywhere. I watched Will wide-eyed as he expertly tied a bandage around the wound in my arm to stem the blood flow, before I passed out.

Chapter 29

February 1

It was the smell that hit me first. Clean, sterile, disinfectant mixed with something floral. I forced my eyelids open and peered around the room. It was small, everything was white including the narrow bed that I was lying in. A cheap print of a cottage by the sea hung on an angle on the wall at the end of the bed, green and gold patterned curtains framed the only window. There were two doors. Both were closed.

"Ah you're awake." A smiling nurse with short highlighted blonde hair came across my vision, picking up my wrist and checking the watch hanging on the chain clipped to her pale blue scrubs. "Water?" she offered.

I nodded, still processing.

"There you are, love," she said, stepping on a button on the floor which gently raised the head of my bed as she held a glass in front of me and angled the straw to my lips.

I took a small painful swallow. The cool liquid trickled over my parched throat. I took another sip and another.

"Where am I?" I whispered.

"The Royal London Hospital, love. You're lucky to be alive. You'd lost a lot of blood when they pulled you out."

"That's enough now," a male voice broke across the conversation. I glanced behind the nurse as two men entered the room. The nurse stiffened, leaned over me and pushed the call button on my headboard.

"She has only just now regained consciousness. You will have to wait until the doctor has seen her before you ask your questions. Now out." She shooed the two men from the room.

I drifted in and out of consciousness as the doctor came and examined me. I was just so tired.

An indeterminate time later, I heard an argument erupt outside my door.

"She might know something," an angry male voice said.

"I have to put my patient's welfare first and she's not up to questioning."

"You could have a hell of a lot more patients if we don't find out what their target was."

A loud sigh and the door opened. "Ten minutes. No more."

I opened my eyes as two men followed the white-coated doctor into the room. The nurse in the blue scrubs followed, concern etched into her face.

The two men introduced themselves as Agent Rob Stevens of MI5 and Detective Inspector Mark Rawlinson.

"How are you feeling, Mrs. McDonald?" Stevens asked.

"Not sure," I replied with a whisper.

Stevens, a tall middle-aged man dressed in a smart suit and tie, stood at the end of the bed. His dark hair was cropped short and he had a small scar above his top lip. He adjusted his glasses. "We're hoping that you're up to talking to us."

"I'll try," I said in a voice that came out as a scratchy whisper.

The nurse rushed forward to offer me more water.

"I'll do that. You may leave," Detective Rawlinson said to her. She glanced at the doctor, who gave her a slight nod. With a disgruntled sigh, she left the room. Rawlinson was a stocky man of mixed race with small shrewd eyes. His head was shaved and he wore jeans and a casual jacket.

"You too," Rawlinson said to the doctor as he handed me the water.

"Now it appears that your husband was part of a terrorist network," Stevens began as the doctor left the room.

I choked on the water. "What? That can't be. Why?"

"That's what we'd like to find out. The explosion that destroyed the warehouse was only the tip of the iceberg. We've found a smaller warehouse close by owned by one of your husband's companies that was stocked with enough C4 to flatten an entire city block."

"God." I gasped.

"Now, do you have any idea where the bomb in the van was headed?" I shook my head. "Did he say anything to you before he put you in the van with it?" Rawlinson asked.

"It's all a bit hazy," I said, struggling to recall what Colin had said. "What about the security guard?"

The two men exchanged glances. "Security guard?"

"When I first went to the warehouse, Colin had a security guard tied up on the floor of his office. I was untying him when Colin came back in. They fought and Colin knocked him out."

"We're still sorting through the rubble, there are a few bodies that we have yet to identify," Rawlinson said.

"Why were you there?" Stevens asked.

"I'm leaving for New York for work," I began. "Well, I was

supposed to be," I added. "I was going to say goodbye and to tell him that I was leaving him."

Stevens raised an eyebrow.

"Is he really dead?" I asked. Stevens nodded. "I feel relieved. Isn't that awful?"

"No, Jess. He planned to kill a lot of people."

"How did you get to the warehouse so quickly?"

"We've had an agent monitoring him for a number of months and he arrived shortly after you did."

"How could I not have known?" I said. "I thought he was a dirty businessman. I'd been gathering information to that effect since my father died." I broke off. "Do you think he killed Dad?" I asked in a whisper.

Rawlinson shrugged. "We'll look into that," he said.

The doctor stuck his head back around the door. "Time's up, gentlemen."

Rawlinson held up one finger. "Mrs. McDonald..."

"Jess, please," I croaked.

"Jess, obviously we'll need to talk to you some more, but for now we just wanted to see if you had any clues as to his target."

I shook my head, bringing on a wave of nausea. "No." I closed my eyes. "How could I have not known?"

"He fooled a lot of people. Fortunately, your suspicions in recent days focused our attention and may have saved hundreds of lives," Stevens said, giving me a kind smile.

"But, I hadn't gone to the police." I was really beginning to flag. Nothing was making any sense. "How do you know that I wasn't involved?" The men exchanged uncertain glances. Stevens nodded and Rawlinson went to the door and spoke to someone. "Will," I said, my memory of what happened before the explosion, coming back in flashes and my subconscious joining the dots. "He was there. Can I see him?"

"Now, Jess, there are some things that you don't know and some things that you can't know. What I can tell you is that Scotland Yard's Counter Terrorism Command and MI5 have been undercover ever since we suspected that an unknown terrorist organization, with links to Al Qaeda, had established a base here in London," Stevens said.

I nodded, not understanding as Rawlinson returned with someone behind him.

"Jess, this is one of our agents, Charlie Matheson. You know him better as William Johnston," he said.

Will stepped into view carrying flowers. His left arm was wrapped in a bandage and one cheek shone with a dark bruise over which little cuts intersected each other like a two-tone tube map. Despite his injuries, his eyes shone and his mouth curved into a wide smile.

"Hey, you look a lot better than the last time I saw you," he said.

I looked at him in complete confusion. "Will, is it true? You are not really who you said you were? All this time?" I whispered, not really wanting to hear his reply. He nodded. The pain was immediate. It started in my chest and spread upwards towards my throat and downwards into my stomach. "No," I whispered, tears pouring down my cheeks, their saltiness stinging the cuts on my face. "Was it all lies?"

"No," Will said in a soft voice, shaking his head. He opened his mouth to say something further, but was interrupted by Stevens.

"We can't discuss any details of the mission at this stage, you understand, so I will have to stop you there."

"Mission?" I asked in disbelief.

Will hung his head and sighed.

"I was assigned to track Colin and his circle, and working with you was the way in."

Stevens cleared his throat.

I stopped listening and sat back against my pillows. I felt numb. My whole life was one big fat lie. I couldn't even start to comprehend that.

"Jess, we'll see you again tomorrow," Rawlinson said, interrupting my thoughts.

"Can I just have a minute alone with her?" Will asked. "Please?"

Stevens nodded. "This is against orders. Make it quick." Both men left the room.

"Jess, it wasn't all lies. I care for you so much. I haven't got time to explain now, but in the flowers is a card with my number. Call me when you are out of here and we can meet and I'll explain.

He leaned down and kissed my forehead.

"I'm so sorry." And he was gone.

II

Part Two

Chapter 30

March 5

The wind cut through the layers I was wearing as
though they were tissue paper and chilled me to the
bone. Not that I felt it. I didn't feel much of anything,
anymore.

I stood on the windswept hill behind the little cottage
above the village of Strathgarvan, looking out over the rugged
Scottish coast, past a small offshore island to the vast ocean
beyond. On top of the ridge beyond the village stood the
ruins of Strathgarvan Castle, what remained of its crumbling
grey walls desolate and unloved, a little like me.

Strathgarvan was to be my escape, my refuge from the
world, their questions and their insinuations. I also hoped
it would provide me with some answers as to just who that
husband of mine had really been. I certainly didn't share
the media's view that he was the leader of a small poorly
organized group of misfits. Colin was way too smart for that.
He had been involved in something much bigger. Of that
I was sure. The agent from MI5 had mentioned a terrorist
network. And this place, this cottage that he liked to escape

to, seemed like the best place to start looking for answers.

I dreamed last night that I was at an airport. I was waiting near the departure gate. Dad was there and a man was helping him with his bags. He looked up, saw me and walked over.

"Jessica, my darling girl." He hugged me to him. "I have to go now."

"I will see you when you get back," I said.

"No, darling, I'm not coming back this time." He kissed my forehead and returned to his travelling companion. I frowned. This made no sense. I watched as they strolled towards the departure gate and turned to wave.

Dad's travelling companion was Will. They disappeared through the security checkpoint leaving me all alone.

Chapter 31

April 1

I closed the door behind me and dumped the heavy basket of firewood by the fireplace. Although it was supposed to be spring, it was still cold. I'd lit the fire each night for the last month which warmed my new home. The cottage was tiny. Just four rooms – kitchen, living room, bedroom and bathroom. It was sparsely decorated, if that's what you could call the very masculine, plain decor, but I was starting to warm it up with a few feminine touches like a big vase of wild flowers on the old wooden dining table and another on the mantel above the fireplace. I had painted the wooden shutters in the kitchen a sunny yellow and thrown out the dusty old curtains and rugs, replacing them with fresh new ones.

My London belongings looked odd here, although most of my lovely china now resided on the open shelves in the kitchen. It didn't seem like there would be much call for my crystal or slow cooker, so they stayed boxed up in the shed. My espresso machine, however, stood gleaming at one end of the small bench. After all, there were limits to my new country existence.

The cottage was about the only thing that Colin left me. The authorities had scooped up everything else that belonged to him as evidence, but they seemed happy to let me have this once they had been all over it. I suppose it wasn't worth anything, a little cottage in the middle of nowhere. I'd also managed to hold on to the London flat since Colin had been too busy to sign the sale and purchase agreement when we bought it; it had been lodged in my name.

Colin had acquired this cottage somewhere along the line. I had never been here. It was his weekend getaway, and his alone. He would come up several times a year to have a golfing, shooting and fishing weekend with the local lads that he was friends with, but otherwise it stood empty. It was showing some signs of neglect, but nothing that couldn't be rectified. I needed a project, so this was it for now.

I wandered into the kitchen to switch on the coffee machine. A heavy bump against my leg made me jump.

"Buffy," I admonished the large shaggy black and white English Sheepdog Collie cross, who stood looking up at me, her big brown eyes deep and soulful. I scratched behind her ears and she leaned into me, enjoying the attention. I had adopted Buffy from a neighbor in London, who had pleaded with me to take her when she heard that I was moving to the country. I had been reluctant, but acquiesced, and it turned out to be the best decision. We had quickly bonded. Buffy, named by my 1990s-loving neighbor after the TV show *Buffy the Vampire Slayer*, turned out to be just what I needed. She was loyal and fun. Most days she was the only living thing that I talked to. I cuddled her on the sofa at night during the long lonely evenings, and although she had a basket in the lounge, she slept at the foot of my bed.

The cottage didn't have a TV, so I was catching up on all the reading that the long hours working in the corporate world had curtailed. I also didn't have a computer or the Internet. I didn't own a radio and never bought a newspaper. I was thoroughly sick of reading some journalist's twisted view of what had been my life. My days as a news junkie were well and truly over. My only technology allowances were an iPhone with a new number and my Kindle, which I loaded at a café with free Internet in Ayr once a week. I had switched off the internet browsers on both devices and only checked my messages at the Internet café. Marie, Rachel, Jimmy and Dave emailed most weeks, but I had resisted their invitations to go and stay with them in London and had refused their advances to visit me.

I spent days at MI5 once I'd been released from hospital, answering questions and trying to get to the bottom of Colin's actions. I was as honest as I could be. I spoke at length to the agents and profilers about my marriage. I knew Colin and I had been growing apart, but I had thought we were just like any other busy young professional couple. But after these sessions, I came to see just how much he had controlled me and I accepted that I hadn't loved him in a very long time. Long before Will had come along. I mean, I had loved the man I married, but Colin had changed or perhaps he just allowed his true self to come to the fore. I was now not sure that I had ever really been 'in love' with him, especially when I compared my feelings for him with how I had felt about Will.

I was very conscious not to discuss my affair with Will in any detail with the agents. My interview sessions were all recorded and I was aware that whatever I said could be misconstrued and be embarrassing for him. I'm not sure why I even considered his feelings. In some ways his betrayal cut deeper than Colin's, but I had put those emotions in a box and pushed them to the back of my heart and hadn't allowed myself to take them out. I wasn't sure that I ever would. Yes, what Colin had done, what he'd made me an unwitting part of, was a betrayal, but somehow, Will's actions, his lies and how he had used me, hurt even more. I saw him several times during those days, standing in the foyer or waiting for me in a stairwell of the MI5 building, but I refused to speak to him. I just didn't know what to say.

I explained over and over to the agents how my suspicions that Colin was up to something had taken hold, but that never in my wildest dreams had I considered anything like this. After picking through the wreckage of the explosion at the warehouse, they had confirmed a direct link to the bomb used in the Cheapside attack and similarities to the smaller Trafalgar Square and Windsor incidents. It was incomprehensible. I'd been living with a man who was responsible for all that death and injury all that time and had no idea. What did that say about me? By the end of the interrogations, I just felt numb.

Once the authorities were satisfied that I was not involved, I was released. The media intrusion had been brutal. I refused to comment or give any interviews. I was portrayed by some journalists as the simpering ignorant wife and by others as a sex-crazed double agent who jumped anything that moved, and everything in between. They camped outside the flat and chased me down the road, pushing cameras and microphones in my face.

I tried going back to work. Of course, the New York job was

off the table, but they hadn't replaced me in my old role, so I slipped back into that, but it was dreadful. Colleagues whom I had thought of as friends avoided me, and I could silence a room by just walking in. Marie, Rachel, Dave and Jimmy were loyal and kind, but I knew that my presence at the bank was making their work lives difficult. After a fortnight, my manager pulled me into his office and slid an envelope across the desk. I was offered twenty-four months' full redundancy to leave. I signed it on the spot and within half an hour had cleared my desk and was sitting in a taxi on my way back to the flat.

After that, the decision to leave London had been easy. At first, I wasn't sure where to go. I didn't want to go home to Mum, as she wouldn't have been able to cope with the media frenzy. I toyed with the idea of disappearing to a Spanish island for a while, but the unanswered questions around Colin bothered me and as far as I was concerned my father's death was still very much unexplained. Colin simply couldn't have planned all of the things that he was accused of, on his own. Something or someone had turned him and made him fanatical or maybe it was already there when I met him. Either way, he was answering to someone, but who? Certainly, Scotland's First Minister and the MP for Ayrshire, whom Colin knew well from his student politics days, had both publicly distanced themselves. After all, it was political suicide to be linked to a terrorist. I assumed that they'd been questioned too, in the wake of the warehouse explosion.

Colin's comments during those last moments at the warehouse also haunted me. It seemed that I had been part of his cover. Young, malleable, Scottish. Except that I hadn't been as malleable as he had intended. Gullible, definitely, I mean, I had no idea what my husband was up to and to make things worse I'd fallen for the man sent to spy on us. The pain that was a constant presence, just under my ribs, intensified with the thought.

Those first couple of weeks at the cottage had been hell. I operated on auto-pilot most of the time, forcing myself to even remember to eat. I was grateful to fall into bed at night and had to drag myself out of bed in the morning. My only visitors had been the local minister and Alastair, the publican who was an old mate of Colin's. They left knowing that I didn't want company. I wasn't ready to play nice with anyone. Alastair continued to check on me though and as the days passed, the ice around my heart started to thaw.

The coffee machine grunted and hissed, shaking me out of my reverie. I ground the beans, steamed the milk and took my cappuccino to the table.

"Okay, Buffy. Once I've had this, we'll set the fire, then go and shoot some rabbits," I said. Buffy's ears pricked up at the word rabbit and she gave a single low bark of agreement.

When I'd moved into the cottage, I'd found a set of keys on a hook in the kitchen which unlocked the padlock on a small shed adjacent to the house. The door had creaked open and I'd peered inside with some trepidation. But the shed didn't contain anything sinister, in fact it was tidy with several fishing rods propped up against one wall, an ancient hand-pushed lawn mower, a set of golf clubs, and two rifles racked on the far wall. I locked the shed again, but a few days later I'd decided that I wanted to learn how to shoot the rifles that Colin had left and was unlocking the shed again when a car pulled up. I turned to see Alastair, climbing out of his four-wheel drive.

"Hey, Jess," he said, scratching at his mane of wild red hair, but keeping his distance, a wary look on his face as though he were approaching an untamed animal. "Thought I'd drop by and see if ya needed anything?"

I studied him for a moment before replying. "Actually, yes I do."

Alastair looked surprised. Up until now I had turned down all offers of help.

"I need you to teach me how to shoot one of these," I said, returning to the shed, picking up the closest rifle and stepping outside again.

"Whoa, easy, tiger," Alastair said. "Point it away from me, in case it's loaded."

"Oh, sorry." I swung the barrel towards the sky as he rushed towards me and snatched it from my grasp.

"Not loaded," he said, sounding relieved.

"So?" I asked.

"So?"

"Will you teach me?" I gave him my most winning smile.

Alastair was easily six foot five, with a scruffy beard to match his hair and I was trying not to be intimidated by him. He looked me over for a moment before he smiled, transforming his features into that of a teddy bear. "Alright then, lass."

He pushed past me into the shed and returned carrying a smaller rifle and a box of cartridges. "We'll start with this one, Jess."

"Okay."

Alastair turned out to be a gentle, patient coach. First, he checked and cleaned the gun, then he showed me how to hold it, how to stand and how to aim. We lined up a number of tin

207

cans on a board on the ground in front of the drywall stone fence at the base of the hill at the back of the property, well away from anyone. I stood as he instructed with my feet apart and the rifle tucked in against my shoulder.

"Now, Jess, this one will give you a kick back unless you brace yourself properly."

I nodded and eased the trigger back. The rifle gave a loud crack and slammed into my shoulder.

"Holy shit," I exclaimed much to Alastair's amusement. I glared at him, after which he kept his laughter to himself.

My shot, of course, had gone wild, but I kept at it and an hour later, I was hitting more than I was missing. He showed me how to clean and store the rifle. So, for the next couple of weeks, I had locked Buffy in the house and lined up the cans to practice. Now I didn't miss.

I had started shooting rabbits almost by accident. I was your typical city girl, who didn't like giving too much thought to where the meat that we ate came from. I certainly wouldn't eat rabbit or venison (Thumper and Bambi), but one afternoon as I set up my cans, I noticed a number of rabbits sunning themselves on the rise behind the fence, so I adjusted my shot and lined one up in my sights. The crack echoed and the bunny fell. And I cheered. I didn't analyze this too much, but I suppose my general numbness inside meant that I no longer had empathy or something. Anyway, I killed four rabbits by the end of that day and had no clue what to do with them.

I drove in to see Alastair. He looked so surprised when I called him out to the car to show him the spoils of my hunting.

"Do you know what I do with these?" I asked.

He studied me, with a new appreciation, it seemed. "Come with me." He led me into the pub's kitchen and gave me a lesson on skinning, gutting and preparing the rabbits. I left him with three and took one home to cook.

Cooking was the one thing that gave me some sense of enjoyment. I had always liked to cook but had never had the time, and Colin's constant demeaning comments had shaken my confidence in my ability. A couple of weeks after moving into the cottage, I started at the beginning of one of my Jamie Oliver cookbooks and worked my way to the end, making every recipe. Accessing some of the ingredients in the village proved challenging and so I had started driving up to Ayr to the supermarket once a week to stock up. Of course, I was cooking far more food than either Buffy or I would ever eat, but the process seemed to be giving me back something of myself.

It was one afternoon, as I lifted a chicken and leek pie from the oven, that I noticed the local doctor's car pull away from the neighboring cottage. The small whitewashed house was around three hundred meters from mine, down the driveway towards the village. An elderly couple lived there. We often exchanged waves, but they had left me alone, which suited me just fine.

A sense of unease settled on me as I watched the old boy stand at the door waving to the doctor. Not stopping to give myself time to change my mind, I walked down to their house there and then, carrying the pie wrapped in a tea towel and knocked on the door.

The old man cracked it open and peered out.

"Hello?"

"Hello, I live in the cottage at the end of the road. I've just taken this out of the oven. It's a chicken pie." I held it out towards him. "I thought you might like it."

"Och, thank you. Mrs. Gordon has just come out of the hospital. Broken 'er hip, she has. Would you like to come in?" He took the pie from me and stepped back inside.

"Look I won't, thanks all the same."

"Thank you again, Mrs. McDonald, I'm not much of a cook, so this is most appreciated."

"It's Jessica, Jessica Harley now. I've gone back to my maiden name. Please wish Mrs. Gordon a speedy recovery." I turned to leave.

Mr. Gordon nodded. "I will. Goodbye, Jessica, and thank you, lass."

Chapter 32

April 12

There was a knock at my door mid-morning as I lifted a carrot cake from the oven. It startled me. Apart from Alastair, I never got visitors. Putting down my oven mitts, I walked over to the door and pulled it open. An attractive, middle-aged man stood there smiling. His wavy dark hair was flecked with grey, and he wore an expensive looking Burberry jacket over his dark trousers.

"Hello?" I said.

"Mrs. McDonald. I'm Ewan Campbell, from the estate. We met a few years ago," he extended his hand.

I wiped my floury hands on my jeans and returned his handshake. He looked familiar. I had met him before, but I couldn't remember the circumstances.

"How can I help you?" I asked. My experience over the last few months had taught me that people only came to me if they wanted something from me.

"I knew your husband well, and I wanted to offer my condolences," he said, the smile dropping. "However it ended, Colin was a good man."

I stiffened and put my hands on my hips, glaring at him. "You'll forgive me if I disagree with that sentiment."

"I am sorry that I haven't been by sooner, but I understand something about grief and I guessed that you would want some time alone to come to terms with things," he continued as though I hadn't spoken.

I nodded and started to close the door.

"I hear you've been helping to look after the Gordons," he said, moving his foot across the threshold. I couldn't shut the door now, without looking extremely rude.

"I haven't been doing much, just helping with meals," I replied. Buffy had come to stand beside me. She looked from me to Ewan and growled, low in her throat.

"Buffy," I murmured.

Ewan smiled. "I don't know that she'll find many vampires to slay around here."

"Mmm... just a few demons, maybe," I replied, with a wry smile.

"Well, I won't keep you," Ewan said. "If you feel like getting out one night, Alastair does good fare down at the pub on Fridays and Saturdays. Give me a call and I could pick you up." He handed me a business card.

"Sure," I replied. "Thanks for dropping by." My manners finally returned from wherever they had been hiding. I turned the card over in my hands and read it. Of course, *the* Ewan Campbell, Laird of the estate. He'd been at our wedding. Colin's mates from the village had treated him with much reverence. Ewan nodded and walked back to his vehicle, a fairly new Range Rover of some sort. It dwarfed my little Fiat 500. He raised his hand in farewell and drove off down the drive. I leaned against the doorframe, playing with Buffy's ears as I watched him leave.

"That was odd, Buffy, condolences and a dinner invitation all in one."

My mobile rang as I stepped back inside. I checked the caller ID before answering; it was Colin's parents.

"Hello," I answered.

We chatted for a few minutes before the reason for the call became apparent.

"Jessica, the police have returned a rather large box of paperwork from Colin's warehouse. We think that you should have it," his father said.

I didn't have the heart to tell them that I didn't really want anything belonging to their son, because he'd ruined my life already. But they were grieving too. In many ways it was worse for them. They still loved the little boy that they had raised and weren't able to reconcile that little boy with the actions of the man he had become. Whereas I didn't have that problem, I didn't love him. Not at all, in fact, I hated him. The worse thing was that he wasn't here for me to tell him. I often shouted it into the wind off at the top of the cliff near the cottage, hoping that wherever he was, probably the depths of hell, it would reach his ears and he would know.

"How about I drive over to Edinburgh on Monday to collect the box?" I suggested.

"Aye, that would be grand."

I said goodbye and ended the call. I was determined to make the visit as short as possible. They would want to sit and rehash everything and to be honest I didn't think that I could stand doing that again.

For the first time, I realized that I was moving forward. I burst into tears and dropped down on the nearest chair. Oh, thank God. I didn't think it was ever going to happen. Buffy came over and put her head on my knees, licking at the salty tears that fell.

A little while later, having iced the cake, I took it down to the Gordons. I left with their shopping list tucked in my pocket and drove straight to the village store.

I was loading the bags into the car, when I heard my name. I turned to see Alastair hurrying across the road towards me.

"Jessica, just the woman I wanted t' see," he said.

I raised my eyebrows. "Oh yeah, what can I do for you?"

"My barmaid has up and gone to the city and I need a replacement, urgently," he said. I nodded, unsure what it had to do with me. "Can ye help me out?"

"Me?" I laughed. "Oh, I don't think so. I haven't worked in a bar before," I said shaking my head and closing the boot.

"Yer a smart gal, you'll pick it up in no time," he said.

"I'm not sure I'm ready to be out in public, Alastair, ya know?" I replied.

He put a big hand on my shoulder. "Jess, it's been a couple of months. It's time. And people round 'ere, they keep to their own business. No one'll bother ya. I'll make sure o' that."

"Aw, I don't know," I hedged.

"I'll see you tonight, six o'clock." He grinned and loped back across the road.

Chapter 33

April 13

The drive to Edinburgh on Monday took just over two hours. I decided to stop at Colin's parents first and get that over with, before spending the night with Mum.

The previous night had been an experience, and not an entirely unpleasant one, I was forced to admit. The time had flown by as I learned to pull pints, collected and washed glasses and cleaned down tables. Alastair had patiently taken me through the various tasks, and at the end of the evening declared that I was hired, whether I wanted to be or not. So somehow I had found myself a part time job, or a part time job had found me. I was to work four evenings, Thursday through to Sunday. I decided that I'd give it a go. It would be an interesting addition to my CV at the very least, although most people do the bar work before the career, not after. The irony was not lost on me. My mother would be horrified, her daughter working as a barmaid. I couldn't wait to tell her.

Colin's mother, Maggie, looked old and tired when she opened the front door. Their small terrace house was neat and tidy but crying out to be redecorated. I felt like I was stepping back into the 1970s every time I visited. A handmade macramé plant holder hung from a hook in the ceiling by the door trailing green foliage down to the floor.

Maggie McDonald embraced me and led me into the front room. She was a short round woman with a kind face and soft auburn hair streaked with silver. Colin's father John was the opposite, stooped and willowy. He was standing looking out at the street from behind a net curtain which covered the front bay window. He turned and nodded to me as I walked into the room. I crossed the floor and hugged him.

"Come and sit, Jessica, I'll make some tea," Maggie fussed and hurried from the room. I could hear the clatter of china coming from the kitchen.

The events of the past few months had very clearly taken their toll on them. John also looked old and grey. I knew that the media had hounded them too for a time. I swallowed a painful lump in my throat and I told myself not to rush my visit.

I dropped my bag beside the brown and orange paisley patterned sofa and sank down onto it. John retrieved a box from behind the sofa and set it down beside me. A whiff of smoke brought an immediate flashback to that terrible day. I pushed the mental images aside.

"This box of papers is from Colin's office at the warehouse," he said. "They don't mean anything to us, so I thought you might know what to do with them…" He trailed off and waved his hand in the direction of the box. "The forensic teams have been through and taken copies of everything they need. I don't quite understand what it all is, you probably will better than me, but they said something about the proceeds of illegal activities like selling weapons was being used to fund his terrorist activities." He rubbed his hand across the back of his head, a mannerism that I'd seen Colin do many times. "I just don't understand."

Despite not wanting to be, my interest was piqued. When I had been trying to make sense of the information that Dad had left in the safety deposit box, I had been unable to find anything at home to tie Colin to any of the companies Dad had identified. And my one attempt at accessing that information from his office had only raised my suspicions further without providing any real answers. Perhaps the information in the box would help to fill in some gaps.

Maggie bustled back into the room carrying a tea tray with cups, saucers and a tiered cake plate, which she placed on the coffee table separating the sofa from two matching armchairs. She left the room and returned with a large teapot.

"You didn't have to go to all this trouble," I said, smiling at her as she poured the tea.

"It's no trouble, love," Maggie said. She glanced at John. "It's nice to have a visitor."

I must have looked surprised.

"People have been avoiding us like the plague," John explained.

"Oh, I'm so sorry," I said.

"It's not your fault, love," Maggie said pushing one of the cups towards me and handing me a plate. "Please help yourself."

I selected a small round savory and a little egg sandwich from the platter.

"Take more than that, you've lost so much weight. Are you sure that you're eating properly?" she fussed.

"I am," I assured her. "In fact, I've been cooking rather a lot. One of my elderly neighbors is unwell and I've been cooking for them."

Colin's parents were keen to talk about Colin, as I expected.

"He was such a bonny wee boy when he came to us, standing there on the doorstep with his wee suitcase, trying not to look afraid." Maggie's tired blue eyes filled with tears.

"Standing on the doorstep? I thought you adopted him as a baby?" I asked, sitting up straighter.

"Oh no, Jessica, he was six, the poor wee man. His mother had just died and he was being so brave," she explained, standing and reaching up to the mantelpiece to pick up a bundle of photos.

And just like that a little piece of the puzzle fell into place. It wasn't a piece that I had realized was missing, but it explained the death certificate in the safety deposit box. I had never investigated that properly. Now I would.

"Funny, your dad thought that too," John said.

"My father?"

"Yes, it came up in conversation when he dropped around just before he died. He thought we were generous setting Colin up in business, but I had to explain that the money didn't come from us, but from his substantial trust fund," John said.

"Trust fund?" I echoed.

John looked uncomfortable. "Jess, I just assumed that Colin would have told you. He had a trust fund which amounted to £750,000 by the time he was twenty-one, a fortune."

I shook my head, my brain whirring. I knew he'd used an inheritance to buy a small local courier firm and had bank funding to expand it, but I didn't realize that he had that much to begin with.

"What about Colin's birth father?" I asked, frowning.

"No one knew who he was. It was left blank on his birth certificate. She was a single mother, an only child, whose parents were dead, so there was no one to ask," John explained. "The lawyers for her estate organized everything. There were a few stipulations. We had to agree to send him back to the village he came from for his holidays to stay with an old couple who were friends of his mother, and to use some of the trust fund to ensure that he had a good education, so there must have been some money somewhere."

"Was it a closed adoption?" I asked, sitting forward on the sofa.

John and Maggie exchanged glances.

"I suppose it doesn't matter now. It was a private adoption. We were considered too old to adopt through the usual channels, so I made some enquiries through contacts of mine. We thought we might have adopted a child from overseas. You can imagine our delight when we got our own wee Scotsman," John explained.

"So—" I paused, unsure how to ask the next question, without sounding rude. "Was it legal?"

John gave a short laugh. "Well, we didn't follow the normal adoption process. But there were lawyers involved who ensured that the paperwork was correct. So, yes, it was legal."

I nodded. My mind was busy processing this new information.

"We didn't use his trust fund. We wanted to pay for his education. He was our son. He got the fund when he turned twenty-one. That's how he bought and expanded the business," Maggie added.

"So, Colin would have remembered his mother?" I said.

"Oh yes, he cried for her on and off for many months. He understood that she'd died."

"He never spoke to me about her. I always assumed that you'd adopted him as a baby from a teenage mother. I didn't realize that he lived with her for the first six years of his life."

"I expect it was too hard for him to talk about," Maggie said. "I always thought that was the reason he bought the little cottage down in Strathgarvan."

"I don't understand."

"That's where she lived, and died," John said.

Maggie patted my hand and poured me another cup of tea, although at that point, I would have preferred something stronger. The lying bastard, what else hadn't he told me?

I left them a couple of hours later, still poring over old photos. I hated Colin even more. All those two ever did was love him unconditionally and to see them in such pain, was unforgiveable.

The drive across Edinburgh to Mum's house took ages. Detours and road blocks were starting to be set up ahead of the G7 conference in a week's time.

Mum was delighted to see me and was horrified, as I'd expected, to learn that I was working as a barmaid. I reassured her that it was all above board and while she started making dinner, I slipped into Dad's study to make some phone calls. I closed the door behind me and stood for a moment surveying the room. I closed my eyes. Nothing had changed. I almost expected him to be sitting behind the desk waiting to chat with me. I shook my head to dislodge the morbid thoughts threatening to crowd me and strode over to his bookcase. I selected the large vintage world atlas where I'd hidden a set of copies of the items from the safety deposit box before I moved to the cottage. I laid it on his desk. It fell open to the page containing the large brown envelope. I opened it and retrieved Catriona Mackie's death certificate and pulled out my mobile.

I wanted to check the *Ayrshire Post* from around the time of her death and I supposed that Scotland's newspaper archive was located in Edinburgh. Sure enough, after a quick Google search and one phone call, the Edinburgh Public Library put me through to the City Chambers. I made an appointment for 10 am the following day.

Chapter 34

April 14

The City Chambers are located in the heart of Edinburgh's historic district. Again, the roadblocks and detours made getting there a nightmare and I ended up parking about twenty minutes away and walking. The building itself is impressive, a grey brick three-story structure arranged around a central courtyard. I wandered past a large bronze statue of Alexander and his wild horse in the center of the front quad and through the arched colonnade. I followed the signs for the newspaper archive and introduced myself at the reception desk.

"Welcome, Ms. Harley," the pleasant receptionist said. "If you could just show me some identification, sign the visitor's book and note what you're researching.

"Sure," I replied, digging out my driver's license from my wallet and entering my name followed by the words 'newspaper archive' in the large book.

"Now if you go through that door, one of the archivists will be able to assist."

"Thanks."

I pushed the sturdy wooden door open and entered a large hushed, cool room with a high ceiling and opaque windows. A number of people were sitting at wooden tables perusing books and documents. Along one wall was a bank of ten computer screens. Several researchers were perched on high stools in front of the first six terminals scrolling through documents on the screens.

"Can I help you?" A man in his fifties approached and peered at me through black framed spectacles.

"Yes please, I would like to see the *Ayrshire Post* for the two weeks beginning 30th May 1998."

The man nodded and led me to a vacant seat at one of the computer screens. "Wait here and I'll see if we've digitized that year."

A few minutes later he returned, confirming that it had been scanned, and showed me how to open a file containing images of the daily newspaper.

"Thank you."

"Let me know if you get stuck or need anything further," he said and stepped away to assist someone else.

I scrolled through the newspaper on the screen for the 30th and the 31st of May, but wasn't until the June 1st edition that I found what I was looking for. A small article at the bottom of page nine caught my attention.

Death in Cliff Plunge

The body of a 23-year-old woman was recovered from the wreckage of her vehicle at the bottom of a cliff near the village of Strathgarvan yesterday afternoon. The car appears to have lost control during a rain storm the previous evening and plunged over the cliff. Police are yet to release further details until next of kin has been notified.

I gasped as I reread the article. Colin's parents were right, the accident happened near where I now lived. I continued scanning the *Post* for the following days, and sure enough on June 3rd a small column confirmed my suspicions.

Victim Named in Cliff Death

The woman who died as the result of a car accident near Strathgarvan on May 30 has been named as local resident Catriona Mackie. There were no witnesses to the incident which happened on a remote stretch of the coastal road south of the village. DS Jones of the Ayrshire Police said that poor visibility at the time appeared to be the cause of the accident and that no other vehicles were involved. Ms. Mackie is survived by her six-year old son. Her funeral will be held on Saturday.

I sat back; so that was how Colin's birth mother had died. I wondered why he'd never told me. I caught the attention of the archivist and he hurried over.

"Would I be able to get copies of two pages emailed to me?" I asked.

"Yes," he said. "I just need you to complete a request form."

Ten minutes later, having completed the necessary paper-work, I thanked him and left the reading room.

"Excuse me," the receptionist called as I walked past her desk.

I paused.

"I just need you to sign out," she said.

"Sure, sorry I didn't realize," I said, reaching for the book at the same time she pushed it towards me. It went flying off the desk and landed face down on the floor. "Sorry," I said, stooping to retrieve it. I placed it back on the desk and opened it. Dates in October of the previous year showed at the top of the page, I reached to turn the pages to get to back to today's date when a name caught my eye. Don Harley, my father. I gave a sharp intake of breath and gripped the edge of the desk until my knuckles turned white as I read his entry.

"Is everything okay?" The reception was looking concerned.

I nodded and turned the pages to sign myself out. I raced down the stairs and back out into the courtyard before I stopped, bending over, hands on my knees and took some deep breaths, my head spinning.

Dad had been to the archives looking at newspapers the day before he'd died. What had he found? Was that why he'd been killed?

Chapter 35

April 14

I was mentally exhausted when I arrived back in Strathgarvan late that afternoon. Buffy came bounding up the drive behind my car as I passed the Gordons', where she'd spent the night, and leapt around me barking her greeting as I climbed from the car. The cottage was cold, so I lit the fire and after taking Buffy for a quick walk, I heated a bowl of soup to eat. I curled up on the sofa with my Kindle and Buffy beside me with her head resting on my legs.

I woke a few hours later with a stiff neck. My Kindle had fallen to the floor and the fire had burned itself down. I slipped my legs out from under Buffy's weight and added a few logs before placing the fire guard in front of it. Buffy jumped off the couch and padded into the bedroom. I followed, walking to the window to pull the curtains closed. It was windy outside, and the dark sky was overcast, no stars visible. A flickering light caught my attention, then another, at the edge of the cliff. I paused and watched. More lights. Several trucks were driving along the road on top of the cliff. I glanced down at my bedside clock. It was just after 2 am. I cracked open the window and listened. The drone of the engines grew louder, followed by the grating of gears changing as they climbed down the cliff road. I counted the red tail lights of four trucks which disappeared from my view as they turned down towards the little harbor.

What would be being transported to or from the harbor at this time of night that needed four large lorries? I closed the window, pulled the curtains across and crawled beneath the covers.

I woke late the following morning. The sun was making a welcome appearance so after breakfast, Buffy and I headed out for our morning walk. I decided to change my usual route and tramped across the fields beside my cottage, towards the cliff road and the harbor to see if I could work out what the activity from the previous night had been.

Buffy danced in front of me, returning to my side every so often to make sure that I was still coming. I was out of breath by the time I crested the rise to the road. I crossed over, calling to Buffy who'd run ahead. I stopped on the far side and looked down into the village's little harbor expecting to see a number of vehicles, but the parking spaces were empty. Four fishing boats were moored along the jetty, with five others anchored in the bay.

I watched as a group of men loaded wooden crates from the jetty onto one of the fishing boats. When the load was on board, the boat was untethered from its mooring and chugged out of the harbor and across the bay towards Campbell Island, the home of Ewan Campbell. I shaded my eyes and gazed out across the water. The approach to the island was rocky, with just a single safe passage ending at a wharf jutting out into the water. There had once been a causeway out to the island but the sea had long since washed it away. The circular island was dominated by a large austere grey brick building in its center, partially hidden by the tall trees that covered the island. The house was three-storied with four chimneys, all of which had plumes of smoke curling skywards. A number of outbuildings were scattered around the house and hidden among the trees. A red and white striped lighthouse stood on the northern edge of the island and had protected boats along the coast for many years. I could see the sun glinting off solar panels attached to the sides of its roof dome.

A car pulled up beside me.

"Alright, Jess?"

I turned to see Alastair in the driver's seat leaning his elbow out of the window.

I smiled. "Yes, lovely day."

"What are ye lookin' at?"

"Just the harbor. I heard a convoy of trucks last night and I wondered if they were still here," I said.

"A convoy, eh?" he said. "Some of the fleet arrived back last night, so they were probably picking up the catch. I'm off to see what they've caught. Fresh fish on the menu tonight."

"Do they sell directly from the boats?"

Alastair grinned. "To me they do."

"Alastair, you knew Colin for a long time, didn't you?"

Alastair's grin dropped and a wary look crossed his face. "Aye."

"Did Colin live in the village until his mother died?"

A slight frown formed on his brow. "Aye, in the cottage."

"Which cottage?"

Alastair looked at me as though I was a little simple. "Why, your cottage, of course."

228

"My…" I began as another piece of the Colin McDonald puzzle slotted into place. Colin didn't buy the cottage while he was at university, it was always his. "Of course," I said nodding.

"Must keep movin'. See ya." Alastair gave a nod and pulled away.

I turned to look back out to sea. The fishing boat had made its way across the bay and was pulling alongside the wharf on the island. I watched as two men strode onto the pier and began helping to unload the cargo.

"Come on, Buffy," I called and started walking again.

My next destination was the cemetery. If Colin's mother had lived here and had been killed near here, then she was sure to have been buried in the local churchyard.

I followed the road down into the village, past a row of pretty stone fishermen's cottages, lining one side of the harbor, once home to the fishermen who plied their trade on this part of the coast and their families, but now sought after historic holiday cottages with their picturesque views of the tiny harbor and the castle ruin on the hill. Most of the cottages had been brought into the twenty-first century with indoor plumbing and modern kitchens added. In many cases the tiny back gardens had been turned into stylish courtyards. At the end of the row of cottages, I turned and walked along in front of the pub. Several of the overnight guests were sitting at tables on the footpath in the sun, enjoying the view across the harbor to Campbell Island as they sipped their morning coffee. Buffy trotted over to scavenge for any stray breakfast items that might be surplus to requirements and was rewarded with half a sausage for her troubles by a middle-aged woman whose portly husband was tucking into a large cooked breakfast. I smiled my thanks at her and continued walking.

The Strathgarvan Presbyterian church stood at the northern corner of the harbor as the land began to rise away from the sea. Its tall steeple could be seen for miles along the coast and from out at sea. The church itself was a sturdy, unadorned structure, built using local quarried stone. It was surrounded by a solid drywall fence. I pushed through the main gate and passed between two large stone columns and into the churchyard. A gravel path meandered through the old graveyard towards the main doors of the church. An elderly parishioner was already hard at work, weeding and sweeping. He raised a finger to his cap in greeting before going back to his work.

The gravestones in front of the church looked old and worn, so I headed towards the back. Here, the graveyard continued into a meadow behind the drywall where rows of neat charcoal colored headstones were lined up like soldiers on parade, with splashes of color provided by floral tributes left by mourners dotted here and there. I walked through the rear gate and over to the nearest row of graves and stopped to read the inscription on the first headstone. The date was 1975, too early. Colin's mother had died in 1998. I crossed to the plots three rows over and tried again. This time the dates were from 1997. I took my time and wandered along the row, stopping every so often to read the sad memorial to someone's loved one. The graves of three men lost in a fishing boat capsize at the end of 1997 gave me pause and I found a lump rising in my throat and tears stinging my eyes.

Buffy had bounded away, chasing something into the trees at the far end of the meadow. As if sensing my sadness, she returned and leaned against my leg, panting. I reached down and gave her head a scratch, before she raced off again and I continued my search. I reached April 1998 at the top of the row and found myself holding my breath as I turned to walk back down the adjacent row. Catriona Mackie had died on May 31, 1998, so her final resting place must be near.

An elderly women and a small child had died in May and then the next headstone was for a man in August. I frowned and retraced my steps, double checking as a thought came to me. Maybe she was cremated. I couldn't see a memorial garden, so perhaps it was time to ask the minister and see if he would check the church records.

"Buffy," I called as I walked back towards the church. She gamboled back to me, tail wagging and ears pricked. "Good girl."

I came across the gardener, who had moved his wheelbarrow and was now working at the side of the church.

"Excuse me?" I said as I walked over to him. "I'm hoping you can help me. I'm looking for the grave of my mother-in-law, Catriona Mackie. She died in a car accident near here in 1998."

The man straightened and pushed his cap back on his head. A look of sympathy crossed his weathered face as he registered who I was. He leaned his broom against the wheelbarrow. "Aye, lassie, I knew her folk well. Follow me."

He turned and trudged towards the rear of the church, a little hunched and walking with a slight limp. Buffy trotted beside me until we reached a grave tucked in beside the wall. It was made of expensive looking black marble, rather than stone like the ones around it.

"She was buried with her folks, God rest their souls.

231

Tragedy has stalked that family," he said. "John and Ethel both succumbed to cancer within months of one another, then poor Cat and now young Colin gone too. Are you going to inter him here?"

I stared at the headstone, surprised to find tears blurring my vision. "There wasn't anything much left of him to inter." I could hear the bitterness creeping into my voice, but I couldn't stop it. As if I'd desecrate this lovely churchyard with the remains of a terrorist. The man patted my arm and nodded his head as if he understood my pain, before ambling back to his wheelbarrow.

I sat down on the grass beside the headstone. Buffy crouched beside me and put her head on my lap. According to the inscription, Catriona Mackie had lost her parents when she was sixteen and had been killed just seven years later. I reached over and ran my fingers across the words.

Catriona Ethel Mackie 1975-1998
Much loved daughter and mother
Safe with God and Forever missed

I pulled a handful of dead flowers out of the vase set into the concrete in front of the headstone and dropped them onto the grass. Someone was still visiting and leaving flowers on occasion.

Buffy's ears pricked up and she lifted her head off my knee, sniffing. A low growl emanated from deep within her as a cloud moved across the sun. The temperature seemed to plummet and the church threw shadows across the graveyard. Buffy leapt up and started barking.

"What is it, girl?" I asked, rising to my feet and looking

around.

There was no one there. The gardener had moved his wheelbarrow and disappeared from sight. Buffy continued to growl, looking in the direction of the trees beyond the church. I shivered and looked at the sky. The sunny morning was gone and rain clouds threatened.

"Come on, girl, time to go home," I said, walking back to the front of the church and hurrying down the path, Buffy at my heels, still growling.

I knocked on the Gordons' door on my way past.

"Come in," a cheery voice called.

I gave Buffy instructions to wait and opened the door. Buffy curled up on the doorstep and put her head on her paws, exhausted after the morning's adventure.

Mrs. Gordon was sitting at the kitchen table reading the newspaper, a walking frame parked within easy reach of her chair.

"Hello, Jessica," she said, smiling at me.

"Hello, Mrs. Gordon, it's good to see you up and about," I said.

"Aye, can't spend all day in bed," she said with a smile. "Would you like a cuppa? Mr. Gordon is down in the village."

"I'll make it," I said and moved to the bench, picking up the kettle from the stove and filling it from the tap over the kitchen sink. I lit the gas and placed the kettle on the hob before taking a seat opposite Mrs. Gordon, who'd closed the paper.

"Been for ya walk then, love?" she asked.

"Yes, actually I stopped by the church and found the Mackie's graves. I didn't realize until yesterday that Colin's mother and grandparents lived in the village."

"It's their cottage that you're livin' in," she said.

"I realize that now. Did you know them well?"

Mrs. Gordon smiled, her cheeks crinkling. "I knew them very well. Lovely couple and Catriona was such a beautiful, kind young woman. And the wee bairn." She stopped speaking and gave me a wary look. "So much tragedy."

The kettle whistled and I jumped up to lift it and extinguish the flame. I busied myself making the tea while I framed my next question. I placed two cups of tea on the table and sat down again.

"I read recently that Catriona died near here in a car accident. Do you remember what happened?"

Mrs. Gordon studied me for a long moment. "She had met a nice young man from the city and was going to a concert with him up in Edinburgh that evening and staying overnight. He had a good job working for the government. Her parents had long since passed, and we often helped out with young Colin so he was spending the night with us." She paused and took a sip of her tea. "We answered the door to her young man the next morning, looking for her. She hadn't made it to Edinburgh. The police found her car that afternoon at the bottom of a cliff."

"Do you recall if there was any suggestion that it was anything other than an accident?"

"Why would you ask that?"

"I just wondered. I figured that she would have known the roads around here well. So there was nothing unusual?"

Mrs. Gordon paused again and looked uncertain. "We thought we heard shouting up at her cottage the night she left, but the police looked into it and said that I must have imagined it."

"Well, I think I'll take some flowers up to her grave tomorrow."

"That would be grand. I usually do, but with this silly hip, I haven't been over to the church for several weeks now."

We chatted a little longer and I finished up my tea. I washed our cups and left them on the draining tray.

"I'd better get Buffy home for something to eat," I said, walking across to the door.

"Pop in anytime, dear."

"Thank you," I said. "One other thing, do you know who Colin's birth father was?"

I could have sworn that an emotion resembling fear crossed the old lady's face. She shook her head. "No, she never said."

Chapter 36

April 15

Buffy and I arrived back at the cottage just as the first large drops of rain fell. So much for the promise of the beautiful sunny morning. I stood on the threshold of the cottage and looked out across the fields to the village and harbor beyond. I wondered how many times Catriona had stood here doing the same thing. I tried to imagine her living in the little cottage and failed. It was beginning to feel like my home now and I couldn't imagine Colin or anyone else here. I wished that I had a photo of her; perhaps that would make her seem real.

I stepped inside and closed the door behind me. Perhaps there might be something in the box of papers that I'd brought back from Colin's parents in Edinburgh. It was still sitting where I dumped it beside the table in the kitchen and seemed to beckon to me. I sighed and kicked off my trainers. No time like the present.

I spent the next two hours emptying the box and sorting its contents into piles. I jumped up at one point to open a window, as the odor of smoke from the fire that followed the warehouse explosion seemed to have infused the paperwork.

The box contained mainly bank statements. As I lifted them out I realized that they weren't just for bank accounts owned by L-FLI. There were other companies too. Companies whose names I'd only seen in one other place; on the company chart that Dad had drawn. I recalled John saying the previous day that the police forensic experts had already been through them, but it wouldn't hurt for me to take a look.

I jumped up and shifted the coffee machine and using a bread knife from the kitchen drawer, levered a brick out of the wall behind it. It was half the size of the other bricks and meant that there was a good sized empty space in the wall cavity behind it. I'd discovered it by accident when I was moving my belongings into the kitchen. Inside the wall cavity I'd hidden a cake tin with all of my important documents, passport, spare cash, a credit card and a packet with the information that my father had left in the safety deposit box.

I brought the package to the table and sifted through until I found the company chart that Dad had drawn up. I set it in the center of the table and sorted the papers from the warehouse into piles for each company beside their name on the chart. I grabbed a blank sheet of paper and began trying to trace any large money transfers through the various companies.

After an hour, I was ready to give up. There were gaps between the amounts paid and not showing up as received and even if the date of a transfer did coincide, the amount received was never the same. I threw my pen down in disgust. Who was I kidding? The police had smarter forensic people than me who'd probably already pieced together the money trail.

I decided to concentrate on L-FLI's parent company, CMEC

Limited. I counted twenty-four bank statements for this company going back six years. I worked backwards, trying to trace the deposits and withdrawals, with little success until I reached the first statement dated from around the time of our wedding. The account had been opened with a deposit of £10,000,000 and £5,000,000 had been transferred to L-FLI the following day. I did a double take. I recalled how tight things were for us when we were first married and Colin was setting up the business. Yet it appeared that he not only had a trust fund worth £750,000, but he also had £5 million to play with.

I reached for my iPad before remembering that I no longer owned one. Instead I grabbed my phone, tapped the settings app and enabled mobile data. I hoped I could get a signal out here and sure enough up it popped. I searched the company's details on line. CMEC was in the export business and Colin was listed as its only Director. Clearly the Companies Office hadn't caught up on the fact that a dead man was running the company. However, to my surprise, Colin wasn't listed as the shareholder. Another company was, one that I'd never heard of called Little Boxes Limited.

I searched its details online. Its sole director was none other than Ewan Campbell. I clicked on the shareholding. It was owned by an offshore trust with an unpronounceable name, registered in Guernsey, which meant the end of the road in terms of discovering its ownership. Despite the European Union's best efforts, it was still nigh on impossible to get behind the walls of that tax haven, but if Colin and Ewan were directors of each company, then it was a good chance that they were among the shareholders too.

The question was, where did they get ten million pounds?

Something tugged at my memory and I sorted through the piles of paper on the small table to find the package with the information that I'd gathered in London. I retrieved the details on Mendelson and ran my finger down the list of shareholders. Ah, there it was, Little Boxes Ltd had a 30% shareholding in a weapons manufacturer who had a contract with the British government. I looked back at the company chart. If Little Boxes Ltd owned 30% of Mendelson, and Tartan Warriors, Scottish Wanderer and Highland Avengers owned 7% each, then the four associated companies between them owned and therefore controlled a majority shareholding in one of the UK's leading weapons manufacturers.

I sat back, closed my eyes and let out a deep breath. Perhaps I had discovered the source of the explosives found in Colin's warehouse.

I drew a box above CMEC on Dad's chart and wrote the words 'Little Boxes' in it and joined the two with a solid line. On the opposite side of the page I wrote 'Mendelson' and drew lines from each of the companies on the chart which owned shares in it and the percentage.

I returned all of the bank statements to the box that Colin's father had given me, leaving those documents relating to CMEC and Little Boxes out to store with my dad's information. I replaced the lid and lugged the box out to the shed, balancing it on one knee while I unlocked the padlock. I didn't want the burnt smell inside the cottage any longer. The sensory memory it provoked was just too strong. Returning to the kitchen I folded the company structure diagram up and went to push it back into the package with the rest of Dad's safety deposit box material. I hesitated, remembering that Dad had included a copy of Catriona's death certificate in the box. I tipped the packet up, emptying its contents onto the table. The photo of a teenaged Colin with the group of boys dressed in fatigues with semi-automatic rifles landed face up. I narrowed my eyes as I scooped it up, studying the boys. Colin was definitely in the center looking up at the older guy whose face was obscured, but I now recognized two more of the group. To Colin's immediate left was a young Alastair, with his wild hair and sarcastic grin and beside him was Harry the postman, who really looked no different than he did now. I turned it over; the words 'The Unit' were written in pen on the back.

I tucked it into my pocket and returned all of the other items to my makeshift wall safe, taking care to replace the brick and the coffee machine.

* * *

I drove down into the village after dinner and parked beside the harbor opposite the pub. Although the rain had stopped, the heavy dark cloud blanketed the sky. Light and laughter spilled from the pub's front window, becoming louder and brighter as I pushed open the door and went inside. The usual crowd of locals were in attendance. A replay of the weekend's football match between Celtic and Aberdeen was playing on the large flat screen on the wall at one end of the room.

Alastair glanced up from the pint he was pulling as I entered, and looked surprised to see me.

"Hey, Jess, what brings you out tonight?"

"I wanted to ask you something," I replied, hoisting myself

up onto a stool at the end of the long wooden bar.

"Okay, gimme a minute," he said, placing the pint of beer in front of a young guy further down the bar, taking his money and giving him change.

"Can I get ya a drink?" he asked, returning to my end of the bar.

"Half of cider, thanks."

Alastair shook his head, refusing the note that I held out to pay for my drink.

"So what can I do for ya?" he said, placing the glass in front of me a minute later and leaning on the bar opposite me.

I pulled the photograph from my pocket and slid it across to him.

"I found this today when I was going through some of Colin's things. I recognized you and Harry in it and I hoped you could tell me who these other guys were."

A look of discomfort crossed Alastair's face before being replaced with a grin. "God, that was a long time ago, Jess. We must have been about fifteen at the time. That's Alwyn, the local mechanic and those two, Mac and Donny, they're on the boats."

"Who's that?" I asked, pointing to the older man.

Alastair glanced at me before answering. "That's the Laird," he said.

"What? Ewan Campbell?"

"Aye," he said handing the photo back to me.

"What were you doing, dressed up like that?"

"Probably rabbit shooting. The old Laird, Ewan's father, used to let us shoot out on the island as long as Ewan was with us."

I nodded. "Why was Colin with you? Didn't he live in

Edinburgh by then?"

"Aye, but he came down most holidays."

"Ah, so what did The Unit mean?" I asked, turning the photo over.

Alastair shook his head. "Dunno, Jess. Why the sudden interest? I thought you hated him."

"Oh, I do. I'm just trying to figure out what made this kid," I said, tapping my finger on Colin's face in the photo, "turn into that monster."

Chapter 37

April 16

After my morning walk over the cliffs with Buffy, I set off on my weekly grocery trip to Ayr. The village store contained all of the essentials, but for anything other than basics, a trip to the larger town was required. My new cooking habit needed feeding, so to speak, and there were a number of ingredients that neither I nor Jamie Oliver could get in the village. I left Buffy asleep in her basket with the promise that I wouldn't be too long. She raised her head to acknowledge me and went back to sleep. She hated being left in the car while I was in the supermarket, so it was better to leave her at home. She was worn out from our walk, so she wouldn't even notice that I was gone. I called in at the Gordons' on the way past to see if there was anything that they needed.

The day was overcast, but it didn't detract from the beauty of the drive along the coastal road. Sea birds circled over the cliffs and seals played around the rocks. I hardly passed another car. Most traffic used the busier A road, which bypassed the coastal settlements, but I preferred the seaside route which wound its way through a couple of sleepy fishing villages and past several more castle ruins. This part of Ayrshire coast had been well fortified in its day. Forty minutes after I left Strathgarvan, I pulled into the carpark behind Waitrose.

I had my weekly treat of coffee and a cream-filled griddle scone at a local café, using their free Internet to answer an email from Marie, with Rachel, Jimmy and Dave cc'd, who were all clearly worried about my self-imposed isolation. Once again, I went to push back on her overtures to come and visit. I wasn't ready. My fingers hesitated over the keyboard ready to click send, when a sudden wave of loneliness came over me. Perhaps a visit wouldn't be so bad. They were my friends after all and didn't seem to be judging me, like the rest of the world. Without giving myself any more time to dwell, I hit the backspace key erasing my excuses and instead typed, 'So, do you still fancy a weekend on the Scottish coast?' I hit send before I could change my mind.

After spending half an hour wandering up and down the aisles of the supermarket, I paid for my purchases and loaded the groceries into my car before making the return journey along the coast road. The rain started about fifteen minutes before I reached the village and was coming down in sheets as I turned into my driveway.

There was no sign of anyone at the Gordons' cottage as I drove past. I continued on with the wipers working overtime. I rounded the bend at the top of the drive, sensing that something was amiss. I pulled to a stop in front of the shed and switched the engine off. Through the rain, I could see a large dark shape on my front porch. I frowned. I had left Buffy inside, since rain had been forecast, so it couldn't be her.

I opened the door of the car and stepped into the downpour, squinting at the object on the porch. Despite the rain, my instincts screamed caution, so I edged towards the house rather than hurried.

I'd only taken a few steps when I realized that the shape was indeed Buffy. I could have sworn I'd left her locked inside and now the poor girl was crouched on the porch trying to shelter from the rain. I broke into a run for the final few steps. She didn't move as I approached and as I got closer I stifled a scream. Buffy was lying on her right side across the doormat her back legs hanging off the step, getting wet in the rain. Blood coalesced around a large wound on the left side of her head, just below what was left of her ear and was dripping off the step, turning into a coppery puddle at my feet. Her eyes were open and glassy. I crouched down in front of the step and put my hand on her side. She was still warm, but not breathing.

"No, no, no," I cried.

The sound of a footstep behind me made me jump up again and as I went to turn in that direction a muffled male voice stopped me. "Don't turn around, Jess."

Horrified, I started shaking and raised my hands in the air facing the door of my cottage. "Please don't shoot."

Laughter sounded behind me and I braced, waiting for the pain of being shot. "Let the dead rest in peace, Jess, unless you want to join them."

I started sobbing, streams of salty tears running down my face. I don't know how long I stood there in the rain with my hands in the air looking down at my poor dead dog. When I finally pulled myself together, I lowered my hands and cautiously turned around. There was no one there. I sank to my knees and buried my face in Buffy's side and cried.

After several minutes, I stood up and wiped my eyes with the back of my hands and walked over to the shed. I fiddled with my keys trying to unlock the padlock, dropping my keyring twice. When the lock finally clicked open, I entered the shed and I grabbed a shovel and an old blue tarpaulin. I ran back over to Buffy. My tears started again as I covered her with the tarp. I looked around for the best place to bury her and spied an area at the top of the small rise at the edge of my property, where the drywall ended. She would wait there for me to catch up when I let her out for our walk each morning.

I climbed the slope and started digging, so engrossed in what I was doing that I didn't hear the van pull up, so when a voice behind me called my name, I swung around brandishing the shovel like a weapon and almost snacked it across the head of Harry, the postman, standing there in his red Royal Mail raincoat.

He held up his hands in a gesture of peace and took a step backwards. "Are you okay?" His voice was wary.

My shoulders slumped and I dropped the shovel.

Harry took a tentative step forward taking in my tear-stained face. "What's wrong?" he asked.

"Oh, Harry, someone shot my dog and threatened to shoot me."

Harry looked horrified. "Who?"

I shook my head. "I have no idea."

Harry held out his hand. "Come on, show me."

I led him back down the slope to the cottage and lifted the tarp off the front porch, giving a hiccupping sob seeing Buffy lying there.

"Bloody hell." Harry pulled his phone from his pocket and made a call. "Jess," he said rejoining me, "Why don't you go inside and dry off. I've got help coming."

I shook my head and sat down on the step beside Buffy and stroked the soft fur on her side, keeping my eyes away from her ruined head.

The rain had eased to a light mist a few minutes later when a truck came bumping up the driveway at speed and Alastair stepped from it. Harry walked out to meet him and they spoke in low voices for a moment before Alastair came over and helped me to my feet. He pulled me into an awkward bear hug.

"I'm so sorry, lass," he said, his voice thick with emotion. "Let us help ya ta bury her."

I nodded. "I've dug a hole." I gestured towards the fence line.

Alastair bent down and scooped Buffy into his arms. "Bring the tarp, Jess."

I followed him and Harry back up the slope. Following Alastair's instructions, I laid the tarp on the ground and he placed Buffy in the center of it, taking care not to drop her. He picked up the shovel and continued digging the hole that I had started. When he determined that it was deep enough, he rested the shovel against the fence and turned to me. "It's time, Jess."

I sighed and crouched down beside Buffy, patting her for the last time. "I'm sorry, girl." I wrapped the tarp around her and with Harry and Alastair's help eased her into the hole. Harry picked up the shovel and started filling in the grave. I couldn't watch that part so I wandered across to my vegetable garden and broke off large handfuls of rosemary. Returning to the grave, I saw that Alastair was fashioning a rustic cross from the fallen twigs of the silver beech tree in the yard.

Harry patted down the mounded earth on top of the grave with the back of the shovel and stepped back. Crying once again, I spread the handfuls of rosemary across the top, while Alastair pushed the cross into the ground at one end.

I stood up and looked at the two men. "Thank you."

"Come on, let's get you inside for a nice warm cuppa," Harry said, leading the way back to my cottage.

After a final look at Buffy's grave, I followed.

I wasn't surprised to find my front door unlocked. Someone had to have let Buffy out.

The men took their boots off and hung their wet raincoats on the hooks beside the door and followed me into the kitchen.

"You get ya self into some dry clothes and I'll put the kettle on," Alastair said.

I nodded and wandered over to my bedroom closing the door. I was wet to the skin. I pulled off all of my clothes and grabbed a clean towel from a shelf in the wardrobe and dried off as best I could before pulling on clean underwear, jeans and a long sleeved t-shirt. I wrapped the towel around my head for a moment to squeeze out the excess water before combing my fingers through my hair to push it back off my face and try to tame it.

When I stepped back into the lounge, I could see Harry and Alastair sitting at the kitchen table, heads together, talking in low voices. They stopped as I entered the room and Alastair jumped up and pulled out a chair for me.

"Feel a bit better?"

I shrugged. "Drier anyway."

248

Harry pushed a cup of tea in my direction. "I've added some sugar, s'posed to help with shock," he said.

"And I've grabbed my emergency supply of whiskey from the truck," Alastair said splashing a generous nip of amber liquid from a small flask into each of three glasses. "To Buffy," he said, raising his glass.

"To Buffy," Harry and I echoed. The whiskey burned all the way down to my stomach, but I was surprised to find that it helped to settle me until a loud knock on the door made me jump and spill my tea.

"It's okay, it'll be Constable Jones," Alastair said, leaping up to let the police officer in.

I stood as he walked into the kitchen behind Alastair, removing his hat and tucking it under his arm.

"I hear you've had some trouble, Mrs. McDonald," he said.

"Ms. Harley, but please call me Jess," I said. "Someone killed my dog and left her on the front porch."

Harry motioned to the kettle, offering to make Jones a cup, but he shook his head as he pulled a notebook from his pocket.

"Maybe it was a hunting accident and they brought her back for you?" Jones suggested.

I stared at him. "Except for the fact that I left her locked inside when I went to Ayr earlier in the day."

"Harry said that a man threatened you with a gun," Alastair said. "Did you see who it was?"

I shook my head. "No. He wouldn't let me turn around."

"Did he say anything?"

"Just not to turn around, then he went away."

Jones frowned and scribbled in his notebook. "Are you sure you didn't just imagine that?" he said closing his book and sliding it back in his pocket. "Shock does funny things, y' know."

I opened and closed my mouth for a moment before I trusted myself to speak. "I think I'd remember someone threatening me. Aren't you going to take fingerprints? Someone broke into my home and killed my dog," I said.

Jones looked at me with pity. "I know you've been through a lot, Mrs. McDonald, I'll look into it."

"Harley."

"Excuse me?" he said.

"My name is Harley, not McDonald."

"Good day, Ms. Harley." He exchanged a look with Alastair before turning to leave.

Alastair saw him to the door as I sank back down onto the chair.

"It's his job to be skeptical and look at things from all angles," Harry said.

"It's not his job to be rude, though," I replied.

"Don't worry about workin' tonight or tomorrow for that matter, Jess," Alastair said closing the front door behind the police officer.

I nodded. "Okay, thanks."

Chapter 38

April 17

I parked the car in the center of Ayr and started looking for a payphone on High Street trying to look nonchalant. But my heart was beating at a million miles an hour. I wasn't sure whether I'd just worked myself up into an anxious knot or whether it was nerves from the call that I was about to make. I located a payphone booth part way along the busy shopping street. Its glass walls were grimy and I was careful not to touch anywhere more than I had to as I entered the tiny booth. On the wall behind the telephone a patchwork of business cards and flyers were arrayed, most offering services of the professional kind. Ignoring the images of scantily clad women, I lifted the receiver, taking care to hold it away from my ear, slid my credit card into the slot and keyed the number written on the card that Will had left me at the hospital.

"Leave a message after the annoying beep," Will's voice message said. Startled, I slammed the receiver down, disconnecting the call. For some reason, I wasn't expecting to hear his voice sounding so normal. Breathing deep and slow, I tried again.

"You can do this, Jess," I told myself. I lifted the receiver, redialed and waited for the annoying beep.

"Will, ah, Charlie, it's Jess. I think I need your help. Text, don't call."

I left my new mobile number, hung up and rushed out of the booth and across the road to a small coffee shop where I ordered a latte. I sat at a table in the window, placing my mobile in front of me and stared at it. Part of me willed it to beep, another part hoped it wouldn't. It chimed with an incoming text almost as soon as my coffee was delivered. The message came from a withheld number and simply said, 'Call again'. I drained my coffee and hurried back to the phone booth and called the number on the card again.

"Jess." Will answered on the first ring.

"Yes." It came out in a whisper, as the memories that his voice conjured up, crowded me.

"What's wrong?" His tone was businesslike, which brought me back to the present with brutal force.

I cleared my throat. "Ah, I've been looking into Colin's past and I must have found something, because someone shot my dog and threatened to kill me," I said, the words rushing out.

"I'll come to you," he replied. "Where are you?"

"No, a stranger would be noticed. Can you meet me in Ayr in Scotland?" I asked.

"Sure, tomorrow?"

"Yeah, but it'll need to be around lunchtime, as I'm working in the evening."

"Where are you working, Jess?" His voice softened.

"In a pub."

"Aw, Jess."

I didn't reply. I couldn't speak past the lump that had

suddenly formed in my throat.

"Okay, where shall I meet you?" he asked after the silence became uncomfortable.

"There's a coffee shop called Bette's on the high street," I said, looking across the road at the café on the opposite side . "Midday tomorrow." I managed to say before hanging up, my heart pounding. I was surprised to find my face wet.

I figured if someone was watching me, I would need a reason to come back to Ayr again so soon, so I dropped into M&S and ordered some new bedding to collect the following day.

On the drive back to the village, I began to second guess my decision to call Will. Surely I was just being paranoid, but then again someone had shot my dog and threatened me. It was hearing Will's voice again that had rattled me, I decided. I supposed that I could just do a no show, but then if I didn't meet him, he would come looking for me and that would most certainly attract more unwanted attention.

It was late afternoon by the time I pulled up to the cottage. I hesitated at the front porch. Despite having scrubbed the doorstep in the morning, I could still see the stain that Buffy's blood had left. I closed my eyes and said a silent prayer for my faithful companion. She didn't deserve to die like that, not when she'd kept me going over the past few months. I unlocked the door and stepped inside as the tears rolled down my cheeks.

I changed my shoes and headed out to a nearby field where there were patches of wildflowers blooming. I gathered as many as I could carry and returned to the cottage, covering Buffy's grave with them. I stood up and brushed myself down, before heading back indoors, locking the door behind me. I turned on some music and began preparing dinner. I gathered an armful of firewood before the sun set and locked the front door, shooting the bolts across the top and bottom. I double checked that each window was secure as I pulled the curtains across and leaned the rifle within easy reach against the wall by the door.

I sat by the fire to eat my dinner and after washing the dishes and putting them away, I curled up on the sofa to read. After a page, the words became blurry as once again tears poured down my cheeks. Buffy had cuddled up to me every night on the sofa. Wiping my cheeks with the backs of my hands, I stood and walked into my bedroom to retrieve a warm throw from the end of my bed. Buffy's basket was in its usual place by the fire, which made me cry harder. The irony that I was crying more over the death of a dog that I'd only known for a few months than for my husband of six years, was not lost on me.

Unable to settle, I retrieved the stack of information I'd hidden in the kitchen. I moved my coffee machine away from the wall and pried out the loose brick. Reaching in, I pulled out the biscuit tin. I returned to the sofa and sorted the most relevant paperwork into a logical order and scribbled a long handwritten note explaining my research, conclusions and noting the gaps. Satisfied, I grabbed a new envelope from a drawer in the kitchen, slid the stack of documents inside and sealed it. Bending the envelope in half, I added it to the tin before replacing the lid and pushing it back into my kitchen wall safe, replacing both the brick and the coffee machine.

Chapter 39

April 18

Will was sitting in the café, when I finally arrived in Ayr. I couldn't quite put my finger on it, but I had a prickly feeling on the back of my neck, as though I was being followed. There had been very little traffic in either direction on the road from Strathgarvan, so I figured that I was once again being paranoid. Someone threatening you with a gun tends to do that to a person.

I wandered along the high street towards Bette's, making a pretense of stopping and looking in various shop windows before entering the café. As I pulled the door open, I saw a reflection in the glass door, of a man watching me from across the street. I managed to resist the urge to turn, but in the distorted view on the glass, he looked somehow familiar. I was glad that I hadn't planned on staying to chat in the coffee shop. Will looked up as I stepped inside and rose from his seat. I gave him a single shake of my head and he instead modified his movement to grab the newspaper off an adjacent empty table and sit back down to read, ignoring me. He looked just the same as I remembered. His dark hair was shorter but still flopped across his forehead. He had discarded his jacket on the back of the chair and the blue t-shirt pulled across his broad shoulders accentuating his muscular arms. The only indication that he wasn't actually relaxing and reading the paper was his clenched jaw, which gave a little twitch. He knew I was watching him. I blushed, took a deep breath, told myself to get a grip and ordered my coffee to go. This, after all, was the man who lied to me for months and broke my heart. There was no coming back from that. As I turned to leave, coffee in hand, I walked past his table and dropped a small piece of paper onto his newspaper. Will flipped the page over, covering it.

Half an hour later, having picked up my new duvet and dropped it back to the car, I took myself to the cinema.

The matinee screening was almost empty, only half a dozen other people, all elderly. I slipped into a seat in the back row, just as the trailers began. Five minutes later, the lights went fully down and the opening credits of the feature film rolled. I glanced around the cinema. No one new had arrived and the closest people were sitting eight rows away.

Out of the darkness, Will slid into the seat beside me.

"Hey, you," he whispered. "No one followed you in here, I've been watching, so you can relax. There's a guy sitting in an SUV across the road, though, who looks out of place, so you might want to avoid him, when you leave."

"Thanks. I'm a bit out of my depth here." I grimaced.

"You did great today; the cinema was a genius idea. If you ever want a job..." He trailed off.

I was glad it was dark so that he couldn't see my face. I rummaged in my bag and handed him the envelope of documents and notes that I'd taken out of my kitchen hiding place that morning. "I think I've been asking too many questions. I've felt like I'm being watched the last few days, particularly at the cemetery."

"Is that where Colin is buried?"

"No. I wouldn't waste my time visiting his grave, if he had one," I scoffed. "It's his mother and grandparents. I found their graves."

"You said on the phone that someone killed your dog."

"Yeah, she was shot in the head and left on the doorstep for me to find." My voice caught on the last word. "And the person who shot her was still there and gave me a warning to let the dead rest in peace unless I wanted to join them."

Will's eyes widened as he absorbed that.

"Could you identify him if you saw him again? I could have one of the team do a Photofit," Will said.

I shook my head. "He told me not to turn around," I whispered.

"God, Jess, you must have been terrified."

I tapped the envelope that I'd given him. "You need to look into Mendelson some more."

"Mendelson? We've already checked them and they're clean. There's no evidence of additional weapons being produced," Will said.

"Remember the companies chart that Dad drew up? Most were shell companies, but the only thing that I can find that they have in common is that they each have shareholdings in Mendelson, which if you add them together, could give someone a controlling interest."

That got Will's attention. "Interesting."

"Was there anything else in your safety deposit box that you didn't tell me about?"

I nodded. "Yeah, a note telling me not to trust anyone, ironic really, Colin's mother's death certificate, a photo of Colin and some boys as teenagers, some old newspaper clippings from Colin's student politics days, along with some cash; an emergency fund." I drew air commas around the word emergency.

Will frowned.

"I have this feeling that Colin's mother's death was suspicious, just like my father's, but I can't prove it. It's all there, you can make of it what you will."

"God, Jess. I'm so sorry." He reached out to squeeze my hand, but I moved it.

Will cleared his throat. "We'll take a look at this. In the meantime, lay low and don't do anything further to provoke unwanted attention. Do you need protection?"

"I think that would draw attention," I replied.

"You could have someone come to stay. I know a couple of women who would be great."

I shook my head. "No, it would look strange. I haven't had anyone to stay at all since I moved there."

"What? No one? Not even Marie?" I shook my head. He gave me a long look. "Okay, I'll be in touch." He rose to leave.

"Hey," I started.

Someone further down the theatre gave a loud *shhh*. Will stopped and sat down again, turning his body toward me.

"Uh, what should I call you?" I whispered.

"My real name is Charlie," he replied. An awkward pause followed. "I'm sorry, Jess. I never meant for you to get hurt."

I forced a bright smile. "No problem, Charlie. Bye." I turned my attention to the movie. It was a nineteenth century drama and I had missed all of the opening scenes, so I had no clue what I was going on.

Charlie paused a moment longer and drew in a breath as if to speak, but stopped himself, rose and was gone.

I felt the tears pricking my eyes as the warmth left by his body vanished with him. Only when I raised my fingers to my face to stop any tears spilling onto my cheeks, did I realize that my hands were shaking.

It took until the end of the movie to get my emotions under control again. I sat in the darkness and let the sadness engulf me. A black SVU with tinted windows was still parked opposite the cinema entrance when I left an hour and a half later. Anger and annoyance replaced my sadness and grief, and I crossed the street walking straight towards it. The driver gunned the engine and pulled away before I could get a good look at him, but not before I noted the number plate with a shock. The last three digits were the exact same as those captured by the surveillance cameras outside Dad's office in Edinburgh the day he died. It was the same vehicle that was at the warehouse the day before the explosion. I hoped that Charlie would move fast, I didn't know how much longer I would be safe.

Chapter 40

April 18

Business was steady at the pub that night. In a break
between wiping down tables and collecting empties,
I chatted to one of the regulars sitting in his usual
position at the end of the bar. He was a lonely figure. Late
fifties at a guess, overweight with thinning grey hair that was
desperately in need of a good cut. Alastair had introduced
him as Douglas on my first night and he'd sat there quietly
nursing a pint or two every night that I had worked since,
before shuffling off when Alastair called last orders.

I gathered from my brief chats with him that he'd lived in
the village all his life and that he lived alone. This particular
Thursday night, he was chattier than usual.

"You're Colin McDonald's widow, are ya not?" he asked.

I nodded. Douglas was silent for a while as I emptied the
dishwasher that had just finished washing the first round of
glasses.

"I knew his mother." It was a closed statement, but not one
that I was going to let rest. Apart from my neighbors, no one
spoke about her.

"You knew Catriona?

He nodded and sighed. "Aye, she was a beautiful lass. Kind-hearted too."

I gave him a smile of encouragement and put down the cloth that I was using to polish the glasses, so that he knew he had my full attention.

"Loved that wee bairn, she did."

"Colin, you mean?" I asked. I couldn't think of Colin as a wee bairn, more a wee bastard in more than one sense of the word.

Douglas nodded.

"Who was his father?" I asked, leaning forward so that the question was just a whisper.

Douglas shook his head. "Cannae say I know. She ne'er said, although I have my suspicions."

The bell above the door leading from the hotel's accommodation upstairs jangled making us both jump. Four strangers ambled in chatting and laughing. Silence settled over the pub as the locals took in the interlopers, four men in their late twenties, dressed in jeans and checked shirts or jumpers. Alastair greeted them from behind the bar.

"Good evening, gentlemen," he said in his broad Scots accent. "I trust your rooms are to your liking."

"Yeah, mate, they're great," said one of the men, a Yorkshire-man by his accent, pulling his wallet from his back pocket as he approached the bar. He was a large fit looking man, tall as well as broad. He turned to his companions who were headed towards a table in the front window. "What do you want to drink?" he called.

"Brew Dog, Freddy," one of the men answered.

"Four pints of Brew Dog, then please," he said.

"Coming right up," Alastair replied. "What brings you boys to town?"

"Ah, a bit of fishing, golf, few beers, ya' know," Freddy answered with a grin, handing over a £20 note. "Chance to escape the missus."

Conversation resumed around the pub as the men took a table by the window. The chef gave a shout from the kitchen, my cue to collect the next meals that were ready to be served. I loaded a tray with cutlery and condiments and stepped backwards into the bar carrying the tray. I don't know what made me glance at the table in the front window, but I did and almost dropped the tray as I recognized one of the strangers. Charlie was sitting with his back to the window.

I managed to hide my surprise by bending and setting the tray down again. Further down the bar, Alastair was chatting to a couple of the locals, whilst keeping a wary eye on the newcomers. He glanced at me and raised his eyebrows silently asking if there was a problem. I smiled at him and carried the tray to a table at the back of the room.

I was wiping down the bar a little while later, when a second guy from Charlie's group came up to the bar. He was dark skinned with his head shaved.

"Another round of Brew Dog and whatever you're having," he said, giving me a cheeky wink.

"That's very kind, thank you," I said as Alastair came to stand beside me and started pulling the pints.

"I'm Sean," he said.

"Hi, Sean, I'm Jess," I replied, although since he was with Charlie, he would already know that.

"I'm sure our visitors would like to see menus," Alastair said.

I gathered four laminated sheets of paper from a pile at the end of the bar and handed them across.

"Grand idea," Sean said, accepting the menus from me.

I was on edge for the remainder of the evening, but they left at closing time, climbing the stairs to their rooms without Charlie even making eye contact with me.

Chapter 41

I expected to see Charlie the following day and hung around at the cottage in case he stopped by. But he didn't and I chastised myself for being so lame. It wasn't until the four of them breezed into the pub for dinner that I saw him again. As with the previous night, Sean ordered the drinks and collected the menus from me. Alastair took their dinner orders a little while later and it was only when I delivered their meals did Charlie actually look at me. He gave me a warm smile along with a polite thank you, as I placed his meal in front of him.

Douglas was propped up at the bar again. I was pleased, as I hoped to continue the conversation that had been interrupted the previous night by the arrival of Charlie and his mates.

As soon as Douglas's glass was nearing empty, I pulled him another pint and placed it in front of him.

"On me," I said in quiet voice. "Or actually on our visitors who bought one for me, but I'm giving it to you." I smiled at him.

Douglas nodded his thanks and sank back into his reverie.

"I was sorting through some old photos after we talked last night," he said the next time I came near.

"Was Colin's mother in any of them?" I asked. "I would love to see, as I've never seen a picture of her. I don't know if Colin even had one." Douglas looked surprised. "You mentioned that you might know who his father was?" I asked. Douglas nodded.

"Can you tell me?"

"Jess, the table at the back needs clearing," Alastair said from behind me. I jumped. I hadn't even heard him approach.

"Sure, Alastair," I replied.

"I'll talk to you later," I said to Douglas, turning towards the food hatch to pick up an empty tray and cloth.

"Do you have a pen?" Douglas asked. I dug my hands into the front pocket of my apron and produced one.

"There you go," I said, sitting it on the bar in front of him and watched him turn over a beer coaster and start writing on the back.

"Now," Alastair added. "Not next week."

I spun around.

"Sorry? Remind me why I'm working here again? It's not like I need the money and I certainly don't need to be spoken to like that. You do that again and I'm done," I snarled at him in a low whisper.

Alastair glared at me and for a moment I felt frightened. Then he sighed and ran a large hand through his hair. "Aye, you're right. I'm sorry, Jess, it's been a long day." He gave me a sheepish grin and moved away to serve another customer.

I shot a glance at Charlie's table. Charlie had a dark look on his face. He'd clearly overheard.

When Alastair called time, Douglas drained his glass and

265

stood pulling on his coat and hat. He stopped beside me, as I loaded a tableful of empty plates and cutlery onto a tray, and reached out to give my hand a squeeze. As he did, I felt him press a round piece of cardboard into my palm.

"Come and see me in the morning," he said.

I nodded, tucking the beer coaster into my jeans pocket. I carried a tray of dirty dishes into the kitchen and set them on the bench.

"That's the last of them," I said to the young guy loading the dishwasher.

"Thank God."

Glancing over my shoulder to make sure I wasn't being watched, I pulled the coaster from my pocket and looked at it. Written in block capitals was an address two streets over from the pub.

I left the minute I could, still fuming at Alastair's words, despite his apologies. I jumped into the Fiat and floored it out of the pub carpark. As soon as I turned onto the main road which curved around the harbor, I realized that I was not alone. I gave a sharp intake of breath and hit the brake. The car skidded to an abrupt stop.

"Don't be frightened, it's just me," Charlie spoke from the back seat.

"For God's sake, you almost gave me heart failure. Don't ever do that again."

"Sorry, Jess, but I need to discuss some things with you away from prying eyes."

I nodded in the darkness and accelerated up the hill and out of the village. "I'll park close to the door, so that you can get out under the cover of the porch."

A few minutes later I let him into the cottage. The embers

of the fire were glowing orange in the fireplace, so I added a handful of kindling to get it going again. I walked around each room, checking the window locks and closing the curtains before returning to the kitchen and closing the shutters.

"Tea?" I offered.

Charlie nodded. "I like your cottage. It's cute," he said.

"Thanks, I've been slowly doing it up. It had been pretty neglected over the years, but it's the closest thing to a home that I have now."

"Did you sell your London flat?"

"No, it's rented out. Surprising what some people will pay for the privilege of living in the home once occupied by a notorious terrorist," I said with a bitter laugh.

Charlie smiled and sat down at the wooden kitchen table. I poured the boiling water into a yellow china teapot and carried it to the table. I grabbed two matching mugs from the open shelves and a bottle of milk from the fridge.

"Do you want anything to eat? I have cake."

Charlie nodded his head. "Cake sounds great. You appear to be doing well, Jess– most people would have crumbled after what you've been through," he said.

"I nearly did."

We looked at one another for a long moment before Charlie broke eye contact and looked around the room. His eyes came to rest on the rifle propped up beside the door. He looked back at me and raised an eyebrow.

"Protection."

"Do you know how to use it?" he asked, frowning.

I grinned. "I do now."

"Do I want to know?" he asked.

I shook my head. "Probably not." My voice caught as I

thought about the manner of Buffy's death and I took a deep breath, letting it out as I reached into the pantry cupboard for the tin containing the carrot cake that I'd made earlier in the day. I cut two wedges and laid them on matching plates with little forks beside them.

"Thanks." Charlie smiled at me and reached into the pocket of the jacket he'd draped across the back of the chair.

"We're obviously not just here for a few days of fishing and golfing," he said.

I nodded and poured the tea. "Yeah, I figured that much."

He laid several photos on the table. "Can I get you to identify each person?" he asked.

"Sure," I said. "That's Alastair the publican, who you've already met, those guys are fishermen, I don't know their names. There's a fleet of around twenty boats which go out from here. That is the local cop, who's a bit useless," I said, tapping the next photo, "and that guy is a mechanic. He runs the garage out on the main road."

"What about this man?"

"That's Ewan Campbell, the Laird. He lives out on the island with the manor house just offshore. Wealthy gentleman farmer, from what I can gather. Owns most of the land around here. Colin knew him."

Charlie nodded. "So we know that Colin's mother is Catriona Mackie, do you know who his father is?"

I shook my head. "I'm working on that. She was still a teenager when she fell pregnant, so I guess it was a local boy, but as you have seen, she didn't name him on the birth certificate."

"This is the village that Colin came to for his golfing weekends, right?" I nodded. "Did you know that from the age of ten, he came back here every summer to attend a boys' camp run on the estate?" Charlie asked.

"Yeah, his adoptive parents recently told me that it was a condition of his adoption that he came back here each holiday. I'm not sure why, maybe to keep the connection with his mother. But it seems that he knew the local lads really well, better than an occasional visitor would," I said, suppressing a yawn that crept up on me. "Sorry, I think the stress of the last few days has caught up with me. I'm not sleeping very well without Buffy."

"Buffy?"

"My dog." Tears filled my eyes and I stood, taking my plate to the sink.

"Jess, I'm so sorry. Do you need anything?"

I held on to the bench and sighed. "Just answers."

Charlie was silent for a moment. "You know what we had was real, don't you?" he said. "I was never supposed to get involved with you. As soon as I did, I tried to get reassigned from your case, so that I could continue to see you. But it was too late to get anyone else involved."

"And then Frankie came along."

"No. You and I were found out by one of my bosses, who was furious with me. I was told in no uncertain terms to terminate our relationship in a way that there was no coming back from. Frankie was that way." He put his head in his hands. "I'm so sorry, Jess, I hate myself for hurting you like that."

I turned away from him, the tears I'd been holding back now rolling down my face. What a waste of lives and love this had all been.

"Well, I have no faith in my ability when it comes to men,

one was a terrorist and I didn't know, and the other was lying to me the whole time," I replied, sniffing.

"Not the whole time, Jess."

"Whatever. I'm involved in an entirely different relationship now."

Charlie's eyes flashed and he glanced down at the photos. "Are you dating one of these guys?"

I laughed without humor and shook my head. "No, what I mean is, I was in the middle of something before and I didn't know. Now I know and I am really scared. Someone killed my dog, Charlie. Actually, I'm just going to call you Will, if that's okay." I shook my head. "You're never going to be Charlie to me."

He grinned. "That's fine by me, Jessica." He pitched his voice low.

It was my turn to smile. "Sorry, Will, I'm immune to your charm nowadays."

He pulled a face. "Sorry, Jess. I wasn't meaning anything." He looked annoyed with himself.

"Can you answer some questions for me?" I asked.

"I'll try."

"What's your full name?"

"Charles William Matheson."

"Where did you grow up? How did you end up doing this job?"

"I grew up in Sussex until my parents were killed in a car accident when I was fourteen. I bounced around the foster system for a while before getting a scholarship to Harrow and the rest you know."

"When were you recruited?"

"By MI5?" I nodded. "While I was at UCL."

"So you've been doing this for years then?"

"No, this was my first full undercover assignment. Up until now, I've been working as an analyst. I can't really tell you any more than that," he said with a shrug.

"Or you'd have to kill me. It's all very James Bond."

"Well, Moneypenny, I must take my leave," he said, putting on a terrible Scottish accent as he pushed back his chair and stood up.

This time I laughed for real.

"I'll see you tomorrow." He let himself out into the night and I bolted the door behind him. I checked the rifle but left it by the door. I felt safer knowing that he and his team were somewhere nearby.

Chapter 42

April 20

I woke to a thick misty rain the following morning. Without Buffy to nudge me out of bed to take her walking, I rolled over and tucked my duvet around me and thought about the events of the previous day. I understood Will a little more, although I would never forgive him for deceiving me. God, I had been so naïve. First Colin and then Will.

I finally forced myself out of bed and got ready to go and visit Douglas after breakfast. I pulled on my coat, put up an umbrella and walked into the village. Low cloud had rolled in overnight and it was only just possible to make out the outline of Campbell Island. Douglas's cottage was two streets over from the pub. The front gate was open and I walked up to the door of the little stone house, admiring his well-tended garden. The front door was ajar and I lowered my umbrella and knocked. After several moments of silence, I knocked again and called out.

"Douglas, it's Jessica, from the pub."

There was still no response. I looked behind me at the quiet street. There was no one around. Perhaps he'd popped out to the shop. People in the village left their houses unlocked all of the time. It wasn't like the city, here there was no theft.

I leaned my dripping umbrella against the doorframe, pushed the door open and stepped into a small reception area. In front of me a narrow flight of stairs led to the second floor. The walls in the hall and stairwell were covered in framed black and white photos. I recognized Strathgarvan Castle and the Campbell Island lighthouse in a number of them. The photographs were stunning capturing shadows and light. Whoever had taken them was very talented.

As I turned to admire the photos further, I noticed a pair of slippered feet in the front room. Peeking into the room, I could see Douglas slouched in an armchair. I smiled. The walls of this room were also lined with framed photographs.

"Good morning, Douglas," I called. I didn't want to frighten him by just appearing at his side.

When he didn't respond, I walked further into the room and stifled a scream. Douglas had a pistol lying in his lap and there was a single bullet wound to his right temple. The back of his head was a bloody mess. At his feet, a large box had tipped over and photographs were strewn across the floor. On the table beside him sat a half empty whiskey bottle and a single glass. I forced myself to step forward and reached out to touch his hand. Cold. He was dead and had been for a while. I shivered with unease. I stepped back and pulled my phone from my pocket to call the police, when I noticed a muddy footprint across several of the photos on the floor. Someone else had been here.

I raced outside and up the path to the house next door. A grey-haired woman wearing an apron answered my urgent knock. Her hand flew to her mouth when I explained what I'd found and she shouted out to her husband. They returned to Douglas's house with me.

"Poor Dougie. He's been a bit low, but I never thought it would come to this," the old man said, stepping back out onto the porch taking deep breaths.

"Did you hear anything last night?" I asked the woman.

"No. I'll go and call the police," the woman said, hurrying back down the path and into her own house.

While she was gone, I looked at some of the photos on the floor. Whoever, the photographer was, he had a gift. Mixed in with beautiful scenic black and white photos were a number of pictures of people I didn't recognize. I looked at Douglas again. He looked peaceful, his eyes staring into space, his features relaxed. Something wasn't right, though.

Constable Jones arrived a short time later. His jacket was stretched around his wide girth and the buttons looked to be under enormous strain. He removed his hat and wiped the back of his hand across his sweaty forehead.

"Ms. Harley," he said. "You're not having a good week. Did ye find the body?" I nodded. "Suicide," he stated and turned as Doctor Stevens, an older man in a dark suit whom I'd met on several occasions at the Gordons', arrived carrying a black leather medical bag. He hurried over to examine Douglas.

"Looks that way," he agreed. "Hi, Jess."

"Hi, Doc."

"Poor old Douglas. I didn't think he was suicidal," the doctor said.

I thought back to the previous evening. Douglas hadn't wanted to talk to me in front of anyone else about Colin's parentage, so he'd invited me here to show me something, but what? I recalled him writing before slipping me the coaster with his address on it. That was it. That's what was bothering me. He wrote with his left hand.

Doctor Stevens was bent over the body.

"Hey, Doc. Wasn't Douglas left-handed?" I asked.

Doctor Stevens straightened up and looked at me. "I think perhaps he was. Jones?"

The policeman shook his head. "Dunno. Why?"

"Wouldn't it be a little hard for a left-handed man to shoot himself in the right temple?" I asked.

Both men looked from me to Douglas. "What are you suggesting, Jess? That someone helped him?" Doctor Stevens asked.

I shrugged.

The policeman laughed. "I don't think anyone would have any reason to kill Douglas." He stepped across the photos on the floor, destroying any evidence as he did.

I opened my mouth to say something further when my phone buzzed. It was Will.

'Where are you?' The text message read.

"I'll get out of your way," I said. "You know where I am if you need to ask me anything."

"Why were you here anyway?" Jones asked.

I indicated towards the photos lying scattered across the floor. "He was going to show me some photos of Colin as a kid."

The two men exchanged an unreadable look but said nothing.

"Right, I'll get the stretcher," Doctor Stevens said, heading back through the front door. In a village as small as Strath-garvan, the doctor often doubled as the paramedic and the undertaker.

I took one final glance at Douglas. When Jones had shifted his arm to check his pulse he'd set it down in a different position on his lap and I could now see the edge of a photo sticking out of his dressing gown pocket.

"Can you give me a hand, Jones?" the doctor called.

As Jones shuffled to the door, I leaned over and extracted the photo from Douglas's pocket and slipped it into mine.

I said goodbye to the two men as they maneuvered the stretcher through the narrow doorway and into the front room. Raising my umbrella to shield me from the rain, I hurried away. I didn't stop walking until I was outside the post office around the corner. I stepped into the shelter of the doorway and slid the photo out of my pocket. It was of a young couple gazing at one another. They were standing on a beach, with the water lapping at their feet, wearing jeans and raincoats. Two tall chimneys could be seen above the trees in the background. The photo looked old, especially if their hairstyles were anything to go by, long and messy. The young man had a scruffy beard and was wearing a type of cowboy hat. The woman's coat was open and the man had his hand resting on her rounded belly. I assumed that the young woman was Catriona, Colin's mother. The family resemblance was there in the shape of her nose and mouth and Colin had inherited her coloring; Catriona had long thick auburn hair. She was very striking.

There was something familiar about the man, but his head was turned to look at the woman, so I only had a side profile to go on and the brim of his hat hid most of that. I slid the photo back into my pocket, retrieved my phone and replied to Will's text.

'Something's happened. Meet at mine.'

Will was waiting around the side of the cottage, out of sight, when I arrived, out of breath from the quick walk uphill. He wasn't alone.

"This is Jake. He'll keep watch while we talk."

I smiled at Jake, the short stocky fourth member of Will's team whom I'd served at the pub the night before. He nodded and then eased back into the shadows at the side of the cottage. Will followed me inside.

"What's happened?" he asked as I closed the door and removed my wet jacket and shoes. He did the same.

"Coffee?" I offered.

"Thanks."

"And Jake? I could pass one out the bathroom window."

"I'm sure he'd appreciate it."

I switched on my espresso machine and opened the fridge for the milk.

"There's been another death."

"A suspicious one?" Will asked.

"I think so."

"What do the police say?"

"The policeman's an idiot."

"Who died?"

"Did you notice the old guy that I was talking to at the bar last night?" Will nodded. "I found him, this morning. Single gunshot to the head," I said, gripping the edge of the bench.

"Jess, are you alright?" Will reached for me, but I stepped away.

"I just hope it's not my fault that he's dead."

"Why don't you sit and tell me."

I made the coffee and handed a cup out of the bathroom

window to a grateful Jake, then returned to sit opposite Will at the small kitchen table where I explained about chatting with Douglas at the pub and his invitation for me to visit him this morning.

"I think he was going to tell me who Colin's father was, as though that would explain everything," I said, jumping up and retrieving the photo from the pocket of my raincoat. "Jones, the police constable concluded that he'd taken his own life, but the thing is, left-handed people don't normally commit suicide by shooting themselves in the right temple."

"You're right, they don't."

"Now I know you'll probably reprimand me for tampering with evidence, but after Jones trampled over everything and dismissed my theory that it wasn't suicide, I didn't think there would be any evidence anyway, so I took this out of Douglas's dressing gown pocket. I can't help but wonder if this was what he intended showing me?"

Will held out his hand for the photo. "I'm not going to reprimand you. Can you give me the address? I'll get one of the boys to drop by. I trust your judgment on this. It doesn't smell right." He studied the photo. "It looks like it could have been taken in the late 1980s, or early 90s, judging by the clothes. Do you have any other old photos that we could compare the people to?"

"Only one of Colin as a teenager with the group of boys."

"And you don't recognize either of these people?"

"Well, I'm almost certain that the woman is Colin's mother Catriona and there's something familiar about the guy, but I can't pinpoint it. If he's Colin's father, then maybe it's just the familial similarity." A thought formed in my mind. "Hang on, I'll get the other photo."

I jumped up and moved the espresso machine and got a knife out of the drawer. I wriggled the brick out of the kitchen wall and reached into the cavity, pulling out the tin. When I turned, Will was watching me with a bemused expression.

"I know. I'm paranoid."

"Perhaps not without reason."

I placed the tin on the bench and removed the lid, lifted out my passport, spare credit card and the envelope of cash that Dad had left me, before I found what I was after. I handed Will the photo of Colin and his friends.

"It could be the same guy," I said, laying the two photographs side by side and pointing to the older man standing among the group of teenage boys.

"Could be," Will agreed. "Bit hard to tell without the beard."

"If it's the same guy, it would mean that Ewan Campbell was Colin's father," I said. "That would make some sense. Colin's mother died when he was six or seven. He was adopted by the people who brought him up," I explained.

"I wonder why the secrecy? Do you think he feels guilty for not taking Colin on after she died?"

"I don't know. Catriona's family was poor. This cottage, which belonged to her parents, was all she had."

"Perhaps she wasn't 'good enough' for Ewan," Will said.

"Maybe, but when Colin arrived at his new family he had a large trust fund and I'm talking hundreds of thousands of pounds."

Will frowned. "How did she die?"

"In an accident, she drove her car over a cliff near here," I said. "Hang on; I want to check something else." I reached into the safety deposit package and pulled out the newspaper clippings from Colin's student days and shook my head in disbelief. I placed them on the table in front of Will and moved to stand beside him.

"No way," I said. "I haven't looked at these since I came here, but look who that is in the background." I tapped on the image of a man standing off the podium at the edge of each photo. "Ewan Campbell. He's been there the whole way."

"Careful not to jump to conclusions," Will said. "Can I take these with me?"

I nodded as a loud bird whistle sounded.

"We've got company. I'll let myself out through your bathroom window," Will said.

I repacked the tin, adding the new photo, and pushed it into my hiding place, replacing the brick, just as a loud knock sounded at the door. I hurried to open it.

"Alastair," I greeted the giant standing on the porch.

"Just checkin' you're okay what with Douglas killing himself," Alastair said as blunt as ever.

"Yeah. It was a shock though."

"What were ya doin' there, Jess?"

"I was taking him some baking. Poor old thing on his own, I don't think he was feeding himself properly," I rambled.

"So long as yer okay." I nodded. "Any chance you could work tonight?" he asked. "I have a feeling it will be a busy one."

"Sure."

"Great. See you then." He turned and strode back to his truck.

I returned to the kitchen and washed the coffee cups, drying them and putting them away. I retrieved the photo from its hiding spot, pulled my raincoat on and set out to visit the Gordons. If anyone could confirm the identity of the man in the photo once and for all, they could.

* * *

Mrs. Gordon answered the door using her walking frame for support and invited me in.

"Would you like a cup of tea, dear?"

"No thanks, I've just had one. I was having a clear out of Colin's things and I came across a photo of his mother," I said, wiping my feet on the mat and entering their kitchen.

"Ah, the poor lass. Let me see," Mrs. Gordon said.

I handed her the photo and watched as her expression changed. She looked up at me with an uncertain look in her eyes. "Where did you say you got this?"

"It was tucked into a book of Colin's," I said. "Who's the man?"

"It's the Laird," she said with a whisper.

"What? Ewan Campbell?" I asked, wide-eyed.

She nodded. "Don't be showing this around, Jess."

I sent Will a text as I walked back to my cottage.

'It's confirmed. The man in both photos is Ewan Campbell.'

Chapter 43

April 20

I t was as though everyone in town had congregated at the pub for an impromptu wake for old Douglas that evening.

Will, Jake, Sean and Freddy arrived early for dinner and ended up leaning on one end of the bar chatting to some of the locals as the evening wore on. Now that I knew who Will's three mates were, I could see that they were law enforcement, alert and watchful. I couldn't believe that other people didn't see it too, but their cover of a lads' weekend away seemed to be holding.

While I was taking their dinner order, standing at their table, notepad in hand, Will murmured to me. "We need to talk. I have some new info."

"Okay, after work."

"Great, I'll have the steak," he replied in a louder voice. "Medium please."

"I think you'll find, you'll take it how it comes," I replied, laughing.

I was run off my feet pulling pints and nips, so I got a fright when I looked up into Ewan Campbell's face.

"Good evening, Jessica."

"Good evening." *You're Colin's father,* screamed across my mind. Now that I knew, I could see the resemblance. They had the same wavy hair, hazel eyes and high cheekbones.

"I've been meaning to invite you over to the island," he said, smiling.

"Have you?" I said, surprised.

"How about tomorrow night?" he said. "I'll pick you up around seven?"

"I think I might be working," I replied, looking around for Alastair, hoping that he would back me up.

"I'm sure that can be changed," he said, handing me ten pounds. "I'll have a whiskey please."

Further down the bar, Jake looked up and caught my eye. He said something to Will, who turned and gave a slight shake of his head.

"Alastair, Jess needs the night off tomorrow," Ewan instructed.

"It's your night off anyway, Jess."

I glanced at Will again. A look of concern crossed his face.

* * *

"We ran a background check on Ewan Campbell. He's squeaky clean, too clean if you ask me," Will said, several hours later as he made himself comfortable in an armchair by the fire in my cottage. "We're digging deeper."

"Really?" I handed him a glass of red wine and sat down in

the armchair opposite.

"Yeah, interesting political views though," Will said. "He's very much a Scottish patriot."

"As was Colin after a few drinks, although I think we all secretly hate the English," I joked. "It's in our blood."

"No, this is more than patriotism. We're still digging into his financials. They are very much a maze of trusts and companies, much like Colin's were. He has funneled a large number of donations through some of these companies into parties and organizations which support Scottish independence and more recently we've linked payments from one of his offshore trusts to the extremist Scottish Homeland Society."

"Never heard of them," I replied.

"That's because they are operating under the radar, but their military arm has been linked to the terrorist attacks in Trafalgar Square and at Windsor after the Brexit referendum. But nothing confirmed. Unlike other terrorist organizations, they don't claim responsibility for their actions."

"So he's involved with some dangerous people. Is that what you're telling me?" I asked.

"Yeah."

"And I'm going offshore with him tomorrow night to have dinner. Great." I took a large gulp of wine. "Is Jake or anyone watching outside? They could come in. It's miserable out there."

"No. It's just me tonight, Jess. I told the others that I'd be staying here."

I pulled a face. "That's incredibly presumptuous of you, Will."

"Not sleeping with you, Jess. But I will be right here all night. It's not safe for you to be alone. You've rattled someone's cage."

284

I blushed. Now who was being presumptuous?

"We need to pack you up and get you away from the village first thing tomorrow," he continued.

"No," I replied. "I'm not running away again."

"Jess, I'm not exaggerating how dangerous these guys are."

"I'm not afraid."

Will sighed and pulled his hand through his hair. The old mannerism tugged at my heart. "Jess, I've told you too much already, but there's been intercepted chatter and we believe that another attack is imminent. The G7 summit is in Edinburgh the day after tomorrow."

"Yeah, I know. It was impossible to drive anywhere in Edinburgh without encountering a detour or roadblock a few days ago when I was there."

"When you have the leaders of the seven largest Western economies attending, there cannot be any security issues. However, we think that the British Prime Minister is a target," he said.

"And you think the terrorists planning an attack are here in this area," I added finishing for him.

"Jess, we've got heat signatures for at least thirty people out on the island. There are not many farms that require a work force of that size to live on site."

"How?" I began. "Actually, never mind."

"There have been a number of boat trips under the cover of darkness from the mainland to the island over the past few days, with trucks coming into the harbor each night and unloading cargo. It's odd for such a small island with only one house on it, albeit a large one."

"I know. I heard a convoy the other night. Alastair told me that it was trucks arriving to pick up the catch from the fishing fleet."

"Did he? Interesting."

"So you don't know what they are transporting? Maybe Ewan's planning a party or something?"

Will shook his head.

"Perhaps I could find out tomorrow night?"

"No. You won't even be here tomorrow night."

I glared at him. "I think that's my decision to make. If I want to go ahead with my date, then I will."

Will's eyes narrowed. "You don't want to date him." He spat the word.

"I don't know, I've dated liars and terrorists before. The only difference this time is that I know." I looked him in the eye. He winced.

"Jess..."

"Look, something or someone turned Colin into a fanatic. If that person is Ewan Campbell, then I need to know. That bastard ruined my life."

I jumped up and walked into my bedroom returning with a spare pillow and duvet. I dropped them on the end of the sofa. I brought out a towel and new toothbrush still in its packaging from the little bathroom and set them down on the coffee table.

"And," I continued. "If he's planning something like attacking the G7 meeting, then maybe I can find out something to help stop it. Make up for being so blind for all those years."

"If Ewan Campbell is the mastermind behind this, then you'll be walking into an extremely dangerous situation," Will said, standing up and rolling his shoulders. "I can't allow you to do that. I want you away from here, somewhere safe."

"You can't allow me?" I said. "I think you'll find it's not up

286

to you. I'm off to bed. And I'm not leaving." I pushed past him. He reached out and grabbed my arm.

"Don't do this. I can't protect you out there. You could get hurt."

"Can't you see that I need to do this? I need closure. My life has been completely derailed. If I'm to properly start again somewhere I need to know everything that went on under my nose in London and perhaps earlier at university." I removed his hand from my arm and held it for a moment. "Use me, Will. You've done so before. I'll go tomorrow night and see what I can find out. I have nothing to lose."

Chapter 44

April 21

I was standing in front of the mirror in the cottage's tiny bathroom fiddling with my hair when I heard the car pull to a stop outside. Abandoning my attempts to tame the strays that refused to join the rest of the strands in a topknot, I gave myself one last glance and strode towards the front door, just as a firm knock sounded. I grabbed my coat from a hook on the wall and slipped it on before unlocking and opening the door.

Ewan Campbell was illuminated by the porch light dressed in a knee length navy blue overcoat, with a tartan scarf looped around his neck, the ends tucked beneath the collar of his jacket. There was a definite chill to the night air and I was glad that I'd opted for a woolen dress with knee-high boots and tights to keep me warm.

"Jessica, you look lovely," he said stepping forward to kiss my cheek. I stiffened beneath his advance and had to force myself to not shove him away.

"Thank you, Ewan," I murmured.

He stepped back, the warmth in his smile not quite reaching

his eyes. I shivered.

"It's cold," he said. "Let's get you to the truck."

I nodded and pulled the door of the cottage shut behind me, hearing the deadbolts engage. Ewan walked ahead of me toward his Range Rover as I wrapped my scarf tightly around my neck and pulled on the gloves from my coat pocket. I nodded my thanks as Ewan held the passenger door open and waited for me to climb up before shutting it and closing me in. I battled my immediate fight or flight instinct with several deep breaths before Ewan climbed in behind the wheel and started the engine.

"I hope you're hungry," he said. "Chef has been preparing all day."

I forced a smile. "Sounds lovely."

"Beautiful night," Ewan said as we drove past the Gordon's cottage and turned onto the cliff top road leading down to the harbor. I saw their curtains twitch and Mrs. Gordon's concerned expression as we passed.

I turned my head to gaze out to sea. It was a clear night; the stars were plentiful and stretched across the sky like a net. The moon cast a silvery trail across the calm waters.

"It's stunning," I said. "I'm still getting used to seeing the night sky without the light pollution of the city."

Ewan turned his head and rewarded my attempt at conversation with another smile. I took a deep breath. I needed to relax and try to act normal or he would suspect that I was up to something.

"Any word on who shot your dog?" he asked.

I snapped my head around to look at him. I wasn't expecting that question. "Ah no, Constable Jones seem to think that someone shot her accidentally and couldn't bring themselves to tell me, so brought her back to the cottage so that I could bury her," I said. I didn't tell him that the gunman had spoken to me.

Ewan gave me an odd look as he maneuvered the car down the steep part of the road towards the harbor. "And do you agree with that?"

I nodded. "It seems the most likely explanation."

Ewan pulled the car into the carpark beside the harbor. A small powerful speedboat was tied up alongside the jetty. We climbed from the car and walked towards the boat. Again, I was overcome by a powerful urge to run, but instead I placed one foot in front of the other and continued walking beside Ewan. The even tap of the heels of my boots echoed on the wooden boards as though I was a soldier marching into battle; which in some ways, I guess I was.

Ewan untethered the rope holding the boat in place and leapt aboard. He held out his hand for me to follow. I stepped across the gap between the jetty and the boat just as a small swell passed and I landed off balance up against Ewan. He steadied me with both hands on my shoulders and looked down with an unreadable expression. He released me and turned to start the engine,

"You can sit there," he said, pointing to one of two seats on the boat.

I had only just perched on the edge of the seat when we pulled away. Ewan navigated the small boat through the harbor entrance and along a twisting passage between dark rocks slick with water towards the island. As we picked up speed, he turned to look at me and I got the most genuine smile of the night so far. Ewan clearly enjoyed travelling at speed across the dangerous channel to his island. I squeezed my eyes shut and prayed that the journey would be over soon.

Moments later, the engine slowed and we glided alongside the island's wharf. Ewan threw a line to a man waiting on the pier and turned to me, once again offering his hand. "Here we are." I accepted his hand and gave the relative safety of the mainland a final glance. What on earth had I been thinking last night to consider this a good idea? We stepped from the boat and made our way onto the island. A golf buggy was waiting at the end of the pier.

"Your chariot awaits," Ewan said with a grin. He strode around to the right-hand side and slipped into the seat behind the wheel. I sat beside him and hung on to the handrail beside the seat as Ewan drove the cart up a steep gravel path. We rounded a corner at the top and the house came into view. It was set back from the cliff edge nestled in a semi-circle of tall trees. A driveway curled around a large flat expanse of grass, at the center of which was a floodlit fountain containing a stone statue depicting William Wallace, in a kilt, brandishing a sword.

The house itself was deceptive. As we drew closer the size of the illuminated grey brick structure became apparent. There were turrets, steep gables and castle-like crenellations covering the expansive roof line. I must have gasped, because Ewan chuckled.

"Yes, it's quite impressive the first time you see it up close," he said pulling the golf buggy to a stop in front of a large bay window surrounded by the ivy which crept up one side of the house.

Ewan led me beneath a massive stone porch and into a wood paneled foyer. The head of a large stag looked down from its mount on the wall above a carpeted staircase which led up into darkness. The only light came from a large hanging lamp which cast eerie shadows across the space. I shuddered. It was as though I'd stepped into a gothic novel. Ewan threw his gloves on a hall table crowded with framed photographs and strode through a door to our left. I followed him into a long reception room filled with clusters of seating and a welcoming fire crackling in the enormous hearth. The room was lit by side lamps and my attention was drawn to the French doors at the far end which appeared to open out onto a large garden. Ewan helped to remove my coat and scarf before taking them from the room. I wandered through the space taking everything in; the large gilt-framed landscape paintings, vases of artfully arranged dried twigs, soft cashmere throws in earthy tones and a wide floor-to-ceiling bookshelf covering one wall, with a ladder resting against its shelves.

I turned as I heard Ewan return to the room.

"This is a beautiful room," I said.

He nodded in acknowledgement before taking my elbow and leading me towards the French doors. "You'll have to come in daylight next time so that you can see the gardens," he said, opening the door and stepping out onto a flagstone patio. What I could see of the garden under the moonlight was magnificent. Large established trees and shrubs framed beds of flowers arranged in straight even rows. I sensed that we were being watched from beyond the trees at the edge of the lawn and shivered.

"It's lovely," I said.

"Let's get you back inside," Ewan said, ushering me through the door and closing it behind us. "Now can I get you a drink?"

"Yes, what are you having?"

"I have a bottle of red open."

"Perfect."

I accepted the glass he poured and turned my attention to the bookcase. After perusing a few shelves, I realized that almost all of the titles were concerned with Scottish history and politics.

"I'm something of an amateur history buff," Ewan said, coming to stand beside me.

"How long have you lived here?" I asked.

"I was born here. Literally. In a bedroom upstairs," he said.

"Really? Did you have brothers and sisters?" Ewan shook his head.

"That must have been lonely."

Ewan shrugged. "Not really. We had a lot of staff in those days who either lived in the staff quarters or in cottages on the estate and their children were my playmates." His expression was distant for a moment before he turned and walked over to the fireplace. I followed, grateful for the warmth it provided.

"Where did you go to school?"

"I was home schooled by my mother until I was twelve. Then it was boarding school and university in Edinburgh. Unfortunately, my father died when I was twenty, so I had to come back and run the estate as soon as I'd completed my degree."

"So no Mrs. Campbell? No children?" I tried to keep my tone light.

Ewan gave me a hard stare as if trying to understand what I was really asking. "No," he said. "Enough about me, tell me about you. Where does Jessica McDonald come from?"

"Jessica Harley," I corrected, "hails from Edinburgh. Like you I was an only child and I too, have lost my father."

"I'm sorry to hear that, especially as you have also lost your husband prematurely."

I took a sip of wine.

"You said that you knew Colin."

Ewan nodded. "Yes, he used to spend his summers in the village when he was a teenager. Our paths crossed from time to time."

"Did you also know his mother?" I said. "Catriona."

Ewan's glass froze halfway to his lips. "Aye, she was a local lass," he said, slipping into a regional accent.

"Dinner is ready, sir," a voice called from the doorway.

Ewan's frown was replaced with a grin. "This way," he said taking my free hand and leading me from the room, back across the entrance foyer to a dining room on the opposite side of the house.

A long polished wooden table with high-backed chairs was in the center of the large room. Two places had been set at one end of the table which could easily seat twelve people. A picture rail ran at waist height around the circumference of the room with wood paneling below the rail and wallpaper covering the wall above. Large framed paintings of rural scenes were hung around the walls at regular intervals. Heavy damask curtains covered the windows. There was an enormous fireplace in the center of one wall, which was set, but unlit. The table held two large candelabras, with more flickering candles set in sconces on the walls, casting shadows across the room. Two casserole dishes and a carafe of red wine sat on a heavy wooden sideboard against the wall.

Ewan held out a chair for me. I sat my wine glass on the table as I slid into the seat. A man in chef's whites emerged through a doorway behind me and placed a bowl of steaming soup in front of me and one at Ewan's place setting.

"Thank you," I said, smiling at the man.

He gave a curt nod and left the room.

I picked up my spoon and tasted the clear broth. Its warmth trickled down my insides, thawing me out somewhat.

"Why did you come to the village, Jessica?" Ewan asked after a few moments silence.

I sipped another spoonful of soup and put my spoon down. "I wanted to see where Colin grew up."

"That was in Edinburgh surely."

"Perhaps I should rephrase. He talked about this village a lot. I wanted to see what it was about this place that attracted him so and try to understand why he did what he did."

"And what have you discovered?" Ewan asked.

"Well, I didn't know that his mother grew up and died here. I guess that goes some way to explaining the attraction to the area."

"But I got the impression that you no longer cared about him."

"Oh I don't. In fact, I hate him, for what he became, for what he made me an unwitting accomplice to. He has ruined my life. I just don't understand what made him fanatical and how he hid it so well. But I intend to find out."

Ewan opened his mouth to reply when the door from the foyer opened and a man in dark clothes entered. He strode straight over to Ewan and bent to speak in a low voice in his ear. I watched as Ewan's posture changed and his gaze slid sideways to me.

"Thank you, Ben," he said dismissing the man. Ben left the room, closing the door behind him.

"Is everything okay?" I asked.

"We have an ongoing battle with poachers on the estate and it would appear that tonight is no different," he said.

The chef reappeared and cleared away the soup. Ewan stood and topped up our wine glasses from the carafe before the chef returned carrying two plates of salmon, dauphinoise potatoes and a medley of vegetables, which he placed in front of us. My murmur of thanks was once again met with a single nod.

"Freshly caught this morning on the estate," Ewan said as I took a bite.

"Wow, it's delicious," I said, savoring the mouthful.

We ate in silence for a few minutes until Ewan's phone buzzed. He pulled it from his pocket and glanced at it.

"I'm sorry, Jessica, but you'll have to excuse me for a moment."

"Of course," I said, putting my cutlery down and picking up my wine.

Ewan pushed back his chair, stood and hurried from the room, towards the entrance foyer.

I sat back and had just lifted the glass to my lips to take a sip when there was a loud crash behind me. I jumped, spilling some of the wine on my hand. I grabbed my napkin as I spun around in my seat and looked behind me. A stooped man stood in the doorway leading to the kitchen, the light behind him forming a halo around his outline. A figure was sprawled at his feet, holding his shoulder and groaning. A booted foot connected with the torso of the person on the ground, kicking him further into the room so that he came to rest in a pool of candlelight. I gasped as the man looked up at me through swollen eyes and a bloodied face. Will. I leapt up, dropping the napkin and rushed forward, as he croaked out a low, "No."

"Stop." The man in the shadows spoke with a slur. "Step away from him."

I hesitated and peered towards the voice before I turned and shouted. "Ewan."

Footsteps approached the main door and Ewan burst into the room. He quickly assessed the situation and came to stand beside me.

"Well, this is unfortunate," he said. "I take it you are acquainted with our trespasser."

"No," Will rasped.

"He wasn't asking you," the other man slurred, stepping forward and silencing Will with another kick.

"Stop it," I yelled.

The man stepped into the light and I gave a little scream before I could stop myself. He walked with a pronounced limp and was missing an arm, but it was his face that horrified me the most. On one side the skin was puckered and shiny, like a melted piece of plastic had been pressed into his cheek. The side of his mouth was misshapen and between his lips I could see gaps where there should have been teeth. His scalp was an angry pink, bald in parts and covered in thin wispy strands of hair in others.

"No," I whispered. "You're dead."

"Oh no, darling wife," he spluttered. "As you can see, I'm very much alive."

Chapter 45

April 21

I took a step backwards and looked at Ewan. He gave Colin a gentle smile before turning to me.

"Despite your best efforts, my son didn't die in that explosion," he said. "You couldn't leave it alone could you?" He gripped my arm, his fingers digging into my bicep, sending shooting pains through my body.

"Why?" I forced myself to look back at Colin. "You are responsible for the deaths of all those people."

"It's a long story," he said, his words whistling as though he had a bad speech impediment. "Why did you come here?"

"Tonight?"

"No, to Strathgarvan?"

"To find out what made you a fanatic."

Colin laughed. "I'm not a fanatic, just a realist. As I told you many times, if you'd actually listened, it's time that the English gave Scotland back to us."

I stared at him. "And setting off bombs and killing innocent people is the way to get them to do that?"

"It worked for the IRA, right, Dad?" Colin looked over at

Ewan, before looking back at me. "Jess, why wouldn't you just take a hint and go away? I thought when I shot your dog you would leave."

"It was you," I whispered. "How could you?"

"You loved that bloody animal more than you ever loved me. I watched you going out each day with it, talking to it, cuddling it," Colin snarled.

"You're mad," I breathed. My eyes dropped to Will, who was struggling to maintain consciousness.

"Ewan, surely you don't condone this," I turned to him and pleaded.

"You've been a thorn in our sides for months, girl," he said. "First your father, and then you interfering."

"My father?"

"Your father was this close to uncovering our plans," Ewan said, holding his fingers millimeters apart.

I started shaking my head and trying to pull away. I could feel my anger rising. "No."

"He had to be dealt with," Ewan said.

"No wonder you didn't want to be at his funeral," I spat, looking to Colin.

He shrugged. "That would have been hypocritical," he conceded.

"Were you really in Dubai?"

Colin laughed. "Nah, I was here."

"You bastard."

"Maybe, but then you brought MI5 into our lives. Did you know or were you so stupid that you were caught in his honey trap?" Colin launched his boot into Will's side again.

"Stop it, you're killing him," I cried, wrenching myself free of Ewan's grasp and rushing to Will's side, crouching down beside him, running my hand over his head.

Colin gave a hearty laugh. It was an awful sound, wheezy and wet. "That's the plan."

He pulled a revolver from the waistband of his jeans and aimed it at Will. I rose to my feet, putting myself between Colin and Will.

"No."

"Aw, ain't that sweet, she still cares about him."

I looked to Ewan for help. He shrugged. "You can't blame the guy. Look what you've done to him."

"What I've done to him? He was the one building bombs in his warehouse."

"Yes, but it was you who brought the police and it was the police whose shots caused the explosion that did this to my son," Ewan said.

"That's a twisted way of interpreting events," I said. I looked back at Colin. "How did you survive?"

"I managed to crawl into the canal, where I hid. Several of our men pretended to be with the emergency services and in the chaos after the explosion, they managed to get me away," Colin said. His words whistled through the side of his disfigured mouth. He gave another crazed laugh. "They must have left my arm behind." He waved his bandaged stump at me.

I swallowed as a wave of nausea rose from my stomach and turned to look at Ewan. "What I don't understand is why? You were born into all of this?" I waved my hand gesturing to the house. "Why support terrorists?"

"The Scottish people have been under the rule of Westminster for too long. The Brexit result was the final straw. Scotland voted to stay with Europe, yet here we are being forced to leave. It's time that we took full control of our own affairs and history has shown that England only responds to force."

I must have looked incredulous, because he laughed. "Surely that's up to the population as a whole to decide, not just you," I said.

"Sometimes the population doesn't know what's good for it and needs a little help making the right decision," he said.

"What about the arms dealing?" I asked. "Didn't you think someone would find out about your little side deals with Mendelson?

Ewan gave a slow clap and almost looked impressed. "Clever. You or your father? Not that it matters. I inherited a large portfolio of shares including Mendelson, and it was so easy to just keep buying more through my various companies until I controlled the board and the staff. It's amazing what the workers will do for a little extra cash. Manufacture a few extra items here and there off the books. But soon I started making serious amounts of money from it. Various organizations worldwide were seeking me out." He sounded proud of his achievements. "It has allowed me to finance our activities undetected."

"Where did Colin fit into this? What about Catriona? Why didn't he grow up here with you after she died?"

"Ah, the beautiful Catriona. Her family were tenants of ours and my parents forbade me from seeing her, a commoner. After her parents died, she fell pregnant; we wanted to marry, but my father refused to allow it and he refused to acknowledge the baby."

Will stirred at my feet and opened his eyes for a moment. I stayed silent, waiting for Ewan to continue.

"Catriona got tired of waiting and started spending weekends away in Edinburgh and suddenly I was no longer welcome to spend nights at her cottage. Somehow, she learned of my little side deals and she was horrified. I had her followed to Edinburgh one weekend and found out that she was seeing another man, who happened to be some low-level government official. The worst type of betrayal. She knew how I felt about the British government. I learned that she was planning to take Colin and leave the village to be with this man." Ewan's fists were clenched at his side at the memory.

"I confronted her as she was leaving Strathgarvan one night to be with her lover and we argued. I knew that she had left Colin with the Gordons for the night, so I jumped in my car and followed her. She was driving too fast to get away from me, lost control and went over a cliff. There was nothing I could do."

I gasped and looked at Colin. His expression was impassive.

"Don't you care that he killed your mother?" I asked.

"She was going to take me away from him."

I shook my head in disbelief before continuing. "What about Douglas?"

"Douglas?"

"Why kill him?"

Ewan looked surprised.

"Left-handed men don't normally commit suicide by shooting themselves in the right temple."

"That was careless," Ewan said, looking at Colin. "Douglas was about to tell you that I was Colin's father. My reputation would be ruined if that gets out now that Colin's name has been dragged through the mud. It had come to my attention that Douglas had been taking photos where he shouldn't, so

God only knows what else he was going to show you. I cannot afford for my name to be tarnished. The only way to further our cause is if I maintain my standing in society."

"Your standing in society?" I asked, incredulous at what I was hearing. Ewan was just as crazy as Colin.

"I had big long-term plans for Colin, which ultimately involved him becoming the head of a free Scotland. He had everything: the charm, looks, smarts. We were playing a long game. I needed him to be a successful self-made businessman first with a happy marriage, which is where you came in and unfortunately turned out to be not such a great choice. Then Brexit happened, and the Scottish people voted to differentiate themselves from England, which accelerated our timetable." He thumped the table. "Back in the nineties I watched the IRA push the British to the point that they were willing to make compromises in the rule of Northern Ireland and Meibion Glyndwr waged a successful bombing campaign in Wales. I decided that the only way to make the British take notice of Scottish demands for independence was to adopt some of their methods."

"I don't think it was the IRA's campaign of violence that led to peace talks," I said, horrified at the direction of his twisted thoughts.

Ewan stopped pacing and stared at me. "That's where you're wrong."

I looked from Ewan to Colin. "So you were responsible for the London bombings."

Colin laughed. "Yeah."

"Why Cheapside?"

"Cheapside was a test run for a larger device. The Trafalgar and Windsor devices were smaller, designed to grab attention, but we wanted to make sure that the message got through, so we needed a public figure involved," Ewan said, his mouth twisting. "I'd watched Catriona's lover rise through the ranks of the British government over the years and I decided that it would be symbolic if the first attack of this campaign took out that man. I found out that he drank at the same pub with friends every Wednesday night, so boom."

"Are you talking about Sir Maurice Jefferson? But didn't he leave before the bomb went off?"

Ewan nodded. "Unfortunately. Perhaps he won't be so lucky next time."

"So where was the warehouse bomb going to?"

"Westminster. That's when we were going to announce ourselves."

"How? You'd never get close."

"Ah, see that's where you're wrong. Colin's firm was on the approved courier schedule for Westminster Palace, so his team could drive a van in there any day of the week."

"But don't they search all delivery vans, even if they're approved? Don't they have sniffer dogs who hunt for explosives?"

Ewan laughed. "Yes, but even the smartest sniffer dogs can't detect explosives housed in the type of airtight container that we designed. They're always having problems with their air conditioning units, so it wasn't hard to hack the system to put out a request to have one delivered."

"My God, you are quite mad," I said, shaking my head.

"No, just focused."

"But what about all the innocent people you have killed and maimed?"

"Jess, my dear, there is collateral damage in any war. And

let me make it clear. We are at war," Ewan said.

Colin laughed again, a rattling hiss that turned my stomach. "And at war the soldiers get to have fun with their captives." He shoved the gun into the back of his jeans and came at me with a lascivious look in his eye.

I backed away from him and bumped straight into Ewan, who grasped my shoulders and held me in place. Colin leaned close to me. "Oh darling wife, I may have lost my arm and the ability to speak properly, but other bits of me still work just fine and it's been way too long."

I struggled against Ewan as Colin's meaning became clear. Colin pressed himself against me and opened his twisted mouth. His breath was stale with a hint of something rotten. I flinched and struggled. He stuck his tongue out and ran it up the side of my face from my jaw to temple. I gagged and he back-handed me across the face. My head snapped to one side. I put both hands on his chest and shoved at him.

"Get away from me."

"I'm just getting started," he snarled.

He looked over my head at his father. "First, I want to wake him up so that he can watch."

Ewan held me in place as Colin bent down, grabbed one of Will's feet and dragged his prone form across the floor towards the table. Will's head bumped along the boards.

"So what are you planning to do now, Colin? Hide here for the rest of your life?" I asked. "I can't see anyone voting for you to become Scotland's next First Minister."

He dropped Will's foot and pulled a chair away from the table. "Thanks to you, my life is over. I'm going to go out with a bang and take as many English scum with me as I can."

I stared at him open-mouthed, trying to make sense of his

305

meaning. "Not the G7?"

"What better international stage to announce ourselves."

Colin picked up my water glass and emptied it over Will's face. Will groaned and curled into himself.

"Come on, wakey wakey." Using one arm, Colin hauled Will up onto the chair. Will slumped against the armrest. Colin slapped his cheek. "Wake up. It's show time." Will's eyes rolled and he blinked several times. His gaze moved from Colin to me.

"Jess," he managed.

Colin turned and limped back towards me. He pulled me roughly from his father and shoved me towards the table. I turned to face him, my hand reaching behind me for a knife or candle or anything that I could use as a weapon. Colin lunged over me and with a sweep of his good arm, cleared dishes, glasses, and cutlery off the table. They hit the floor with a crash, shattering the crystal and smashing the china. He pushed me against the edge of the table and stepped back to undo the button and unzip his jeans. I leaned my weight against the edge of the table and kicked out with both feet, catching him in the stomach. He stumbled backwards for a moment but maintained his balance. I spun and grabbed for one of the iron candlesticks at the same moment as Ewan moved it out of my reach. Colin grabbed me from behind and pushed my dress up around my waist and ripped at my tights with his hand. Ewan moved beside him and took the gun from his waistband and levelled it at Will's head.

"No," I screamed.

Outside, the silence was broken by the loud crack of an explosion, shaking the house and rattling the glass in the window panes. Colin froze. A second explosion sounded, closer this time, from the direction of the trees at the side of the house. A flash of light filled the room for a moment. The door to the dining room burst open and Ben rushed into the room.

"Sir," he addressed Ewan. "You must come now. We are under attack."

"Colin, with me," Ewan instructed.

"But…" Colin began.

"You can finish with her later. Lock them in."

Colin took a deep breath and grabbed a handful of my hair, pulling my head back so that my cheek was alongside his ruined face. "I'll be back, my darling," he spat. He pushed me aside and zipped up his jeans.

The three men rushed from the room and I heard a key turn in the lock. I pulled my dress down and slumped against the table for a second before rushing over to Will, who had forced himself to his feet. He pulled me into his arms and held me.

"God, Jess."

"What are you doing here? I thought you were on the mainland?" I said, disentangling myself and running to the main door. I grabbed the handle and gave it a shake. It was locked as I expected. I turned and rushed across the room to the chef's entrance, but that door wouldn't budge either.

"You didn't think I'd let you come out here alone did you?" Will said.

I shook my head. "Will…"

"It's okay."

"What are those explosions? Are they your doing?" I asked as the echo of another detonation sounded from outside.

He nodded. "They are distractions only, we don't have much time."

I grabbed one the heavy chairs from the table. "In that case, we're going to have to break a window and make a run for it."

"Campbell has a lot of armed men on the island, we wouldn't get very far. I have a better idea," Will said. "I've studied the schematics for the house. This room has a priest's hole, I think."

He moved as fast as he could towards the enormous fireplace, running his hands over the wood paneling on either side.

"A priest's hole?"

"Yeah, they were common in houses such as this in the sixteenth century to hide Catholic priests from Elizabeth I's priest hunters."

"But won't we just be trapped?"

"Not necessarily," Will said, stepping beneath the mantelpiece and right into the giant hearth. He began tapping the brick surround. "Help me, we don't have much time before they'll be back."

I joined him. "What are we looking for?"

"An opening, a loose brick, a sliding panel, I'm not exactly sure."

We searched the entire fire surround and found nothing. Another explosion sounded outside.

"I think the window is our only option," I said, stepping out of the fireplace.

Will bent over with his hands on his knees breathing deeply. "Okay." He straightened and took a step after me before tripping. I turned as I heard him stumble and reached out to catch him. We saw it at the same time. A large flagstone at the edge of the firebox had a hole in one corner and was ever so slightly raised. Will grabbed an iron poker from a wood basket beside the fireplace and slotted it in the hole, levering the stone upwards. I helped him to slide it sideways. We both looked down into a hole with a narrow stone staircase leading down into the darkness.

Chapter 46

April 21

Will returned the poker to the basket as I ran across the room and pulled a lit candle from one of the candlesticks on the table.

"Come on, Jess, let's go," Will urged. "You go first and I'll pull the stone back over us."

I hesitated for a moment before lowering myself into the hole, desperately trying not to think of what might be waiting in the gloom below. It couldn't be any worse than what we faced if we stayed in the dining room any longer.

"You can do this," he said, taking the candle from me. I climbed down several steps. They were narrow, around half the width of my foot. I let one hand go and reached for the candle. I shone its light below me. I could see the floor a few steps down. I kept easing myself down as Will's feet came over the edge towards me. I reached the last step and jumped onto a dirt floor as a scraping sound echoed above me. I held the candle up as Will started to drag the flagstone back over the hole. I could see that he was struggling, so I set the candle down and climbed back up, squeezing in beside him.

Together we pulled the stone across, both breathing a sigh of relief hearing it slot into place.

"Thanks," he said. "I'm not sure I could have managed that on my own."

"You've taken quite a beating," I said, all of a sudden aware that we were pressed together in a very tight space. I looked into his face and thought for a moment that he was about to kiss me.

He cleared his throat. "You climb back down first."

I nodded, not trusting myself to speak, and scrambled back down the steps, picking up the candle.

Will took his time descending the stairs as I looked around. We were in a large cellar with a low curved brick roof. A gentle breeze blew from somewhere in front of us causing the candlelight to flicker. I cupped my hand around the flame to protect it. Will leaned against the wall at the bottom of the staircase to catch his breath. He was looking very pale. I reached my hand out to caress his cheek.

"Are you okay?"

He nodded and pushed off the wall. "We need to keep moving."

I dropped my hand before it made contact. "Are you sure you can?" I asked. "You could hide here and I'll go for help."

Will shook his head. "No, let's stick together for now."

I nodded and shivered. Will tried to shrug out of his jacket, wincing with pain as he moved.

"What are you doing?" I asked.

"Giving you my jacket. You're freezing."

"Don't be stupid. You're injured. You need it." Will looked torn. "Come on, there's a breeze coming from over there," I said. "That might be a way out." I hooked my arm around his waist. "Lean on me," I said. "You'll keep me warm at the same time."

"Okay," he said. "I'm not too proud to admit that I need you to help me."

"I'm sorry that I dragged you into this. You were right. I should have left this alone," I said.

"Well, whatever happens, you gathered some great intel."

Together we crept across the cellar towards the breeze. Wooden whiskey barrels and empty crates were strewn about. The roof curved further towards the ground as we neared the edge of the room. In the far corner, a low narrow passageway opened up in front of us, sloping downwards and disappearing into darkness. Will let me go and looked around.

"Let's drag some of these across behind us," he said. "It will slow down anyone that follows."

"I'll do it," I said. "You hold the candle." I thrust it into his hand.

I lifted two empty wooden crates in front of the tunnel entrance and then stacked two more on top. I rolled two of the whiskey barrels in front of the crates and scuffed the floor clear of the roll marks.

"That's probably enough, let's go," Will said in a soft low voice, squeezing behind the crates. "I'll go first." He hunched over to avoid hitting his head and disappeared from view down the passage. I froze as I heard footsteps crossing the floor above me. They continued across the boards and seemed to move deeper into the house. With a final glance into the darkness behind me, I hurried after Will.

The passage narrowed until it was really only a crawl space with walls roughly hewn out of stone. Will dropped to his knees and began edging forward. I crawled a few meters before my tights ripped and small stones and pieces of rock scraped at my knees. It was slow going with Will stopping every few seconds, causing me to run into his feet.

"Are you okay?" I called.

"Yeah, trying to conserve my energy," he said.

A sudden wind gust up the tunnel extinguished the candle that he was cradling in front of him, plunging us into darkness.

"Shit." Will stopped again and this time I fell against his legs.

"Sorry."

"It's okay, we're nearly there. I think I can see moonlight ahead of us."

We crawled a little further and the tunnel widened into a cave. A sharp cool breeze swept in from the sea. Will pulled himself to standing and stretched before leaning against the wall of the cave, sucking in shallow breaths.

"Here," he said after a moment, opening his arms. I went straight into them and rested my head on his shoulder being as gentle as I could. His arms came around me and held me for a long moment. The sounds of the waves crashing onto the rocks and then pulling back was rhythmic, almost soothing.

"What now?" I asked.

"Hopefully, your wire is still working and we can call for help," he said.

I reached down and unzipped my boot, reaching inside for the tiny transmitter. I pulled it out and gave it to Will, just as a beam of light swept across our hiding place. We scrabbled backwards into the darkness of the tunnel.

"What was that?" I whispered.

Will eased himself forward and peered out of the cave entrance before coming back to stand with me. "We are just below the lighthouse. That light is its beam sweeping across the entrance to the harbor." He held the transmitter to his mouth.

"Jake, did you hear that? We are at the bottom of the lighthouse on Campbell Island requesting immediate evac."

"How do you know if he heard?" I asked.

"I don't."

"So what do we do now?"

"We wait."

We sat huddled together just out of range of the lighthouse beam, which swept by at regular intervals. In the distance, we could hear men's voices and the occasional round of gunfire, which caused me to jump.

"It's okay, Jess, we should be safe here." No sooner had the words left his mouth than we heard a scraping noise back up the tunnel behind us. Someone was moving the crates I'd stacked in front of the entrance. Our escape route had been discovered.

"Quick." Will climbed to his feet and reached for my hand as a flashlight beam flickered behind us.

We rushed to the cave entrance and clambered across the rocks towards the base of the lighthouse, helping each other move as fast as we could with only the halo from the lighthouse to guide us across the uneven surface. This side of the island was comprised of large sharp boulders sloping down to a gravelly beach. My high-heeled boots were not made for this terrain and my feet kept slipping. Will's good arm latched firmly around my waist was the only thing that stopped me falling a number of times.

Behind the lighthouse, the island rose sharply, an exposed cliff supporting the plateau where the manor house was situated. Powerful flashlight beams danced among the trees along the ridge. They were searching for us.

Then the heel of my right boot caught in a narrow crevasse between two rocks. My knee wrenched painfully as we kept moving.

"Will, my foot," I cried out, pulling against him and forcing him to stop.

Will cursed as he looked over my shoulder back down at the tunnel entrance. He released me, reached down and, wrapping his hands around my ankle, pulled. There was a snap and my leg came free, leaving the pointed heel of my boot wedged in place.

"Come on," Will urged, pulling me around behind the lighthouse as the sound of footsteps thundering into the cave reached us.

Chapter 47

April 21

"I know ya there. I'm coming to finish what we started," Colin called in a strange slurry singsong voice.

I looked at Will, terrified, and stifled a scream as a gunshot rang out, hitting the wall of the lighthouse with a sharp thud. "One, two, three, I'm coming," Colin called.

Will and I edged around the lighthouse until we came to a wooden door. Will tried the handle and it sprung open. He pushed me inside. "Find something to bar the door from the inside and I'll distract him."

"Will, no," I said, reaching for him.

"Help is on the way, I can buy us a little time."

"He has a gun, Will, and we don't know that Jake even heard us."

"Even if he didn't, I have a GPS tracker embedded in my arm. They will be tracking me with that. Listen, I can hear a chopper." He leaned in and kissed me hard on the lips before pushing me away and pulling the door closed between us.

I looked around. I was in a circular room with a spiral stone staircase winding upwards against one wall. A couple of old chairs and a table sat beside a grimy window opposite. I grabbed one of the chairs and wedged it under the door handle, as a shadow passed by the window. I ducked down low, pressing myself out of sight, as the door handle rattled. I bit down on my hand to stop myself crying out in fear.

The rattling stopped and I could hear footsteps moving away from the lighthouse followed by shouting and another gunshot.

I raced towards the staircase and began climbing the stairs. The second floor was empty, so I kept going. The third and fourth floors that would once have been home to the lighthouse keeper were now storage rooms. I was out of breath by the time I reached the top level where floor-to-ceiling windows surrounded a large lamp in the center of the room. A doorway led out onto an external walkway which wrapped around the entire structure, two feet below the level of the light. I ducked and retreated down several steps so that I was hidden but could still see out. The light turned a full 360 degrees, shining across the coastline and beach.

I caught a glimpse of Will scrambling across the rocks towards a cluster of trees. Several meters behind him, I watched a second figure moving at a faster pace after him, before the light moved. I blinked several times and squinted, trying to adjust my vision to the darkness. In the pale moonlight, I could just make out the two figures.

"Come on, Will, run," I urged as my heart raced. I could see that he wasn't going to make it to the trees before Colin caught up with him. In the gloom I saw Colin raise his arm and Will stumble, but keep going. Colin raised his arm again and this time Will fell.

"No," I cried, rushing across the room and opening the door

onto the external walkway, my gait uneven as I hobbled in my broken boots.

The rhythmic thump of a helicopter's rotors filled the air. I looked out to sea. In the darkness, I could just make out the lights of an approaching aircraft. I watched as a dark shape appeared over the island. The noise of the rotors intensified as it passed low over the lighthouse, before swooping around and training a spotlight on Colin. Colin's hunched figure was illuminated as he scrambled across the rocks to where Will had fallen. He stopped and turned his head to the sky, shielding his eyes with his arm for a moment before firing his gun towards the helicopter. I heard a loud ping as the bullet hit the undercarriage. The helicopter hung in the air for a moment, before I watched in dismay as it tilted its nose down and flew away from the island and back out to sea.

The lighthouse beam swept across the landscape once more, this time illuminating me for a brief instant standing at the outside railing. At that exact moment, Colin looked up. He saw me and grinned, before picking his way across the rocks to where Will lay. Colin turned around to make sure that I was still watching as he shoved the gun into the back of his jeans and bent down with one arm, hoisting Will onto his shoulder. He took a few steps to the edge of the boulders and threw him into the churning surf below. I screamed as the tide pulled Will out, before tossing his inert body back onto the sharp rocks. Colin turned and called out to me, but the sound of the helicopter returning drowned out his voice.

I raced back inside the lighthouse looking around for something to use to defend myself. There was nothing. I hobbled back to the doorway and waved my arms at the helicopter, just as a small rocket, fired from the ridge behind me, whizzed past the lighthouse towards the aircraft. The pilot took immediate evasive action and the rocket cut underneath, missing the landing skids by millimeters. The helicopter banked and flew out to sea again, as I heard the door of the lighthouse crash open, followed by footsteps thundering up the stairs. I closed the outside door behind me and scampered to the opposite side of the walkway just as Colin arrived at the top floor.

"Hey, Jessie," he called, spotting me through the window.

The beam rotated again, blinding me for a few seconds, long enough for Colin to cross the floor and join me on the walkway.

"Now, we're gonna have some fun before I kill you, bitch," he said, advancing towards me.

I backed away from him, trying to assess my options. I could get back inside and run down the stairs and out onto the shore where there was nowhere to hide or I could stay out here, where I would be seen if the helicopter returned. Neither option was ideal. The wind up on the walkway was cold and I could feel it seeping into my bones. I kept moving, trying to keep out of his reach until he pulled the gun on me.

"I don't want to have to use this yet, but I will if you don't stop," he said.

I watched as the beam swung again and timed my move for the moment it blinded him. Instead of continuing to move away, I hurtled towards him, catching him by surprise. I grabbed for his hand and smashed it against the railing. The gun fell from his grip and clattered onto the walkway. I lashed out with my foot and kicked it over the edge, but by the time I had regained my balance, he had grabbed me from behind and had his arm tight across my throat. I stamped down on his foot as hard as I could with the heel of my boot and shoved my elbow back into his stomach. His grip loosened as he let out a breath and I twisted away so that I was facing him.

His twisted grin widened. "I didn't know you liked it rough."

"Get away from me, you creep," I shouted.

"It's because of you that I look this way," he said, his lip curling and pure hatred filling his eyes.

"I hate you," I said. "You ruined my life."

"And you ruined mine, so I guess that makes us even," he said, reaching for me.

I batted his hand away and started running, but I wasn't quick enough. Colin grabbed a handful of my hair, pulling me to an abrupt and painful stop. He slammed my head into the lighthouse window and for a moment blackness encroached on my vision. He began dragging me back towards the door. Over his shoulder I could see more flashlights moving around on the ridge and suddenly the sound of two sets of rotors filled the air, drowning out the sound of the waves hitting the rocks. Two large black helicopters rose up from behind the island and flew over the lighthouse.

Colin stopped moving for a moment and turned his head to watch as one helicopter banked right and began firing on the ridge behind the lighthouse, while four dark-clad figures rappelled from the second helicopter before it turned and flew back in the direction it had come. The first helicopter stopped firing and hovered for a moment longer as though assessing the situation. There was no returned fire from the ridge, but the smell of smoke wafted on the breeze. A woman wearing a helmet and camouflage gear watched us from her seat in the cockpit, before speaking into the mouthpiece of her communications headset. Seconds later the aircraft pulled away from the island towards the mainland.

I struggled against Colin's viselike grip on my arm as I watched the four figures make their way towards the lighthouse. A cloud had moved across the moon and it was only the residual light from the lighthouse beam's last pass that allowed them to be seen.

"Don't come any closer, or I'll throw her off," Colin shouted down to the figures, as two crouched behind large boulders and trained their weapons on us. The other two continued to inch closer to the lighthouse, moving through the terrain with a lot less effort than Will and I had expended earlier. Colin pulled me in front of him to shield his body from any gunfire.

"Let her go," one of the men called up.

Colin leaned around me and laughed. "Yeah, right."

I took advantage of his distraction to pull away and twist enough to land a hard kick into the knee of his bad leg. He staggered and released me, reaching for the rail to maintain his balance. I kicked him again, this time in the back of his other knee. There was a loud cracking sound as the railing and part of the walkway gave way. A look of horror crossed Colin's face as he slipped and started to fall. The metal groaned as the rivets sheared off propelled by his weight. Colin clutched at the air for a moment before clasping his hand around a piece of the railing. The walkway shuddered dangerously as the boards beneath our feet began to crack and splinter, pieces falling like hail onto the rocks below. I scrambled backwards, clinging on to the window frame of the lighthouse as the boards under Colin gave way and he swung over the edge, still hanging on to the broken railing.

"Jess, give me your hand," he cried.

I hesitated, then dropped to my knees and holding the remains of the railing with one hand, I reached out with the other. As my fingertips grazed his hand, I saw a shrewd look pass across his ruined face.

"You're coming with me, it's only fitting," he hissed.

I pulled my arm back as though stung, just as the remains of the walkway beneath my feet cracked and the railing supporting Colin gave way. I scooted backwards until I ended up pressed against the outside wall of the lighthouse.

"You bitch," Colin screamed as he lost his grip and plunged from the lighthouse landing with a sickening thud on the rocks below.

The walkway continued to give way and I struggled to my feet trying to find something to hold on to as the boards beneath me broke one after the other, falling in large chunks onto the rocks. Shouts went up from below and I heard running footsteps.

All of a sudden, there was nothing beneath me and I felt myself falling. I made a desperate grab for the ledge of the window and got one hand to it before swinging my body around and reaching up with my other hand, my fingers finding purchase on the narrow frame. I clung to the ledge with my cold fingertips as my body dangled helpless over the edge, high above the treacherous rocks. I tried to steady my breathing, as my heart raced out of control. I glanced down, which was a mistake. In the eerie light cast by the lighthouse beam, the sea crashed onto the rocks below, foaming white before retreating leaving the sharp peaks glistening. I could see Colin's leg twisted at an odd angle below me, being lapped by the waves. A scream of terror escaped from deep within me.

The first camouflaged officer arrived at the top of the internal lighthouse staircase. I was relieved to see that it was Will's mate Sean.

"Sean, find Will," I gasped but he couldn't hear me.

"Hold on for just a few moments longer, Jess," he shouted. "Turn your head away." Seconds later I was showered with broken glass.

"I can't hold much longer," I said, beginning to lose feeling in my fingers.

A second man arrived at his side with a piece of heavy material which he laid over the edge of the broken window. I screamed as the fingers of my right hand slipped from the ledge and lost their grip. I swung precariously just as Sean's hand clamped on to my forearm. The second man grabbed my right arm and they hauled me back inside the lighthouse.

"Will?" I asked as I landed in a heap on the floor.

"If you mean Charlie, we've got him," Sean said.

"Is he alive?"

"Just. Come on, let's get you out of here."

They helped me down the stairs and out through the broken doorway. As we rounded the side of the lighthouse, another man stood with his gun pointed at the ground beside Colin's body.

"Don't look, love," he said when I hesitated.

"I need to, otherwise he will haunt my dreams. I need to know that he is really dead this time," I said, looking down on the bloodied, broken body of my husband, his head twisted at an unnatural angle, his eyes open and unseeing.

"Are you saying this is Colin McDonald?" Sean asked.

I nodded. "He survived the explosion at the warehouse. Have you arrested his father?"

"His father?"

"Ewan Campbell. He's the mastermind behind the recent London terror attacks and they're planning to assassinate the British PM at the G7. He's on the island somewhere."

"Don't worry, we'll get him."

Chapter 48

May 31

"This is quaint," Marie said, peering through the windscreen of my little Fiat as we pulled up to the cottage.

"Wait 'til you see the inside," I said, turning off the engine and climbing out. I dug into the pocket of my jeans for the keys as a second car screeched to a stop behind mine. I grinned as Jimmy and Dave jumped out. Dave leaned on the roof of the car, taking in the vista back down towards the village.

"Great view, Jess," he said.

Marie held the passenger door open and tipped her seat forward, allowing Rachel to alight. She unfolded her long limbs from the tiny backseat and stretched.

"You could have come with us, Rach," Jimmy said.

She gave him a sidelong glance. "Ah, thanks, but I think I was safer with Jess."

Jimmy clutched his chest and attempted to look hurt at her insinuation.

I shifted my gaze from the cottage towards the garden and Buffy's grave. I felt Marie's hand on my arm.

"Do you want to go and say hello?" she said.

I shook my head. "Not right now." I shivered. "It's cold, let's get inside and get the fire on."

I started towards the door as a voice called my name. I turned to see Mr. Gordon hurrying along the driveway towards us. I smiled and went to meet him. "Hello, how are you?"

"Much better than you've been, my dear," he said. "Who would've believed that of Ewan Campbell?" He shook his head. "Now, we emptied out your fridge and kept an eye on things as you asked." He handed me several letters. "These came for you too."

"Thank you," I said, giving his hand a squeeze. "I didn't want to come back to rotten food. How have you been?"

"Good, there's been much excitement here," he said. "The village has been crawling with police."

"I can imagine. Tell Mrs. Gordon that I'll be down for a cuppa tomorrow."

"Will do." He raised his hand in a wave to my friends and headed back to his cottage.

I watched him for a few seconds before turning towards my little house. I unlocked the door and showed my guests inside.

"The tour takes all of ten seconds," I said, tossing the post on the table. "Kitchen, bathroom, lounge and bedroom."

"Ooh, this is cute," Rachel said, dropping her handbag on the sofa. "It's like one of those tiny houses that you see on the Internet."

I shrugged and crouched down in front of the fireplace. Someone, Mr. Gordon I presumed, had emptied the ashes and reset the hearth with kindling and paper. I struck a match and watched the paper catch hold and the flames dance. After a few moments the kindling caught, so I added a few pine cones from the basket beside the fire.

"Do you need more wood brought in, Jess?" Dave asked.

"Actually, that would be great. There's a little covered area beside the shed which is full of wood. Take the basket," I said, standing and handing the empty wood basket to him.

"Shall I make coffee?" Rachel asked.

"Great idea," I said, following Dave to the door. "I'll just get the groceries from the car."

"I'll help," Marie said, following me outside.

Half an hour later, we were gathered around the fire cradling cups of coffee and devouring the tin of homemade shortbread biscuits that Mum had sent with us.

"So this is where you were hiding," Dave said, looking around.

I nodded. "Yeah, I was trying to find out what happened to make Colin do what he did and this seemed like as good a place as any to start."

Marie sat cross-legged on the floor, leaning against Jimmy's legs. His hand rested on her shoulder. Things had progressed there in my absence. I shot her an enquiring look, which she chose to ignore. "And did you find out?" she asked instead.

"Yeah, but it was far more complicated than I had assumed."

"In what way?"

"Well, I thought an event must have driven him when he was in his twenties, but I've come to the conclusion that he became fanatical when he was a teenager, and he'd learned or been taught to hide it well," I said.

"And that's where this Ewan Campbell comes into the equation?" Dave said.

"Yeah, he got him at a vulnerable time and brainwashed him with his extreme political views."

"Which was independence for Scotland at any cost," Rachel said. I nodded.

"So when Colin went away for those fishing and golfing weekends, he was actually visiting Ewan?" Marie said.

"Yeah, I never understood the attraction to the area until I discovered that his mother Catriona lived and died in the village. This was her cottage. Catriona was poor, orphaned at sixteen and pregnant by seventeen."

"But why the secrecy?"

"I think initially because Ewan Campbell's parents were old school and didn't approve of his relationship with Catriona and refused to acknowledge Colin as their grandson. When they died Ewan was free to marry Catriona, but she'd tired of his revolutionary zeal and was concerned about some of his shady business dealings. It seems she wanted Colin away from his influence. I think Ewan all but drove her off the road and over a cliff near here on the night she died."

Rachel gasped. "That's awful."

"Ewan was playing a long game. He saw himself in the role of king maker, with his son as the head of an independent Scotland. I think he loved Catriona, but he couldn't allow her to take his son away from his control. After Colin was adopted, he spent most of his school holidays in Strathgarvan, apparently staying with the old couple at the end of the driveway, although I'm not sure about that now. I think he probably stayed out on the island."

"Why didn't he just live with Ewan after she died?" Marie asked.

"I'm not entirely sure, but I think it was simply that Ewan

didn't actually want to bring up a child. He just wanted a young man ready for him to mold. He ensured through Colin's adoption process that he still had control, but could remain hidden in the shadows in the background. Colin never really felt like he fitted in to his adoptive parents' world, and I think he was impressed by Ewan's wealth. Ewan convinced him that he was destined for greatness if he stuck with him. Colin was desperate for his father's love and attention and believed every word the man uttered. By the time Ewan finally revealed his plans, Colin was already converted. That's my take on it, anyway."

"I read in the newspaper that Ewan was funding his terrorist network by arms dealing through a weapons manufacturer that he largely owned," Jimmy said.

"Yeah, it took me a while to unravel that one. The companies that he and Colin owned had bought small shareholdings that together meant they had a controlling interest in Mendelson, the weapons company. Ewan had guns manufactured off the books which he sold and transported using Colin's freight business to contacts in the Middle East. The sales funded Ewan's version of a Scottish Republican Army."

"So they were behind the London bombings?" Marie said.

"Yeah, in Ewan's twisted mind, he thought the use of terror would force the British government to grant independence to Scotland. In the wake of the Brexit vote, Ewan assumed that the Scottish people would be supportive of independence, if it allowed them to stay in Europe. He just had to keep his methods for achieving this out of sight. His ultimate plan for control relied on having his son, a happily married, charming and successful young Scottish businessman ready to lead the newly independent nation."

"Unbelievable." Rachel shook her head.

"I know, I was just a pawn in their game with no idea what I'd become involved with," I said, standing up and gathering everyone's empty cups. "Anyway, do you want to go for a walk before we think about dinner?"

"Sure," Jimmy said, jumping up, holding out his hand and pulling Marie to her feet. "Then we'll head down to the pub and check in."

I stoked the fire before we pulled on our coats and hats and left the cottage. We stopped beside Buffy's grave on the way off the property.

"She was such a lovely dog and didn't deserve to die like that," I said, my voice catching. Marie put her arms around me and pulled me into a hug.

"He really was a bastard, that husband of yours," Jimmy said.

I smiled at his candor. "Yeah, I sure know how to pick 'em."

"Speaking of which, have you seen Will?" he asked.

"Jimmy," Marie said, letting me go and frowning at him.

"It's okay," I said. "Yes, Jim, I've seen Charlie. I sat by his bedside for two weeks until he regained consciousness. But will I see him again? No."

"Not even after he saved your life?" Marie asked.

"No, he was just doing his job."

"You sure about that?" she asked.

"Very." I turned away.

"I still can't believe that you two were at it and we had no idea," Jimmy added. "I'm usually quite good at picking up on those things."

"Jimmy," Marie and Rachel said at the same time.

"What?" He spread his hands in confusion. "Just sayin'."

I laughed. "I have missed you guys. I'll be sure to give you an extra big hint next time I'm seeing someone, Jim. Now, follow me, we'll get a really good view of the island and the castle from the top of the ridge."

We trudged across the fields to the edge of the cliff. It was late afternoon and the lights were beginning to come on in some of the cottages down in the village and along the edge of the harbor. Spotlights cast shadows on the castle ruin on the hill, majestic in its position overlooking the village and the coast. But it was Campbell Island that had everyone's attention.

"Can we go out to the island tomorrow?" Dave asked.

I shook my head. "No, it's still off limits. The authorities are busy processing the house and grounds. Will be for weeks, I'm told, and the lighthouse needs repairing before it's safe for anyone to visit."

I shivered as I looked out at the red and white striped tower on the far edge of the island, its light still flashing at regular intervals, as though undisturbed by recent events. The image of Colin tossing Will's body into the sea flashed across my vision, but I pushed it aside.

"We can visit Strathgarvan Castle tomorrow, though," I said. "The view along the coast from up there is spectacular."

We walked down into the village and followed the footpath around the edge of the harbor where I counted fifteen fishing boats tied up to buoys.

"There's not usually that many boats in the harbor, I wonder if the fleet has been grounded given recent events," I said.

"It's possible," Dave agreed. "Your old neighbor did say that the village had been crawling with cops."

I showed my friends the gorgeous old church where Colin's mother and grandparents were buried, before we returned to my cottage and piled into Jimmy's car to head down to the pub. The pub was full for a Saturday night. I peered in through the front window, all of a sudden feeling a little nervous. I must have hesitated, because Marie took my arm.

"It'll be fine," she said. "You're with us."

Rachel pushed through the door and strode towards the bar. I started to follow and then froze. It was as though someone had turned the volume switch to mute. You could have heard a pin drop in the room. Forty pairs of eyes stared at me. I fought the urge to turn and run, and instead lifted my head to look over at the long wooden bar. Alastair's eyes met mine and he put down the pint he was pulling.

"Jess," he said, rushing out from behind the bar and charging towards me.

Dave and Jimmy flanked me, ready to step in if necessary, but Alastair scooped me into a bear hug, lifting me off the ground.

"Ah, lass, you're alright," he said, putting me down and holding me away from him with his hands on my shoulders as though he was checking that I was in one piece. "Come on, what are ya having?" He slipped an arm around my shoulders and pulled me towards the bar, giving my friends a flick of his head to indicate that they should follow.

I saw Jimmy and Dave exchange an uncertain glance before they too headed to the bar. Conversation resumed, but much less animated than before. People kept giving us surreptitious glances. I introduced my friends to Alastair as he took our drinks order. He shooed a couple of locals away from a table in the front window, so that we could all sit. He refused to accept payment, and a couple of minutes later he arrived at the table with our drinks balanced on a tray. He set the tray down and pulled a chair across from a neighboring table and sat with us.

"Jess, I'm so sorry," he said. "I don't know what else to say. I never dreamed that Colin would try to hurt you."

"Did you know that he was alive?"

Alastair hung his head. "Yeah, Ewan made us promise not to tell a soul."

"You could have told me."

"I know, I nearly did several times, but you hated him so much, that I didn't think it would do any good."

"Did you know what Ewan was up to?" Marie asked.

"You sound like the police," he said, giving her a wry grin. He ran his hand through his shaggy hair. "I have never answered so many questions in me life as I have over the last couple of weeks."

"But did you know?" I prompted.

"Bits and pieces. I mean, I knew that he was hiding Colin when everyone thought he was dead. And you couldn't help but notice that things were being transported on and off the island at odd times. I suspected that he might have been building an army of sorts out there, but he was always rather secretive, so who knew what he was really up to?"

"Why didn't you say anything? Go to the police?"

"The police?" Alastair looked at me as though I was stupid. "Constable Jones and his father before him were on the Laird's payroll. Many around here were in one way or another. He owned most of the fishing boats, the farms, this pub..."

"So he bought everyone's silence," I said.

"Not so much silence, just that we looked the other way when things happened that we didn't understand," he said.

"So do you believe in an independent Scotland at any price?"

I asked.

Alastair looked weary as he shook his head. "Not at any price. Back when I was young and foolish, we were all part of The Unit, part of the group in that photo you showed me. I believed revolution was the only way, but not as I grew older. Y'know, Ewan had us doing military training exercises out on the island. Several of those boys are now well placed in the Royal Regiment of Scotland."

"Like sleeper agents waiting to be activated," Dave said.

Alastair shook his head. "I don't think so. I think we all grew to realize that Ewan's views were extreme."

"Except for Colin. Why did he continue to buy into Ewan's fanaticism, when the rest of you grew out of it?" I asked.

"Because he was the heir apparent, he wholeheartedly believed in what the Laird was doing. I'm so sorry that you got caught up in it all."

"Me too," I agreed. "Were you told to keep an eye on me?"

Alastair's head dropped again. "Yeah, they wanted to know what you were up to. Neither of them wanted you here. Colin thought when he killed your dog that you'd run back to Edinburgh."

I gulped. "Did you know it was him?"

"I suspected as much when Harry called me that day. I'm sorry, Jess, I didn't think that he was quite that unhinged. He certainly had anger issues, but I didn't think he'd do that."

"Well, he tried to do a lot worse to me out on the island. I don't think I was ever supposed to leave there alive."

Alastair gave my arm a squeeze. "With what I know now, I don't think you were either."

Marie muttered under her breath.

"Did you tell them that I was going to visit Douglas?" I said.

He shook his head. "I didn't know that you were." He paused. "So it's true then, Douglas didn't do it himself."

"No, he definitely had help."

"God." Alastair looked distraught. "Why?"

"He was about to give me proof that Ewan was Colin's father and I'm not sure what else, but something that Ewan didn't want anyone knowing about. There were photos strewn everywhere when I found him."

"Douglas was quite the photographer, so perhaps he snapped something that he shouldn't have."

"I think so, but I guess we'll never know. Ewan is denying any involvement in that death. And Jones ensured that any evidence was compromised."

"What about your father, Jess?" Dave asked. "Didn't Ewan confess to having him killed?"

"Yeah, that night on the island he told me that he'd arranged it, but as for the two men who carried it out, they've disappeared. The truck from the security photos that Dad's assistant tracked down, was found in a shed on one of Ewan's properties last week. I don't know if they'll ever be caught."

"Jess, that's awful." Rachel put her arm around me.

"At least we know what happened now. The day before he died Dad must have found something. I know he visited the newspaper archive in Edinburgh that day, but he made the mistake of telephoning Ewan to confront him. The police have now looked into his phone records which show that they had a ten-minute conversation. It appears that they'd arranged to meet the following day. Dad's online calendar had the afternoon after he died blocked out with Ewan's number as the reference. But Ewan ensured that meeting would never happen."

"I knew he wasn't squeaky clean, but murder." Alastair shook his head and rose.

"You can't help feeling a bit sorry for him," Jimmy said, watching him walk back behind the bar and start serving his next customer.

Rachel snorted. "He's right to feel guilty. It's the likes of him, turning a blind eye that allows evil people to operate in the shadows and get away with awful things."

"The problem is the whole village is guilty on some level," I said.

Epilogue

I hugged my mother goodbye in the hallway of her house in Edinburgh.

"It's just for a few weeks, Mum. I'll be back before you know it," I said.

Mum sighed and cupped my cheek. "I know, but I'm worried that you're not ready."

"It's been two months, Mum, my wounds have all healed. I need to get away, somewhere hot and sunny, and give myself the space to work out what happens next."

"I know you do. I just wish you were taking Marie or someone, with you."

"It's okay, Mum. It's all over now. Colin is definitely dead and Ewan is facing so many charges, that even if they only manage to make a quarter of them stick, he won't be out of prison in his lifetime."

"What about Charlie?"

"What about Charlie?" I replied.

"He's called every day for the past two weeks and you've refused to speak to him."

337

I opened my mouth to reply, but she held up her hand and continued. "I saw how you were at the hospital. You were at his bedside every day until he regained consciousness."

"I just wanted to make sure that he was going to be okay. It would have been my fault if he'd died."

"No, Colin's fault, not yours," Mum said. "Charlie cares about you."

I shook my head. Mum sighed and hugged me again as the taxi tooted outside. I extracted myself and kissed her soft cheek before turning and opening the door.

"I'll call you every day," I said.

* * *

Edinburgh Airport was busy with holiday makers escaping to the sun. I checked my small piece of luggage and proceeded through departures and found the gate for my flight on the digital departures board. After a cursory wander past the shops, I located an empty seat on the end of a row of chairs at the gate lounge and pulled my Kindle out of my bag.

"Is this seat taken?" a voice beside me asked a few minutes later.

I shook my head and kept reading. I felt someone sit down beside me and after a few seconds I realized that they were looking at me. I breathed in a familiar scent, sighed and closed my Kindle. When I looked up, Charlie was smiling at me. He was looking very relaxed in faded blue jeans and a long-sleeved black t-shirt. His cuts and bruises had all healed, although I could see the edge of a red scar emerging from beneath his hairline on his forehead.

"Are you stalking me? Is this even legal?"

Charlie's smiled widened. "I'm not sure that talking to your mother is either stalking or illegal."

"My mother, I should have guessed."

"I know what you said at the hospital, but what we feel for each other is real, Jess. I see it in your eyes and I know it in my heart. Let's start again away from all this."

I took a deep breath and shook my head. "No, I can't."

Charlie reached over and took my hand. "What are you afraid of?"

"Trusting someone again, only to have them betray that trust," I said as a single tear rolled unbidden down my cheek.

"I know," Charlie said reaching out to catch it. "But I promise that I will never hurt you again. It's time to stop being afraid, the worst has actually happened. Life is too short Jess, to spend it hiding. We both could have died, in fact, I almost did." He shrugged.

"To save me."

"Doesn't that tell you something?"

I stared at him for several long minutes, not saying anything. All I saw was love in his eyes, along with concern and hope. There were no shadows, no doubts, no hidden agendas. He was right, the worst had actually happened, what lay ahead wasn't something to be frightened of, it was something to embrace. This was my chance for a new start, out of the shadows and into the light.

I leaned forward and kissed him, a gentle peck at first which morphed into something stronger, more passionate. I felt his hands cup my face and I rested my hands on top of his. When we broke apart his eyes were dancing, but his expression was serious.

I sat back, smiled and held out my hand to him. "Hi, I'm Jessica."

His warm hand enveloped mine and he returned my smile. "Hi. I'm Charlie."

The End

Acknowledgements

First and foremost, thank you to my editor, Gary Smailes, for his continued support, guidance and encouragement. Many thanks to Julia Gibbs, once again, for her detailed proof reading and to my beta readers Sarah and Craig whose time and effort I hugely appreciate. Thanks also to Trevor for his advice on rifles vs shotguns. The cover was designed by Warren Designs and I think perfectly captures Jess looking out towards the lighthouse on Campbell Island.

My advance reader team has once again been massively supportive with their early reads and reviews. A big shout-out to Tres, Shannon, Michaela, Melanie, Judy, Eveie, Roger, Karen, Graham, Eileen, Suzanne and Milena.

Thanks to my husband Craig, father Jack and my boys Jude, Zak and Scott for your love and encouragement. I couldn't do this without you.

And finally, a big thank-you to you, my readers. Thank you for your emails! I love hearing from you.

If you would like further information about me or my books you can check out my website or join my Reader's Group (http://eepurl.com/gtD0EX) to be kept up to date on up-coming book launches, exclusive giveaways and competitions and to receive a FREE copy of *In the Shadows*; a short story told from Will's perspective.

SL Beaumont

www.slbeaumont.com

Author's Note

Did you enjoy this book?

Please consider leaving a review on Amazon, Bookbub and/or Goodreads. As a writer, reviews are critically important. Why?

You probably consider reviews when making a decision whether to try a new author – I know I do. Reviews also help indie authors like me to gain exposure for their work and get advertising opportunities.

So if you enjoyed the book, and would like to help spread the word, I'd be so grateful if you could leave a review (as short or as long as you like) on the site where you purchased it and don't forget to recommend it your friends!

Thank you so much!

S

Also by SL Beaumont

The Carlswick Affair

The Carlswick Treasure

The Carlswick Conspiracy

The Carlswick Deception

The Carlswick Mythology

Made in the USA
Middletown, DE
12 August 2024